DEAD, TO BEGIN WITH

▼

ALSO BY BILL CRIDER

DEAD, TO BEGIN WITH

A SHERIFF DAN RHODES MYSTERY

BILL CRIDER

MINOTAUR BOOKS

A THOMAS DUNNE BOOK

NEW YORK

This is a work of fiction. All of the characters, organizations, and events portrayed in this novel are either products of the author's imagination or are used fictitiously.

A THOMAS DUNNE BOOK FOR MINOTAUR BOOKS.
An imprint of St. Martin's Press.

www.thomasdunnebooks.com
www.minotaurbooks.com

Library of Congress Cataloging-in-Publication Data
Names: Crider, Bill, 1941– author.
Title: Dead, to begin with : a Dan Rhodes mystery / Bill Crider.
Description: First edition. | New York : Minotaur Books, 2017. | Series: Sheriff Dan
    Rhodes mysteries ; 24
Identifiers: LCCN 2017011875| ISBN 9781250078537 (hardcover) | ISBN 9781466890831
    (e-book)
Subjects: LCSH: Rhodes, Dan (Fictitious character)—Fiction. | Murder—Investigation—
    Fiction. | Sheriffs—Fiction. | Texas—Fiction. | BISAC: FICTION / Mystery &
    Detective / Police Procedural. | FICTION / Mystery & Detective / General. | GSAFD:
    Mystery fiction.
Classification: LCC PS3553.R497 D387 2017 | DDC 81

Our books may be purchased in bulk for promotional, educational, or business use. Please contact your local bookseller or the Macmillan Corporate and Premium Sales Department at 1-800-221-7945, extension 5442, or by email at MacmillanSpecial Markets@macmillan.com.

First Edition: August 2017

10 9 8 7 6 5 4 3 2 1

To all the readers who've followed Sheriff Dan Rhodes through the years. The sheriff and I thank you for your support.

Marley was dead, to begin with. There is no doubt whatever about that.

—Charles Dickens, *A Christmas Carol*

DEAD, TO BEGIN WITH

▼

Chapter 1

▼

Sheriff Dan Rhodes was at his desk going over some arrest reports when the phone rang.

Hack Jensen, the dispatcher, answered the call. For a few seconds he listened. Then he said, "You sure about where she's headed?"

Rhodes put down the report he'd been reading, something about a burglary at a house on one of the county roads.

"I'll tell the sheriff," Hack said. "He's right here. Don't worry, Harvey. He'll stop her."

Hack ended the call and turned to Rhodes. "Elaine Tunstall's off her meds again."

"Uh-oh," Rhodes said, taking off his reading glasses and putting them in his pocket.

"Harvey said he thought she'd been takin' 'em, but she's good about pretendin'. She musta got to feelin' so good that she figgered she didn't need 'em. You know how it goes."

Rhodes knew how it went. "I'm just guessing here, but I have a feeling the meds aren't the problem Harvey called about."

"Nope. What he called about is a bad haircut."

"I had one of those once," Lawton, the jailer, said as he walked in from the cellblock. "Wanted to stay in bed for a week but had to work instead. Wore a ball cap all day for a while."

"I remember that," Hack said. "That was a good while ago. Back when you had hair."

"I got hair. More hair than some I could name."

"You talkin' about me or the sheriff? 'Cause he's the one got the thin spot in back. I still got all my own hair. Mostly."

Rhodes knew what they were doing. He'd thought for years it was a conspiracy to drive him crazy, but he'd decided it wasn't, not really. They dragged everything out simply because they couldn't help themselves. Or because they thought of themselves as the Abbott and Costello of Blacklin County, Texas, a duo to whom they bore a physical resemblance.

Or it might have been a conspiracy.

"Let's get back to Harvey," Rhodes said.

"He's been breakin' up an old sidewalk in front of his house," Hack said. "It's got all whomper-jawed, and he's gonna pour a new one and level it."

Rhodes hated to give them the satisfaction of asking what was going on, but if he didn't, he'd never find out. "What does a whomper-jawed sidewalk have to do with a bad haircut?"

"I kinda wondered the same thing," Lawton said.

"Harvey's been usin' a sledgehammer to break up the concrete," Hack said, as if that explained everything.

"I still don't get it," Lawton said. For once he was as out of the loop as Rhodes was in one of these conversations.

"Well," Hack said, "Elaine's left the house, and she picked up the sledgehammer when she got in the pickup to come to Clearview."

The Tunstalls lived in Wesley, a small town about ten miles from Clearview, which was the county seat and the home of the sheriff's department.

"What size hammer is it?" Lawton asked.

"Not a great big one. Eight-pounder, Harvey said."

"I still don't get it," Lawton said.

Rhodes didn't get it, either, but he wasn't going to admit it.

"She got a bad haircut at the Beauty Shack," Hack said.

Rhodes got it then. "She's going to get revenge for the bad haircut. With the sledgehammer."

"That's what Harvey thinks," Hack said. "He says the haircut's fine, and Elaine would know that if she was on her meds, which she ain't. You better get on over to the Beauty Shack before she does. You're just wastin' time sitting there."

Rhodes stood up and pulled on the insulated jacket that had been hanging on his chair. The jacket had the sheriff's department logo on the back, a brown shield outlined in gold with a gold star in the middle. Above the star were the words BLACKLIN COUNTY, and below it SHERIFF'S DEPARTMENT.

"You'd better hope Elaine Tunstall doesn't get there before I do," Rhodes told Hack.

Hack wasn't bothered by the implications of Rhodes's comment. "Harvey tried to stop her," he said, "but she come at him with the sledge. He was gonna call Lonnie and warn him, though. Lonnie'll have the place locked up. He'll keep ever'body inside."

"He won't keep the cars in the parking lot inside," Rhodes said on his way out the door.

"I didn't think of that," Hack said, "but Elaine ain't mad at the cars. Just the haircut."

Hack might have added something to that, but the door closed behind Rhodes, who wasn't listening anyway. He was too busy worrying about what Elaine might do with that sledgehammer.

Luckily nothing in the town of Clearview was far from anything else. The heater in the Tahoe wouldn't even have time to heat up before Rhodes got to the Beauty Shack, which was too bad because a norther had come in overnight and dropped the temperature into the low forties.

The interior of the Tahoe wasn't much warmer than the outside, but at least Rhodes was out of the wind. He started the vehicle and headed for the Beauty Shack. When he got there, he saw Lonnie Wallace and his partner, Eric Stewart, standing outside in the parking lot.

Lonnie was the owner of the establishment. He was togged out, as usual, in pressed jeans and high-heeled cowboy boots. Although boots were practically required footwear for Texas sheriffs, Rhodes had never been able to wear them comfortably, and he wondered how Lonnie managed to stand up nearly all day every day in them. Lonnie also wore a Western-cut leather jacket and a Western hat that Rhodes thought would blow off in the wind if Lonnie wasn't careful. Rhodes didn't wear a hat, either. On windy days like this one, he wished he did.

Eric Stewart was taller than Lonnie, and he wasn't wearing boots. He had on jeans, though, and running shoes. Rhodes thought his feet were probably cold. The wind would go right through the mesh tops of the shoes. Instead of a cowboy hat Eric had on a knit watch cap pulled down over his ears and a puffy gray thermal jacket. Eric managed the combination art gallery and antique store that Lonnie owned. It was only a couple of blocks away, so Eric had probably walked to the beauty shop to help Lonnie out in the current emergency.

Rhodes got out of the Tahoe, and the north wind had found every crevice in his clothing by the time his feet touched the ground. It blew his hair in several directions, no doubt making the thin spot look even thinner. As much as Rhodes disliked hats, he disliked billed caps even more, but lately he'd started taking one with him in case of emergencies. He reached back into the Tahoe and got the cap, which was lying on the passenger seat. It had the sheriff's department logo on the front, and Rhodes felt very official when he put it on and pulled it down tight.

"Glad to see you, Sheriff," Lonnie said when Rhodes got the cap on and closed the Tahoe door. "Harvey told me he'd called you, so I guess you know what's going on."

"I've heard," Rhodes said. "That must've been some haircut Elaine got."

"It was fine," Lonnie said. "Just what she asked for."

"There's just no pleasing some people," Eric said.

The watch cap was pulled down low on his forehead, almost touching his eyebrows. It also covered his ears, and Rhodes, whose ears were already beginning to feel like two blocks of ice attached to the side of his head, wondered about getting a knit cap. He'd never considered it before, but the idea was suddenly quite appealing. Maybe he could order one with the department logo on it.

"How do you plan to handle things, Sheriff?" Lonnie asked.

"I'll talk to her, try to calm her down, try to keep her in the car."

"Sounds good," Lonnie said.

"Where is she, anyway?" Eric asked. "She should've been here by now."

"I don't want to wish bad luck on anybody," Lonnie said, "but maybe she had a flat tire."

"Or ran off the road into a ditch," Eric said. He paused. "Or maybe that's too harsh."

Rhodes wasn't worried about Elaine, but he did wonder where she could be.

They waited a few more minutes, with Eric and Lonnie talking about hairstyles. Rhodes didn't have much to add to the conversation. He was about to call Hack and ask him to see if he could find out anything about Elaine's whereabouts when Lonnie spoke up. "There's a problem with your plan, Sheriff."

"What's that?" Rhodes asked.

"Won't work," Eric said.

"Why not?"

Eric pointed. "Because she outsmarted you and parked down at the antique store. Here she comes."

Rhodes looked down the street. Sure enough, Elaine Tunstall was headed in their direction. She wore carpenter's overalls, and the sledge hung from a loop on the side. The long handle bumped against her leg as she walked, and Rhodes wondered if the hammer might pull her overalls off. It wouldn't be easy, not with the shoulder straps, but it might happen. Or the heavy hammer might rip out the loop.

As if she knew what Rhodes was thinking, after she'd gone a few steps, Elaine pulled the sledge out of the loop and gave it a little swing. Not just anybody could handle an eight-pound sledge as if it were lighter than air, but Elaine was making it look easy.

"The wind's not doing her haircut any good," Eric said.

"It's what we call our classic bob," Lonnie said. "Nice blunt cut, with a side part and just a few layers. The bangs really add a lot to the look, but the wind's messing them up. That's okay, though. It's the kind of cut that'll fall right back into place as soon as she gets inside."

"It suits her."

"That's what I told her."

"Nice color, too."

"We call it sun-kissed brown," Lonnie said. "I think it's perfect for her skin. Don't you?"

"I can't really tell from here, but I guess she doesn't agree with you."

"She would if she was feeling herself. Her husband said it's being off her meds that makes her like this."

Rhodes had nothing to contribute to that conversation, so he kept an eye on Elaine, who continued in their direction, pushing the bangs up off her forehead with her left hand, the sledgehammer dangling from her right. She wasn't wearing a jacket, but she had on a red-and-black flannel shirt and didn't seem to notice the cold. Her eyes were narrowed, and as she got closer, she raised the sledgehammer.

"You two go on inside now," Rhodes said.

Lonnie shook his head. "Uh-uh. You might need our help."

"You don't get paid for this," Rhodes said. "I do. Besides, she's mad at you, Lonnie, not at me. We don't want to rile her any more than she already is, so you need to be out of sight."

"Good thinking," Eric said.

He took hold of the sleeve of Lonnie's jacket and gave it a tug. They turned and went inside, just getting the door closed as Elaine arrived to confront Rhodes, stopping about ten feet away.

"Hey, Elaine," Rhodes said. "I like the classic bob cut you got. Looks good on you."

Elaine squared herself up, pushed her bangs out of her face, and glared at him. "It looks like hell. You get outta my way, Sheriff. I have some business to do here."

"I like the color, too," Rhodes said. "Nice shade of brown. What's it called?"

Elaine looked at Rhodes as if he might have lost his mind. "Who cares what it's called?" She brandished the sledgehammer. "Outta my way."

Rhodes stood his ground. "Harvey says he really likes the way it looks."

"Harvey's required to say that because he's my husband. He'd say he liked it if I was bald. This is worse than bald. I look like I'm hiding under a haystack."

"No, you don't. You look—"

Rhodes didn't get to finish what he'd started to say because Elaine feinted to his right, and when he moved to stop her, she slipped past him on his left, giving him a tap on the elbow with the sledgehammer.

Something like an electric shock ran up to Rhodes's neck and down to his hand. Not for the first time Rhodes wondered why anyone had ever called the ulnar nerve the funny bone. For a second or two his arm was paralyzed. By the time he'd shaken it off, Elaine was rattling the knob of the door to the Beauty Shack. Rhodes was glad that either Lonnie or Eric had remembered to lock it, but Elaine wasn't happy that she couldn't open it. She had a solution, however. She raised the sledgehammer.

Rhodes got to her just before she brought the hammer down on the doorknob. He grabbed the sleeve of her shirt at the elbow and pulled backward. She brought the sledge down anyway, but she missed the doorknob by about an inch. Angered, she rounded on Rhodes.

"You made me miss!" she said, bringing the hammer back up.

"It's a good thing I did," Rhodes said. "You're in enough trouble without destroying someone's property."

As Rhodes finished speaking, the wind snatched the cap off his head and sent it tumbling across the parking lot and into the street. That was just one of the reasons he didn't like wearing a cap. The wind blew his hair in three directions, and it wouldn't fall back into place like it would on someone with a classic bob.

Rhodes ignored the cap, but Elaine didn't.

"You better go get your cap," she said.

"I'll get it later." Rhodes held out his hand. "Right now I want you to give me that sledgehammer."

Elaine looked at the sledgehammer as if she hadn't noticed it before and lowered it to her side. "What do you want with it?"

"I want to put it away where it can't hurt anybody. Hand it here."

"I wouldn't hurt anybody."

Rhodes thought about his funny bone. It had stopped tingling, but that didn't mean it hadn't hurt for a little while. He supposed he could forgive that.

"Just give me the hammer," he said.

Elaine raised the hammer and appeared to be about to hand it to him when Rhodes heard the sound of a siren. He turned to look down the street and saw a sheriff's department car headed toward the Beauty Shack. Hack must have called one of the deputies for backup.

Elaine, unlike Rhodes, hadn't been distracted by the siren. She turned around and knocked the knob off the door with a metallic clang. She shoved against the door and managed to push it open. By the time Rhodes turned back, she was already inside the shop. He went in after her.

"Everybody get outta my way," Elaine said.

She needn't have bothered. Customers and beauticians alike had already run to the back of the shop. They stood between the sinks and chairs and watched Elaine, except for Lonnie and Eric, who advanced on her slowly.

Rhodes warned them off. "Lonnie, you and Eric step back. I'll take care of this."

The two men looked at each other. Rhodes figured they were thinking that he hadn't done such a good job taking care of things so far, and they were right.

Elaine turned to look at him. "You leave me alone, Sheriff. I'll just bust up a few things and teach them not to give me a bad haircut. Then I'll go home."

"I don't think it's a bad haircut," Deputy Ruth Grady said as she came through the door.

Rhodes was glad Hack had called Ruth. She was smart, she was sensible, and she could handle almost any situation. She'd never dealt with a woman holding a sledgehammer before, though, not as far as Rhodes knew.

Ruth pushed the door shut, but it didn't do any good. The wind shoved it open again and sent papers flying off the counter to her right. Rhodes stepped to the door, closed it, and held it shut. The wind hadn't done much to clear out the odd chemical smell of the shop, and he considered opening the door again.

"I'm glad you like the cut," Lonnie said to Ruth. "It's a classic bob. It's really very nice."

"I agree," Eric said.

"What do men know?" Ruth asked. "Right, Elaine?"

Elaine pushed at her hair with her left hand. "That's right. Men don't know squat about haircuts."

Lonnie opened his mouth to protest, but Rhodes raised a hand to silence him. Lonnie shut his mouth.

"I think it's cute," Ruth said. "It just suits you." She took off her hat and shook her head. "See? I have the same cut. Almost, anyway. It just shakes right out. No hat hair."

The wind had ruffled Elaine's hair, and now she shook her head. Her hair fell right into place. Rhodes was envious.

Elaine reached up and patted her classic bob. She looked at herself in one of the many mirrors in the shop.

"It really does work," she said. "I guess maybe I was wrong about it. It's not as bad as I thought. Catch, Sheriff."

She tossed the sledgehammer to Rhodes, who grabbed the handle and barely managed to hang on and keep the head from hitting the floor.

"You gonna arrest me?" Elaine asked.

Rhodes hefted the hammer. "That depends on Lonnie. You broke his doorknob. You going to press charges, Lonnie?"

Lonnie looked doubtful. "I . . . I guess not."

"Harvey'll pay for the doorknob," Elaine said.

"Well, all right then," Lonnie said. "We'll just forget it ever happened, but it better not happen again."

"Harvey will make sure of it," Rhodes said. "I'll talk to him."

"So will I," Ruth said. "Come on, Elaine. I'll take you home."

They left together. Elaine seemed perfectly happy to go with her. Rhodes hoped Elaine didn't have another mood swing on the way back to Wesley.

"Thanks, Sheriff," Lonnie said when the two women had left.

Conversation started up all around the beauty shop as the customers and beauticians resumed what they'd been doing. Rhodes knew that the incident would be talked about all over town within an hour or two. He was glad that Jennifer Loam hadn't been there. She had an Internet news site called *A Clear View of Clearview,* and she also had what Rhodes considered an irritating habit of exaggerating a lot of things that happened in the town and the whole of Blacklin County. He remembered clickbait headlines along the lines of SHERIFF BATTLES JURASSIC TURTLE! and THE CROCODILE FIGHTER OF CROCKETT'S CREEK. It had been an alligator, not a crocodile, but nobody seemed to care. Rhodes supposed it didn't make much difference, but since Jennifer didn't mind making the switch, there was no telling what she'd say about Elaine's little escapade. At least there wouldn't be video, unless someone in the shop had been using a cell phone to take some. Rhodes hadn't noticed.

"That ended better than I thought it would," Eric said. He shook his head. "Nobody got hurt."

"I'm glad," Lonnie said. "I wouldn't want anybody to get hurt, especially me or my customers, and that includes Elaine. Thanks again, Sheriff."

"Deputy Grady's the one you should thank," Rhodes said. "She's the one who got Elaine calmed down."

"Well, you kept her busy until the deputy could get here," Lonnie said. "If it hadn't been for you, I'd have lost more than a doorknob."

He gave Rhodes a critical look that made Rhodes a little self-conscious. He tried to push some of his wayward hair back into place.

"You want a haircut on the house?" Lonnie asked. "I could give you what we call the Brad Pitt cut. Looks tousled all the time but still looks really good. What do you think, Eric?"

"He's definitely the Brad Pitt type," Eric said. "A little taller than Brad, though."

Rhodes didn't think he was the Brad Pitt type at all.

"I don't know about that thin spot in the back of your hair, Sheriff," Eric said. "That might not work with a Brad Pitt cut. Lonnie, you got any of that protein hair fiber stuff you sprinkle on thin spots?"

Lonnie frowned. "I don't carry it. I don't think it looks good."

"Why not?"

"Mainly because it looks like you sprinkled iron filings on your head."

"I'll pass on the sprinkles and the haircut for now," Rhodes said. "I have to get back to crime-fighting."

"And I need to go get a doorknob for this place," Eric said. "I have some nice brass ones in the antique store. I'll be back in a jiffy to install it."

He and Rhodes went outside.

"I had a cap around here somewhere," Rhodes said.

Eric pointed to the street where something lay like roadkill. "That it?"

"That's it," Rhodes said. "Somebody ran over it."

He went to pick it up. The bill had a greasy tire track across it, and gravel and dirt were ground into the crown. Now Rhodes had another reason not to like caps. He slapped it against his leg to get some of the dirt and gravel off.

"See you later, Sheriff," Eric said, and started to walk back to the antique store.

Rhodes looked around for a trash can but didn't see one, so he jammed the cap in a jacket pocket and went to the Tahoe. Before he got settled behind the wheel, the radio crackled.

It was Hack Jensen. "You need to get over to the opera house, Sheriff. Looks like there's trouble."

"What kind of trouble?" Rhodes asked.

"Jake Marley's dead," Hack said.

Chapter 2

▼

The Clearview Opera House was in what had once been Clearview's downtown area. Rhodes supposed it was still the downtown, except there wasn't really a downtown anymore. The businesses that had once made up the central business district had long since either closed for good or moved out to the highway, especially the area around Walmart. That area of the town was lively. There were dollar stores, a big grocery store, and lots of new businesses. Not in the old downtown, though. Some of the buildings still stood, but others had either fallen down or been demolished. For a while the whole place had resembled a ghost town, but now some buildings, like the combination antique store and art gallery where Eric worked, had been what people called *repurposed,* and the area was beginning to take on a semblance of new life.

While most of the old buildings hadn't been restored to their former state of good repair, a couple had, including a flower shop. Others, like a beauty shop, a thrift store, and even a church, were in buildings that had hardly been improved at all in the last forty or so years. There was, however, a new senior citizens' center, and the big white law office that Rhodes called the Lawj Mahal was another recent addition, having replaced four or five of the older buildings.

And there was the opera house. It was squeezed into a narrow space between an empty building that had once been the biggest department store in town and another one that had been a drugstore. Rhodes wasn't sure when the last opera had been performed in Clearview. For all he knew there might never have been an opera in the theater. The name might have been chosen for its grand sound rather than its literal meaning. The building was a relic of Clearview's oil boom days, when the town wanted to appear cultured instead of rowdy and lacking in refinement. After the boom the theater, like the town, had fallen on hard times, closing its doors sometime in the early 1940s.

A couple of years later someone had opened the building again, with a movie screen installed on the stage. The movie theater had been in operation for only a few years before television had come along. Clearview wasn't in an area where TV was easily accessible, so the theater hadn't had any competition until sometime in the middle 1950s. More and more people started putting up tall antennas that brought in stations from Dallas, and they began to stay at home watching old movies that had once been in color on tiny screens that showed them in black-and-white. It didn't seem to matter to anyone that the experience wasn't the same. Business at the theater continued for a while, but then it began to taper off. A new manager came along and tried some gimmicks to bring in the customers, without much success. After a few more years of struggling, the theater closed for good. The front had been boarded up, and what was behind it had been forgotten by just about everyone. Clearview's prosperous times were far behind it now, and the building had sat vacant for longer than a good part of the population of Clearview had been alive.

The previous summer, however, Jake Marley had taken an interest in the old building. Marley was the grandson of one the men who had become wealthy during the oil boom days, the last living remnant of one of the families who'd struck it rich. He had continued living in Clearview, while the other descendants of the people who'd made bushels of money from black gold had either died or moved far away to live their comfortable moneyed lives in other states, or even other countries: California, Florida, Hawaii, the Bahamas.

Marley was widely regarded as an eccentric misanthrope. He was past sixty and had never married. His parents had died years ago, one from pneumonia and one from cancer of some kind, and his sister, who had been a couple of years older, had died in a one-car rollover accident when she was a teenager, nearly fifty years ago. Marley lived a reclusive life in the family home, a large stone house almost ninety years old now, located just outside of town. He'd never taken any interest in civic matters and didn't seem to care a bit about whether the town disappeared or prospered, an attitude that many in the town considered selfish, and maybe it was.

Marley was much talked about but seldom seen around town. He didn't attend church, and when he shopped at Walmart he did it late at night when hardly anyone else was there. Sometimes he was spotted at the Dairy Queen drive-through or sitting alone in the Jolly Tamale having the #1 Dinner, but he didn't socialize or have any friends, not even among the people he'd gone to school with. He'd lived in Clearview all his life, but no one really knew him.

Rhodes had heard several rumors about how Marley had occupied his time before deciding to renovate the theater. Some said he was writing a book about his family history. Others claimed he spent his evenings at nightclubs in a nearby city, romancing younger women. Some claimed that he was addicted to online gambling. Still others believed that under an assumed name he wrote a blog where he published scandalous stories involving thinly disguised versions of certain citizens of Clearview.

Rhodes didn't know whether any of the speculation was true. If anyone had seen the blog, it was always a friend of a friend. No one had ever seen Marley at a nightclub in any other city, except possibly that same friend of a friend.

Why Marley had emerged from his self-imposed solitude after many years was a mystery that nobody had asked him about. They couldn't ask because before he'd started the work on the theater, they never saw him, and now that he was out in public and doing something to improve the town, they didn't want to offend him and send him back into seclusion.

All anyone knew for sure was that Marley had decided to restore the Clearview Opera House and establish some kind of community theater there. His announced plan had been to have Harry Harris, an English teacher at the local community college, write a play for the theater's grand opening, which was to be at Christmas of the following year. The play was to be a Texas version of *A Christmas Carol*. A lot of work remained to be done on the building, but everyone was confident that another year was plenty of time to have it ready for the opening.

Rhodes wondered what would happen to those plans now, since if what Hack had told him was accurate, Jake Marley was lying dead on the stage of the opera house. It was Marley's money that was being used for all the expenses. Rhodes didn't know a thing about Marley's will, but he figured there were likely to be problems.

Rhodes drove the two and a half blocks from the Beauty Shack to the opera house in under a minute and parked in front. There was never a shortage of parking around there.

Rhodes's wife, Ivy, along with some other members of the community, was involved with the restoration of the old building, so Rhodes knew a bit about it and had visited a couple of times to see what progress had been made. The work had started with the front of the building. The theater marquee that had once jutted out over the entrance had long since disappeared and had not yet been replaced, but the box office and entrance doors had been found in fair shape behind the graffiti-covered boards that hid them. The box office and lobby had cleaned up nicely, but that was all that had been accomplished so far.

The interior of the theater was still intact but not in such good shape as the lobby had been. Many of the seats were in terrible condition. Rats had chewed on them, and the old leather had cracked where it hadn't been chewed. The springs showed through the leather in most of the seats. Water had leaked in on some of them. All would have to be replaced.

The movie screen was long gone. The heavy velvet curtain had been in place, but it had been removed for cleaning and repair. The prop room was still filled with old props and clothing, and the scenery flats just needed a good going over to remove dust and grime. Taken all together, it was a job that would require quite some time, even if Jake Marley were alive to supervise and provide the funds, and he wasn't alive, not anymore.

Or so Hack had said. Rhodes needed to find out for himself, so he went into the lobby. It hadn't been recarpeted, but the candy counter had a new glass front, and the old popcorn machine stood at one end of it looking almost ready for business. Just for a second

Rhodes imagined that he could see candy bars lined up behind the glass and smell fresh popcorn popping. The actual smell wasn't so pleasant. A scent of must and mildew still hung in the air.

Doors opened into the theater on each side of the counter. Rhodes pushed open the one on his right and entered the auditorium, with the cold air from the lobby right behind him, not that the interior of the building wasn't cold already. It didn't have a heating system that worked. That was one more thing that had to be remedied. Rhodes let the door swing shut behind him.

The auditorium had a wide center aisle and narrow aisles on each side. A light with one bulb hung above the stage. That light was burning, for reasons that Rhodes didn't want to think about at the moment, but the house lights weren't on. Too much electrical work was needed before they could be used. The first time Rhodes had looked into the theater, some light had come in through small holes in the roof, but those had been repaired. Now several battery-powered LED floodlights sat on the stage. All were turned on. One of them was angled upward toward the grid deck high above the stage, and the others showed a figure lying a little to the left of the center of the stage. A woman sat in a front-row seat on the center aisle.

When Rhodes came in, the woman stood up and turned around. "Is that you, Sheriff?"

"It's me," Rhodes said, walking down the slightly slanted aisle to the foot of the stage. There was a narrow orchestra pit, and Rhodes wondered how many instrumentalists it could have accommodated.

He had a momentary flashback to his high school days when for a time he'd been known as Will o' the Wisp Dan Rhodes, thanks to having run back a kickoff for a touchdown in the opening football game of the season. In those long-gone days he and several of the other football players for the Clearview Catamounts had perfected the art of running down the center aisle of the high school auditorium and jumping onto the stage. Rhodes didn't think it would be a good idea to try that little stunt in this theater now, or anywhere else ever again for that matter. Besides, the stage at his high school hadn't been fronted with an orchestra pit.

The woman who had spoken was Aubrey Hamilton. Hack had told Rhodes that she was the one who'd found the body. He'd told her not to touch anything and not to call the paramedics until Rhodes got there if she was sure Marley was dead.

She'd told Hack there was no doubt about it.

"I'm glad you're here, Sheriff," she said. Her voice quavered slightly. "I didn't know who to call or what to do. I've never found a dead person before, and it's very spooky to sit in an old place like this with one with a dead person in front of me."

Aubrey was a Realtor. She'd worked in an office run by a man named Ed Hopkins for a while and then opened her own one-person firm. She was about forty, and it appeared to Rhodes that she'd been crying. Rumor had it that although she was a good bit younger than Jake Marley, she might have been the only person who had known him even a little bit before he began his theater project. She was the one who'd gotten in touch with the owners of the building and arranged its sale to Marley, and she'd been in touch with him throughout the negotiations. She wore gray pants, a gray jacket, and a white blouse, very businesslike. Her sensible shoes appeared to Rhodes to have rubber soles, but they looked good with the outfit. Her smooth brown hair hung just about to her collar. Rhodes was sure that the cut wasn't a Brad Pitt, and it didn't look like Elaine's classic bob, so Rhodes had no idea what to call it. To him it was just a haircut.

"You did the right thing by calling Hack," he said. "You sit back down, and I'll go have a look."

Aubrey sat down, and Rhodes walked to the right-hand side of the auditorium, where a short stairway at the end of the orchestra pit led to the stage. When he got on the stage, he looked around but saw nothing unusual aside from the body. Some scenery flats leaned against the wall in back. The back door that led to the alley behind the theater was closed. It was a heavy metal door, which was one reason the theater had never been broken into.

Rhodes went to Marley's body, the lights casting his long shadow across the stage. Marley was dead, all right, as dead as the dime Dr Pepper or the five-cent bag of popcorn. Rhodes knelt down on one knee to have a look, careful to keep his shadow off the body. He recognized Marley's profile, the hawk nose, the close-cropped gray hair, and the one bushy eyebrow that he could see. There was what looked like a slight contusion above the eyebrow. The skin was torn, and there was a dab of blood.

Rhodes wondered if he'd ever get accustomed to death. He'd seen many dead bodies, too many of them, and every time he felt a kind of sadness come over him. Some people reached out and embraced life, and some people, like Marley, shut themselves away from it, but they all came to the same end.

It wasn't as if Rhodes had known Marley. He'd hardly ever spoken to him, but the death of any person took something out of the world that couldn't be returned, no matter what the person had been.

Rhodes looked around the bare stage. More and more often these days he was remembering little things from his high school classes. His former teachers would have been proud of him. At the moment he was recalling a play he'd read, something by William Shakespeare, that said people strutted on the stage of life for a little while and then were silent forever after. And besides that, their lives hadn't amounted to anything anyway. Marley hadn't even gotten his chance to strut. He'd waited too long to come out onstage and try to make his life mean something. Maybe Shakespeare had a point, but Rhodes didn't like it.

Rhodes looked back at Marley's body. The most likely cause of death would be a heart attack, but the odd angle of Marley's neck indicated that a heart attack most likely had not been involved. Rhodes also knew why Aubrey had been so sure that Marley was dead. It was obvious from that odd angle that his neck was broken. As a result, his brain would have stopped his heart and breathing, and Marley, while he wouldn't have died instantly, would not have lived long, seconds maybe but no more.

Rhodes felt for a pulse in Marley's neck, though he didn't expect to find one. There was nothing but stillness. Marley's skin was cool. He'd been dead for a while. It was cold in the building, which might make a difference in how fast the body cooled, but that wasn't Rhodes's concern at the moment. He patted Marley's dark blue Levis and felt a wallet in one back pocket. There was nothing in the other.

Rhodes started to turn the body over and heard vertebrae scrape together. The sound set Rhodes's teeth on edge, but he continued. Rigor mortis seemed to have only just begun, but Rhodes didn't try to estimate a time of death from that. Rigor varied too much from person to person. The autopsy would determine the time of death, so there was no need for guessing.

Something in Marley's jacket pocket jingled. Car keys. He wasn't carrying a cell phone, which didn't surprise Rhodes. If there was ever somebody who wasn't the cell phone type, even well into the twenty-first century, it was Jake Marley.

Marley's head was crushed on the side that had hit the stage, but Rhodes didn't see any other signs of harm. He wondered how a man managed to break his neck and mash in his skull in the center of a bare stage.

It wasn't possible, of course. Either someone had broken Marley's neck or Marley had fallen and broken it himself. Rhodes didn't think it was likely that someone could slip and fall on this stage and break his neck. Possible, yes. Likely, no.

There were certain things in a theater that could break someone's neck, however. Sandbags, for one thing. The theater was old, and it used what Rhodes had been told was a hemp rigging system, which meant that the lines used to raise and lower curtains and scenery were made of rope and that the counterweights were heavy sandbags.

Rhodes looked for any traces of sand on the floor near Marley's body. He saw none. He ran his hand over the floor, but his fingers encountered nothing as gritty as sand. He saw no sand on Marley's clothing or face, either.

Rhodes stood and looked up toward the grid deck high above in the fly loft. The spotlights were all in place, not that he'd thought one had fallen on Marley. He hadn't seen any traces of anything like that, and it would have taken several people to move one away from the stage had it fallen. Traces of it would still be there, and Rhodes saw no evidence of it.

Modern theaters had metal grids, but the one here was made of wood. That was something that would have to be upgraded during the theater's renovation, assuming it continued. The grid was at least two stories above the stage. A man falling from up there could easily break his neck. The fall would knock him unconscious even if it didn't break his neck, so he wouldn't be able to get out his phone and call for help for a while. If he had a phone. In Jake's case, help wasn't necessary.

One of the lights on the stage was directed upward, so it was possible that someone had been up in the grid, maybe Marley. Even with the light, it was too dark up there for Rhodes to see much. He'd be able to see better if he pointed all the lights upward, but even with that someone would have to climb up there and look around sooner or later. That someone would most likely be him.

While Rhodes wasn't afraid of heights, he didn't enjoy them, either. Clambering around on the grid wasn't his idea of a good time. He didn't mind at all that it would have to wait.

"You can call the EMTs now," he told Aubrey, "and if you don't mind, call Gene Franklin, too. He's the justice of the peace."

"All right," Aubrey said.

Her voice was steadier now, if not exactly normal. She reached to the seat next to her and got her purse from under a coat that lay on top of it. While she was digging in the purse for her phone, she asked Rhodes what she should tell the paramedics and the JP.

"Tell them that there's a dead man in the theater, and tell them that I'm here. That should be enough."

"All right," Aubrey said.

While she was making the calls, Rhodes got out his own phone and took photos of the body from several angles. He checked to be sure they were sharp and then e-mailed them to himself so he'd have them on his computer at the jail. He also e-mailed them to Mika Blackfield, who did most of the forensics work for the department, in case she could see something that he'd missed.

When he'd taken the photos and was about to leave the stage, he felt a current of cold air move through the auditorium. A couple of seconds later, Ruth Grady came in.

"Hack thought you might need some backup," she said.

"I could use your eyes here, all right," Rhodes told her, "but first go out and bring in some gloves."

Ruth went out of the auditorium and returned with a pair of nitrile gloves that she gave to Rhodes when she joined him on the stage again.

"You're treating this like a crime scene," Ruth said.

"You never know," Rhodes said.

He checked to make sure that it was indeed car keys that he'd heard in Marley's pocket. He also removed the wallet to take a quick look inside it. He saw no credit cards, just a driver's license. There were a few bills, but Rhodes didn't take them out. Satisfied that nothing was unusual, he put the wallet back in the jeans and looked out at the auditorium, where Aubrey Hamilton was still sitting as she watched what was happening on the stage. Rhodes wondered if she thought it was like a play.

"I'm sorry to keep you in this cold building," he said to her.

"I don't mind, Sheriff," she said. "I want to help if I can."

"I appreciate it," Rhodes said. He turned back to Ruth. "Seen anything suspicious?"

"Not so far," Ruth said. "I don't think there's anything suspicious to see."

"Maybe not. How's Elaine Tunstall doing?"

"I took her home to Harvey. He said he'd watch her and be sure she got back on her meds. She was fine when I left. She and Harvey were drinking coffee. I think she'll be all right."

"Did you give Harvey his sledgehammer back?"

"I slipped it to him when Elaine wasn't looking. He put it in the garage and said he'd hide it later, just in case. He's going to have somebody bring his car to him this afternoon, so everything's okay for the time being."

Rhodes hoped so. He told her what he knew about Marley's death, but he didn't know much.

Ruth looked up into the gloom of the fly loft. "You think he could've fallen from up there?"

"I can't come up with a better answer," Rhodes said, "but maybe you can. We have to consider all the possibilities. You look things over some more while I have a talk with Ms. Hamilton."

"All right," Ruth said, and Rhodes left the stage and went to where Aubrey was sitting.

Aubrey had finished the phone calls, and the purse was back in the seat beside her. Rhodes sat in the one next to it. The covering was cracked, and the stuffing showed through in a couple of spots, as did the springs.

"The EMTs and Mr. Franklin said they'd be here quickly," Aubrey said.

Rhodes nodded. He could hold off the EMTs for a little while if Ruth needed more time to look things over. The EMTs would have to wait until Hamilton had pronounced Marley dead anyway.

"Thanks," Rhodes said. "You've already been a big help, but now I have to ask you a few questions."

Aubrey nodded. "May I ask one first?"

"That's okay. Go ahead."

"How did Mr. Marley die?"

"I can't answer that one," Rhodes said. "We'll have to wait for the autopsy. My guess is that his neck is broken."

"That's what I thought. How could that happen? The fall wasn't that bad, was it?"

"I don't know how it happened," Rhodes said, "but I'll try to find out. It could take a while."

"No one else is here. It must've been some kind of accident."

"That's possible," Rhodes said.

Aubrey looked away from Rhodes. "You don't commit yourself, do you."

Rhodes was bothered by that mark over Marley's eye. "We have to investigate. I can't just make guesses and hope I'm right the first time."

"Well, I hope you find out for sure. It's very sad. Jake— Mr. Marley—was really getting interested in this theater and his play. It was wonderful to see how he was changing."

Rhodes saw his chance to get the conversation back on track and asked, "How was he changing?"

Before Aubrey could answer, Rhodes heard the ambulance siren. He stood up. "Hold on. I'll need to talk to the EMTs before you tell me. You'll have to wait here."

"I can do that."

"Good. I'll be right back."

Rhodes walked up the slanting aisle and into the lobby, where he met the EMTs, who were pushing a gurney. He knew both of them, Danny Watson and Fran Jellico. They were both good at their jobs.

"You'll have to wait for a few minutes," Rhodes said. "The JP's not here yet, and my deputy's doing some work on the scene."

"Sure," Danny said. "We can wait unless we get another call. Then we'll have to leave."

"I understand," Rhodes said.

The lobby door opened, and wind rushed in along with Gene Franklin, who wore a topcoat and a golf cap. Not many people in Clearview wore topcoats and golf caps, but Franklin could pull off the look. Rhodes wondered how he kept the cap on in the wind, but it didn't seem to be a problem for Franklin. He was tall and solemn and managed not to look like a member of a 1950s street gang in the cap, not that there were any street gangs in Blacklin County, as far as Rhodes knew.

Franklin nodded to the EMTs and said, "Another body, Sheriff?"

"That's right," Rhodes told him.

"We could just do this over the phone," Franklin said. "You know, like they did for that Supreme Court justice who died out in West Texas. They just certified his death by natural causes over the phone."

"It's probably better that you see the body in this case."

"He was an important person, that justice. We don't have any Supreme Court justices visiting here, do we?"

"It's Jake Marley."

Franklin's eyes widened. "That can't be good." He paused. "Not that it would be good if it were anybody else, either. You know what I mean. If there's anybody in the county as important as a Supreme Court justice, I guess it would be Jake Marley."

"He's an important man, all right," Rhodes said. "Come on inside and take a look."

They went into the theater and down the aisle. Franklin stopped to say hello to Aubrey and then followed Rhodes onto the stage, where Ruth Grady stood beside Marley's body.

"Did you see anything unusual?" Rhodes asked Ruth.

"No," she said, and pointed to the fly loft. "I can't see much up there, though. Too dark."

"We'll get some more light there in a little while. Let's get out of the way and let Gene examine the body."

Franklin pulled a packet of disposable vinyl gloves from inside his topcoat. He opened the packet, pulled out the gloves, and stuck the packet back inside his coat. He pulled on the gloves and knelt down to check the body. The examination didn't take long.

"I can certify that he's dead, all right," Franklin said. He stood up and removed his gloves. "But not the cause of death. Looks like a broken neck, but what caused it?"

"We're still working on that part," Rhodes said.

"Could be an accident," Franklin said. "A fall or something like that."

"Maybe," Rhodes said. "We can't be sure yet."

"When you're involved, it's usually not an accident. I can see why you wouldn't want to handle it over the phone, not that I plan to start doing that."

"My involvement doesn't mean anything," Rhodes said. "I just happened to be close by when the call came in."

"There's no sign that it's anything but an accident," Ruth said.

"Maybe not," Rhodes said, "but it's best to treat it as a suspicious death. That way there won't be any mistakes that we'll regret later."

Franklin put the gloves in an outside pocket of his coat. "That's fine with me. I'll put down that the immediate cause of death is a broken neck but that the underlying cause is undetermined, pending an autopsy. If that's all you need me for, I'll be going. You want me to send in the EMTs?"

"Yes," Rhodes said. "Thanks."

"This is really going to shake things up around town," Franklin said, shaking his head. "It's too bad it happened just when Marley was getting interested in the town and doing something for it."

"Too bad it had to happen anytime," Rhodes said.

"Yes, that's true. I'll guess I'd better go and get the paperwork done."

"If you don't mind, when you give Dr. White a call about the autopsy, tell him that it should be done as soon as possible. Maybe this afternoon."

Dr. White was a retired physician who was a certified forensic pathologist, and he'd worked for the county for as long as Rhodes had been the sheriff. Rhodes thought the county was lucky to have him.

"I'll be sure to tell him," Franklin said. He left the stage, and Rhodes and Ruth watched him walk back up the aisle.

"Wait a second," Rhodes called after him, and Franklin turned back. "Have them drive around to the alley. I'll open the door for them. It'll be easier that way."

"Sure, be glad to tell them," Franklin said, and went on out.

When he was gone, Ruth turned to Rhodes and asked quietly so Aubrey wouldn't hear, "You do think it was an accident, don't you?"

"Let's just say I *hope* it's an accident. How's that?"

"And if it's not?"

"That's what we need to find out," Rhodes said.

Chapter 3

▼

When the body had been removed, Rhodes told Ruth to ask at the few businesses up and down the street to find out if anyone had seen Marley come into the theater that morning.

"That shouldn't take long," Ruth said.

"You can come back when you're finished asking," Rhodes said. "I'll still be here. I need to talk to Aubrey."

They left the stage together. Ruth went on up the aisle to the exit, and Rhodes looked toward the back of the theater and saw the little balcony that overhung the back few rows of seats. Above the balcony were openings for spotlights and the movie projector that had been installed when the opera house converted to a theater. Rhodes wondered if the old projector was still there. He hadn't thought to ask anyone about that.

"Did you ever come to the movies here?" Aubrey asked.

"I'm older than you are," Rhodes said, "but I'm not that old." He sat down in the seat he had vacated earlier. "I'm sure there are people in the town who did see movies here, though."

For a second he wondered what might have played in the old theater. Abbott and Costello movies? War movies with John Wayne? Westerns with Roy Rogers?

"Now we don't even have a theater," Aubrey said.

Rhodes nodded. "People seem happy enough watching movies at home."

"Maybe so, but there's nothing like watching with an audience."

"I was just about to ask you how Jake was changing," Rhodes said, getting back on task. "Now you can tell me."

"It was obvious to everybody who was around him here," Aubrey said. "He was getting out of his house, he was coming to town, he was dealing with people. Before, he was a very private person. As far as I know he hadn't done any of those things."

He hadn't done them as far as Rhodes knew, either, and he wondered what had happened to get Marley on the move.

"Did you talk to him about that?" Rhodes asked.

"No, I didn't want to pry. I didn't know him that well. I'd heard about him, but I don't think I'd ever seen him until he called me and asked about buying this old building."

"I'm curious about that. Did he ever mention why he wanted it?"

"For a play," Aubrey said, as if surprised that Rhodes would ask. "I thought everybody knew about the play."

"I know about it," Rhodes said, "but I don't know why he wanted to do a play, and I don't know why he wanted to do it now. For a long time he didn't seem to care much about the town or anything else."

"He didn't tell me why he wanted this building, other than for the play. I thought that was the only reason."

"Maybe it was," Rhodes said, but he didn't quite believe it. "Tell me what happened this morning to bring you here."

"It didn't happen this morning. It happened last night. Mr. Marley called me and asked me to meet him here this morning. He said he had something he wanted to ask me about."

"He didn't say what it was?"

"No. I just assumed it had to do with real estate, that maybe he wanted to buy another building or something like that. It's not as if we were friends and talked things over. And I've been helping a little with the restoration. Because of my work, I know a lot of the people around town who do carpentry and odd jobs."

Rhodes wondered if Marley might have had other motives for calling Aubrey. Her husband had died a couple of years previously in a pipeline accident, just as she was getting her Realtor's license. She was an attractive woman, younger than Marley by a good many years, but that didn't mean that Marley might not have been interested in her as someone who could be a friend. Or more than a friend. Rhodes looked at her left hand. There was no wedding ring on her third finger, but Rhodes had no way of knowing when she'd stopped wearing it. She wore no rings of any kind.

"Maybe Jake wanted to ask you out," Rhodes said.

Aubrey hesitated. "You mean on a date?"

"I do."

"That's flattering, but you're wrong. He just wasn't interested. Has he ever gone out with anyone?"

"Not that I've heard about."

"There you go, then. He wasn't going to start with me, either."

Rhodes gave up on that idea for the moment, but it was something he'd keep in the back of his mind.

"Did he say what he was going to be doing here?"

"No, but he comes down here often to look things over and see what progress is being made. He was probably checking on something or other."

"What time did you get here?"

Aubrey looked at her watch. Rhodes was surprised she still wore one. A lot of people didn't, not anymore.

"It's almost noon," Aubrey said. "I was supposed to meet Mr. Marley at eleven, but I was early. So I guess I got here about ten forty-five. I came right in, and that's when I saw him. I went up on the stage, and I could tell right away that he was dead. I called your office then."

Rhodes thought about what he'd learned. Not much, but maybe there wasn't anything to learn. Maybe Marley had just had an accident.

"It's funny," Aubrey said, "sitting in an empty theater with a dead man, I mean. A person starts thinking all kinds of things." She shivered. "Do you believe in ghosts, Sheriff?"

Rhodes didn't want to talk about ghosts. "No, I don't."

"Me, neither," Aubrey said, "but sometimes I wonder."

Rhodes stood up, dismissing the idea, and thanked Aubrey for her help. "I'll call you if any other questions come to mind."

"I'll be glad to do whatever I can," Aubrey said. "Mr. Marley was a nice man, not at all like people said he was."

"What did people say he was?"

"You know. Gruff, standoffish. He wasn't like that at all."

"Maybe not with you," Rhodes said.

Aubrey picked up her purse and coat. "Not with anybody. You ask people who worked with him here. You'll see."

"That might not be necessary," Rhodes told her.

"You should ask anyway. You'll find out that he was really a nice man."

Rhodes could ask Ivy. She'd had a little contact with Marley in working on the restoration. Marley had applied to the insurance firm she worked for to get updated coverage for the building, and Ivy had become interested in the project. She'd had more contact with Marley than Rhodes ever had.

"I'll ask around," he said, and Aubrey put on her coat and left the theater.

Rhodes was on the stage arranging the lights not already pointed toward the grid deck so that they all pointed upward when Ruth Grady came back in.

"I didn't find out a thing," she said, walking toward the stage. "Nobody was at the church, and nobody in any of the buildings up and down the street noticed anybody come into the building or leave it."

"Did you ask over at the law offices?"

Ruth stopped walking and didn't speak.

"Okay," Rhodes said. "I shouldn't have asked that. I know you always do things right. I guess nobody there saw anything, either."

"That's right. Mr. Marley was probably in here alone and fell from the fly loft. He could have climbed up there and had a heart attack."

"We don't want to make up our minds before we've checked everything," Rhodes said.

Ruth climbed the stairs to the stage. "I know. I'm just speculating." She stared up at the fly loft. "I can see things up there a lot better now."

She and Rhodes stood quietly for a minute looking up at the grid. It seemed sturdy enough, but a man could easily fall off the edge if he wasn't careful.

"There might be a small gap there, but I don't see any breaks," Ruth said. "Somebody's going to have to go up."

"I know," Rhodes said. "I'll do it."

"I was hoping you'd say that, but before you go, I have a question."

Rhodes didn't mind the delay. "What?"

Ruth pointed to the bare bulb that hung above the stage. "What's that light for?"

Rhodes sighed. He wasn't sure the delay would be worth it. "I wish you hadn't asked me that."

"Why?"

"Your friend Seepy Benton, that's why."

Seepy Benton, or Dr. C. P. Benton as he was known at the local community college where he taught mathematics, was a dedicated amateur sleuth who believed that by virtue of having attended a citizens' sheriff's academy he was practically a member of the department. He was also dating Ruth.

"What does Seepy have to do with a lightbulb?" Ruth asked.

Rhodes was tempted to make a joke about the number of mathematicians it took to screw in a lightbulb, but he knew it wouldn't be a good idea. So he said, "It's a ghost light."

"A ghost light? What's that?"

Ivy had told Rhodes about the superstition, and of course Jennifer Loam had written about the light on her Web site.

"I thought everybody knew about the light," Rhodes said. "Hasn't Seepy told you?"

"He might have, but I don't remember that he's mentioned it."

"It's been written up on *A Clear View of Clearview*."

"The only articles I read on that site are the ones about you."

Rhodes wasn't sure whether she was leading him on, and he wasn't going to ask, so he explained about the ghost light. "It's what they call a light that's left burning in a dark theater."

"I don't see what that has to do with ghosts."

Rhodes didn't want to talk about that part of it because that was what interested Seepy Benton, but he continued anyway. "Some people believe that all theaters are haunted. The ghost light is left on so the ghosts can give performances. That way they'll be happy and won't curse the theater."

"That doesn't make sense," Ruth said.

"I agree," Rhodes said.

Ruth grinned. "Everybody knows that ghosts can see in the dark."

"Don't start with that," Rhodes said. "You've been hanging around with Seepy too long."

In addition to being a math teacher, Seepy Benton had started a ghost-hunting business as a sideline, which was why the ghost light was of particular interest to him. Rhodes had hoped that Seepy would forget the ghost hunting when school started again, and it seemed that he had. Recently, however, he'd taken it up again.

Rhodes had to admit that Benton had been helpful in a previous case involving a ghost, not that anybody had proved it was a real ghost. Rhodes didn't believe in ghosts, or so he kept telling himself and anyone who asked him, including most recently Aubrey Hamilton. Anyway, he didn't want Benton getting involved in this case or looking for any ghosts.

"The light would have had to be on for a long time to keep the ghosts happy in this place," Ruth said. "It's kind of a creepy old building."

The length of time the light had been on was another thing that Rhodes didn't want to talk about.

"All that was in Jennifer Loam's story. You could look it up."

"Or you could just tell me and save me the time."

"Well," Rhodes said, and stopped.

"Well, what?"

"Well, when the building was opened up for the first time, they found the light on," Rhodes said. "It seems that it had been on all the years that the building was closed."

Ruth looked skeptical. "The bulb would've burned out."

"Maybe not. It seems to be a very old one, but somebody looked up the record on the Internet and found out that some lightbulbs have lasted for a long time. There's one somewhere out in California that's burned for more than a million hours. It even has its own home page. Jennifer Loam wrote about it in her story."

"I can never tell when you're kidding me," Ruth said.

"I'm not kidding you. That's something else you could look up."

Ruth shook her head. "I'll trust you. What about the electricity in this building? Are you telling me it's been on all the years that this place was shut down?"

"That's right. The bill was always the minimum charge, and the owners never bothered to have it shut off."

"They must have money."

"Probably," Rhodes said. "If they didn't before, they do now, since Jake bought the building."

"The bulb was really burning all that time?"

"I was told that it was on when the first people came in after the boards were removed from the front of the building."

"That's really odd. I'm going to ask Seepy about ghost lights."

"He already knows."

"He does?"

"He reads Jennifer's Web site. He's been wanting to come in here with his ghost-hunting equipment and check things out. He didn't want to ask Marley, because he was sure he'd get turned down. So instead, he's been trying to get me to ask him."

"He never mentioned it to me," Ruth said.

"He will now."

"Why do you think that?"

"Because," Rhodes said, looking down at the floor where the body had been, "now he'll think there's another ghost."

"Another one?"

"You know what I mean. I don't think there ever was a ghost or that Jake Marley's going to haunt the place. That's just what Seepy will think. I know how his mind works."

"I'm not so sure anybody knows that," Ruth said, "and I'm not so sure you don't believe in them, too. Ghosts, I mean."

"I'm sure, though," Rhodes said. "I don't believe in them."

It was already cold in the auditorium, but as Rhodes spoke, the temperature dropped. He and Ruth turned toward the entrance, expecting to see someone come in, but no one did.

"I thought somebody had opened the front door," Ruth said.

"So did I," Rhodes said. "It must have gotten colder outside."

"That can't be it. It's already gotten warmer in here again. What happened?"

"It's just drafty in here," Rhodes said. "Old buildings have a lot of cracks in them."

That wasn't what Seepy Benton would have said, Rhodes was sure. Seepy would have brought up spectral presences and ectoplasm and things like that, but Rhodes wasn't going to get into that discussion.

"It was nothing," he said. "Let's see about getting up into the fly loft."

"You mean, let's see about *you* getting up into the fly loft."

"Exactly," Rhodes said.

Chapter 4

▼

The only way to get to the grid was by climbing straight up a metal ladder that was bolted to the back wall of the building. Rhodes stood beside the ladder and looked up. He estimated that the roof of the building was about fifty feet from the stage. The grid was lower than that, but Rhodes wondered if someone as tall as he was would have any headroom at all. He didn't think there would be much.

"You could always call Buddy and have him climb up there," Ruth said.

Buddy was another of the deputies. He was smaller than Rhodes, and younger, too.

"I'm already here," Rhodes said. He took one of the ladder's rungs in his hands and tried to shake it. It didn't move. "Marley climbed up there, or we think he did. If he can do it, I can do it."

"I believe it," Ruth said. "There's a lot of stuff up there, pulleys and ropes and stuff. I wonder what Mr. Marley was doing?"

"Inspecting it, probably," Rhodes said. "To be sure it was safe."

"I guess it wasn't as safe as he thought."

"You're just trying to cheer me up," Rhodes said, and he started up the ladder. He was still wearing the nitrile gloves, so he had a good grip on the cold iron rungs.

The climb wasn't bad, and soon Rhodes poked his head through the opening onto the grid. It was colder up there than it had been on the stage, and it was draftier. Rhodes heard the wind blowing across the roof and rattling things around up there.

The illumination from the LED lights came up through the gaps and cracks in the grid and threw shadows all around. Rhodes could make out numerous ropes and pulleys, and he was glad he didn't have to work up there and try to figure out how to use them. He'd probably get tangled up in the ropes and create havoc down below.

He climbed on up and stepped off the ladder onto the catwalk. The headroom was adequate, but only barely. If he'd been wearing a hat, he'd have had to remove it. Even in the poor light, Rhodes could see dust and dirt everywhere, and he could tell that it had been disturbed on the catwalk. Someone had been up there, all right, and it had probably been Marley.

"Are you all right there?" Ruth called from below.

"I'm okay. I'm going to look around a little."

The problem with the catwalk, as far as Rhodes was concerned, was that it lacked a railing. He could imagine some agile young fellow from early in the last century roaming around and handling ropes, lowering scenery flats and pulling them back up, but Rhodes wasn't young, and he wasn't agile. He'd have to be careful, as Marley would have had to be.

The catwalk appeared to Rhodes to be none too sturdy. He didn't like the way it sagged and trembled a bit under his weight, and he didn't like the way some of the boards creaked when he stepped on them. He wondered if any of the boards were rotten. If one of them broke and he fell over the side, he could try grabbing one of the ropes. Tarzan could have done it without any trouble, but Rhodes wasn't too sure about himself. He didn't have a lot in common with Tarzan.

He worked his way to about the center of the stage to check the gap they'd seen from below. A man of Marley's size could have slipped through with room to spare. Rhodes knelt down. The dust and dirt were disturbed, sure enough, and that meant someone could have fallen at that spot.

He saw Ruth below, looking up at him. Dust motes drifted through the beams of light.

"I think Marley did fall from here," Rhodes said. "It's a long way down."

"You know what they say about falls and sudden stops," Ruth said. "It's a sad thing to have happened. Just a stupid accident."

"Maybe so," Rhodes said.

He stood up and made his way back to the ladder. He was glad it extended well up through the opening so that he could step right onto it. He didn't like the idea of having to feel for the rungs below with his feet.

When he was back on the stage, Ruth came over to the ladder.

"Case closed?" she asked.

"We'll have to wait for the autopsy," Rhodes said, pulling off the gloves and stuffing them into his jacket pocket.

"I know, but he did fall, didn't he?"

"Looks that way. Why he fell is another question."

"He could've gotten disoriented and slipped. Or he could've had a heart attack."

"Both of those are good possibilities."

"It could even be suicide."

"That's true," Rhodes said. "Unlikely, but possible. He did call

Aubrey and ask her to meet him here. Suicides sometimes do things like that, I've been told."

"You sure don't like to commit yourself," Ruth said.

"I just like to keep an open mind until we know everything we can know, but I'll give you this much: It was probably an accident."

"I don't see how it could've been anything else."

"Are you sure about that? Give it a little more thought."

Ruth opened her mouth to speak, then shut it. She stood there looking at Rhodes.

"What?" Rhodes asked.

"I get it now," Ruth said. "I didn't miss it. I just didn't think enough about it."

"About what?"

"About that place on Mr. Marley's forehead just above his eye."

"What about it?"

"You know what. You've been thinking about it all along. If Mr. Marley fell from up in the grid, he'd have been knocked unconscious when he hit, most likely, if he wasn't dead already. He wouldn't have turned his head over. So where did that abrasion come from?"

"You're right," Rhodes said. "That's been bothering me. That's the suspicious thing about his death. We'll need the autopsy to tell us more about that abrasion or whatever it is, but I don't want to take any chances."

"He could've hit his head on a board in the grid when he fell off the catwalk," Ruth said.

Rhodes nodded. "A definite possibility."

"He could've had a heart attack up there and fallen because of that."

"Another good possibility."

"Here's a thought. A ghost might've pushed him."

"Don't start that," Rhodes said.

"Just kidding." Ruth said. "I should've thought about that contusion to begin with, though."

"You thought of it now, and that's soon enough."

"I'm not so sure."

"Trust me," Rhodes said. "It's not going to change a thing for Marley or our investigation. For now we'd better put the lights back where they were and then turn them off. I don't know what's going to happen to the theater with Jake Marley out of the picture."

"The show must go on," Ruth said.

"Not unless somebody pays for it," Rhodes said.

A fresh breeze blew through the theater, and Rhodes looked toward the back to see Jennifer Loam coming inside.

"I'm too late for the excitement, I suppose," she said.

Jennifer was young, sharp, and ambitious. Her youth, blond hair, and wide blue eyes might have led some people to think of her as being more decorative than businesslike. They would be badly fooled if they made that mistake. She'd been a reporter for the local newspaper, but it had been sold to owners who downsized the staff to almost nothing and cut the publication schedule from five days a week to three. Rhodes figured the next step would be to make it a weekly.

Instead of leaving town when she lost her job, Jennifer had started her Web site, which at this point was read by everybody in the county who had a PC, a tablet, or a smartphone, and which had an audience in other counties as well. She had a lot of advertisers, probably more than the newspaper, and Rhodes's only problem with the site was her tendency toward sensationalism. She had explained that the tabloid nature of the site was necessary if she wanted to get a lot of page views, and she needed the page views to attract advertisers. Rhodes understood, but he didn't like it, especially when she was exaggerating about him or something he'd done.

"There wasn't any excitement," Rhodes said.

"You must be joking," Jennifer said, walking down the center aisle to stand in front of the stage. "Jake Marley is dead. That's big news."

"Sad, too," Rhodes said, "but not exciting."

"It is for my readers. Maybe not as exciting as the action at the Beauty Shack today, though. I missed that, too."

"You're slipping," Rhodes said.

"I was covering another story. Some kids got into a fight at the high school. If this kind of thing keeps up, I'll have to hire another reporter."

"Seepy Benton might be interested," Ruth said. "He seems to be in the middle of a lot of things around town."

Rhodes suppressed a groan. "I thought he was already a reporter for you."

"Only part-time," Ruth said. "Lately, not even that."

"I need someone who could work full-time," Jennifer said. "Seepy was good, but he has to be in class a lot."

Rhodes relaxed. "I'm sure you can find somebody. Right now, though, Deputy Grady needs to get back on patrol, and I need to get back to the jail."

"You wouldn't deny me an interview, would you? I know you believe in cooperating with the press."

"How long has it been since there was an actual press involved in news reporting?" Rhodes asked. "I'll bet it was before you were even born."

"It's just an expression. The founding fathers didn't foresee computers and coldset printing. We still call ourselves the press, though, even if there are very few presses left. So how about the interview?"

"I can give you five minutes," Rhodes said. "Deputy Grady, you can get back on the streets."

"Yes, sir!" Ruth said, and she gave Rhodes a salute before she turned and left the stage.

"You get a lot of respect," Jennifer said.

Rhodes thought of himself as the Rodney Dangerfield of sheriffs, but he didn't say so. He said, "Let's go down in front and have a seat."

They sat in the same seats that Rhodes and Aubrey had sat in, and Jennifer took her little video camera from her bag.

"You don't need to record this," Rhodes said. "Just take notes."

"This is easier," Jennifer said. "Tell me what happened."

Rhodes sat up straighter, Jennifer started the camera, and Rhodes told her the facts of Marley's death as simply as possible.

"So there's no indication of foul play?" Jennifer asked.

Rhodes hadn't heard the phrase "foul play" in a long time, if ever, but he tried not to smile as he answered. He figured he was as good at clichés as Jennifer was.

"There's no indication of foul play," he said.

Jennifer looked disappointed. "So your investigation into the death is closed?"

"Until we find out the results of the autopsy, yes."

Jennifer perked up. "Do you expect the autopsy to show that there was foul play?"

That was three mentions of "foul play" in under a minute. Rhodes wondered what the record was.

"No," he lied, "I don't."

Jennifer's look of dejection returned.

Rhodes hated to see her look so disappointed. "Look at it this way. Even if Marley died by accident, there'll be an investigation. Other things have to be considered, too."

"What other things?"

"I'll check on this, but as far as I know there aren't any heirs. His lawyer will have a copy of his will and might even be the executor. If that's the case, depending on the lawyer, of course, the sheriff's department might be asked to look into the house to make sure everything's in order."

Rhodes didn't add that he'd certainly be going to the house if Marley hadn't died by a simple accident.

"And if you get into the house?" Jennifer asked.

"Maybe we'll find out all Marley's secrets."

Jennifer was smiling now. "How do you think this will affect the restoration of the theater?"

"We'll just have to wait and see, won't we?" Rhodes stood up. "And now I have to get back to work, serving the community and protecting its citizens from crime."

Jennifer laughed and turned off her camera. "You made me ruin your last comment. Maybe I can clean up the sound before I put it on the Web site, though."

"I hope so," Rhodes said. "I wouldn't want the voters to think you were laughing at me." He stood up. "I have to turn off the lights. You'd better leave now."

"I can wait," Jennifer said. "You might think of something else to tell me."

"I doubt it," Rhodes said.

He went up on the stage and turned off the LED lights one at a time. The ghost light gave just enough illumination for him to see his way back down to the auditorium, and he joined Jennifer at the front row of seats.

"Now let's get out of here and let me get back to work before criminals take over the county," he said.

"No chance of that," Jennifer said, "not with you in charge of protecting the citizens."

"True," Rhodes said, "but it's best not to take chances. And on that subject, you be careful walking up the aisle. The old carpet has some kinks in it."

He started up the aisle, with Jennifer right behind, not bothered at all by the carpet kinks. She caught up with him at the lobby, and they were almost to the door leading outside when Dr. Harry Harris and Dr. Seepy Benton came through it. The blast of cold air was bad enough, but seeing Harry and Seepy made Rhodes feel even worse.

"We just heard the news about Jake Marley," Seepy said. "It's a good thing we're on our lunch hour."

Seepy wore a stained black fedora that had seen better days at some point in the distant past. Rhodes hadn't seen it in those days. Seepy didn't have a thin spot in his hair. He had almost no hair at all on the top of his head, so he needed a hat on cold days and sunny days and most other days. He wore jeans, a plaid shirt, and a heavy black coat, unbuttoned, and his salt-and-pepper beard was neatly trimmed, which wasn't always the case.

"Why are you here?" Rhodes asked.

"You say that like you aren't happy to see me," Seepy said.

"I'm thrilled. Why are you here?"

"Ghosts," Harris said.

Harris was dressed like Rhodes thought a college professor should look. He wore a dark blue wool blazer, slacks, and a white shirt with a light blue tie with some kind of squiggly designs on it. He had a goatee that gave him a scholarly look. At one time he'd gotten in trouble at the college, but he'd repented of his sins and was back in the good graces of the administration. He was also Benton's partner in the ghost-hunting business.

"There aren't any ghosts here," Rhodes said.

"Don't count on it," Seepy said. "Mr. Marley has just died. His spirit is probably still lingering in the theater."

"That's not possible," Rhodes said.

"That's what you told us the last time we helped you out," Seepy said. "You were wrong then, too."

"I wasn't wrong," Rhodes said.

" 'That's, like, just your opinion, dude.' "

"I've seen that movie," Rhodes said. "It's not my favorite."

Seepy's eyes widened. "I didn't know you watched Coen brothers movies. I thought you were more the Adam Sandler type."

Rhodes preferred old movies, especially bad ones. It seemed he never had time to watch movies these days, however, and nobody showed the bad ones on television anymore anyway. Adam Sandler movies were bad, he had to admit, but not in the way that appealed to Rhodes.

"Don't make me hurt you," Rhodes said. "Ms. Loam and I are about to leave now, and you need to do the same."

"I don't think so," Seepy said. "We have permission to be here."

"Who gave you permission?"

"I did," Harry said.

Rhodes was skeptical. "Somehow that doesn't seem right."

"I'll explain." Harris adopted a lecturing tone. "As you may know, I'm writing the play to be presented when the theater opens, so I was working closely with Mr. Marley. He not only gave me permission to visit the theater, he gave me a key in case I needed to check something out."

Harris reached into a pants pocket, pulled out a key on a silver ring, and held it up for Rhodes to see.

"How closely were you working with Jake?"

"It depends on how you define *close*. We e-mailed now and then."

"You didn't meet him in person?"

"No. He even mailed me this key, but I do have it, along with his permission to be here."

Rhodes knew there was no use arguing. Harry and Seepy hadn't dared come into the theater when Jake was alive, at least not for ghost hunting, because they'd been afraid he wouldn't put up with them. Now that he was gone, they hadn't wasted any time in taking advantage of the situation. Rhodes couldn't stop them from going inside, but he wasn't going to let them roam around on their own. He still wasn't convinced that Marley's death was an accident.

"Who else has a key?" Rhodes asked.

"Several people, I believe," Harry said. "We can come and go as we please."

"Is that a key to the front or the back?"

"The front. Nobody has a key to the back except Jake."

"All right," Rhodes said. "You can go in, but I'm going with you."

"What about the criminals taking over the county?" Jennifer asked.

"We'll just have to risk it," Rhodes said.

"It's worth it," Jennifer said. "I'm going in, too. This will be great for my Web site."

"Publicity," Seepy said. "I love it. Let's go, Harry."

The two men breezed past Rhodes and Jennifer and entered the theater.

"Isn't this exciting?" Jennifer said.

"No," Rhodes said.

"What is it, then?"

Rhodes didn't even have to think about it. "Aggravating," he said.

Chapter 5

▼

Seepy and Harry had gone right through the lobby and into the auditorium. Rhodes assumed they didn't think ghosts would be hanging out in the lobby. Maybe ghosts didn't like popcorn.

Rhodes went into the auditorium with Jennifer on his heels. Seepy and Harry stood in the middle of the center aisle, and Seepy was looking at something he held in his right hand. Rhodes knew from his previous dealings with the ghost hunters that the thing Seepy held was a combination EMF meter and thermometer. It could measure both a disturbance in the electromagnetic field and sudden drops in temperature, both of which were associated with ghosts, at least according to Seepy.

Rhodes tried not to think of the temperature change he and Ruth Grady had recently experienced. It was only natural that things like that would happen in a drafty old building.

"Let me turn on some lights," Rhodes said. He wouldn't have admitted it to Seepy, but the place did look a bit like something ghosts would inhabit, with the ghost light casting long, wobbly shadows in the near-darkness.

"We don't need any more light," Seepy said. "We have one. The ghost light is just right. We want the conditions to be as much like they were over the years the building was closed as possible. That way the ghosts will be comfortable."

"Nobody ever died in here," Rhodes said. "Except Jake Marley, I mean. There won't be any ghosts."

"It doesn't matter if anybody died here," Harris said. "Some of the actors who performed here might have had the best times of their lives on this stage. That memory would have drawn them back here after their deaths. They'd want to go on performing in the plays that gave them such enjoyment."

"Ghosts are partial to the places where they were happy," Seepy said. "I think my ghost will haunt the classrooms where I was teaching the ideas from my paper on 'Algebraic Models for Constructivist Theories of Perception.'"

"I have a feeling your students' ghosts won't be there," Rhodes said.

"Always the kidder," Seepy said.

"I don't see how there could be such things as ghosts," Jennifer said. "It's just not logical."

Good for you, Rhodes thought, but Seepy wasn't going to let her get away with that kind of comment.

"Of course it's logical," Seepy said. "It's simple quantum mechanics."

Jennifer gave him a doubting look. "I think that's a contradiction in terms. There's no such thing as simple quantum mechanics."

"There is if you're brilliant," Seepy said.

Rhodes grinned. Seepy wasn't exactly the most modest person in Blacklin County, or even in the state of Texas, for that matter.

"I should have phrased it differently," Seepy said. "Elementary quantum physics, maybe. Let me explain it."

He handed Harry the EMF meter, and Harry wandered off, looking at the dials. Harry had probably heard it all before. Several times.

"It has to do with duality," Seepy said. "Photons and electrons have a dual nature. They act like both particles and waves."

"Stop right there," Jennifer said. "You'll have to explain particles and waves."

"Light," Seepy said, pointing to the ghost light. "Is it a wave or a particle? According to quantum physics, it's both."

"Oh," Jennifer said, and Rhodes wondered if she really understood what Seepy was talking about. Rhodes was pretty sure he didn't, even if she did.

"So," Seepy continued, "if subatomic particles can have a dual nature, why can't there be a duality of the soul and the body, too? Everything has a quantum code, and the information that's written on our brains could be uploaded into what we might call a spiritual quantum field. We die, or our bodies do, but that information—our consciousness—lives on. Thus, ghosts."

Rhodes didn't get it. This wasn't exactly the same explanation as the one that Seepy had given him previously. It was, if anything, even more complex, no matter how much Seepy was simplifying it.

"Let me put it another way," Seepy said. "We like to think that the universe was created first, and then consciousness showed up. What if consciousness came first and created the universe? If that's true, we create the world around us, too."

"How?" Jennifer asked.

Rhodes wished she hadn't. Seepy liked nothing better than an audience for his lectures. Rhodes felt like asking if there was going to be an exam when he finished talking.

"Do you have an office?" Seepy asked Jennifer. "A place where you do the work on your site?"

"Yes, sure."

"Do you know what it looks like?"

"Of course."

"No, you don't, not really, and in fact it doesn't exist until you or someone sees it. It's like the tree that doesn't make any noise when it falls in the forest."

"The tree makes sound waves or whatever they are," Jennifer said. "I remember that from one of my science classes."

"Right," Seepy said, "but the waves aren't sound because there's no receiver to convert them. In your office the light is hitting the computer and whatever else is there and bouncing off. If you were there, you'd be the receiver. You'd see colors and shapes, but you're not there. There's no receiver, so the office doesn't exist. You create it when you see it."

Rhodes thought all this sounded like a lot of baloney, which reminded him that he was hungry. A baloney sandwich would be good, but Ivy bought only turkey baloney. Rhodes didn't believe in turkey baloney.

"What does that have to do with ghosts?" he asked.

"Consciousness creates things, not vice versa," Seepy said. "It doesn't disappear when we die. It just goes somewhere else."

"I think I get it," Jennifer said.

Rhodes didn't get it, and he was about to say so when Harry called out from a spot near the steps up to the stage.

"Over here," he said. "I have a reading."

Seepy hurried over to join his ghost-hunting colleague, and Jennifer asked Rhodes if he thought Seepy could be right about ghosts.

"I didn't understand a word he said," Rhodes told her, "except the part about the tree falling in the woods. I don't believe in ghosts. Do you?"

"Not really," Jennifer said, "but it'll make a good story for the Web site if they find something that resembles one. I don't think I'll record an interview with Seepy, though. My readers would just write 'TLDR' in the comments."

"TLDR?"

" 'Too long, didn't read.' What's that thing they're looking at?"

"Ghosts supposedly affect electromagnetic fields," Rhodes said, recalling what Seepy had told him about the EMF meter at another time. "That thing Harris has measures them. The thing is, though, magnetic fields vary all the time, and lots of things affect them. Cell phones, electric wiring, computers, you name it. It's no big deal."

"They act like it's a big deal."

"That's because they want it to be."

"Are you here, Mr. Marley?" Seepy called out. "Can you hear us?"

Rhodes sighed.

Jennifer looked expectant.

Jake didn't answer. Neither did anyone, or anything, else.

"False alarm," Harry said. "I'll go up on the stage and try it there."

Rhodes didn't want him on the stage, although there wasn't much chance that he'd mess anything up. With Rhodes and Ruth and the JP having been up there, not to mention the EMS team, any evidence of what Jennifer had called foul play was contaminated anyway. As far as Rhodes knew, for that matter, there hadn't been any foul play. It was just that he had a hunch, a feeling that he couldn't explain.

Not that it had anything to do with ghosts. He'd had hunches in the past that had led to things of some importance, and there hadn't been any ghosts around. He was sure of that.

There was nothing supernatural about hunches. Rhodes was sure they were based on things he'd seen or heard but hadn't consciously processed. It just took a while for his brain to bring them to his attention.

Rhodes's cell phone rang.

Benton and Harris turned to look at him as if he'd cussed in church. They must have thought he'd scared off their nonexistent ghost.

Rhodes grinned, shrugged, and pulled out his phone. It was the first time since he'd had it that he could remember being glad that it had rung.

"This is Hack," Hack said when Rhodes answered. "You busy?"

"Hunting ghosts," Rhodes said.

"I thought you didn't believe in ghosts."

"I didn't mean *I* was hunting them. The good doctors Harris and Benton are doing the hunting, but it appears they believe your phone call has disturbed their communication with the spirit world. They aren't happy with you right now."

"I sure am sorry about that, but I had to call. You need to come back to the jail."

"Is it an emergency?"

"Nope, you just need to get back here, is all."

"Are you going to tell me why, or do I have to beat it out of you when I get there?"

"You might think you're funny," Hack said, "but you ain't."

"So you keep telling me."

"Ever'body else does, too. You comin' back, or not?"

Rhodes didn't like the idea of leaving Seepy and Harry on their own in the theater. Jennifer could watch them, but he doubted that she'd try to keep them out of mischief. She might even encourage them.

"I'm not coming unless you give me a good reason," Rhodes said.

"Okay. The reason is, there's two women here to see you."

"Do they have a reason for wanting to see me?"

"Yeah," Hack said.

"Well, what is it?"

"They want to discuss your sex life," Hack said.

Chapter 6

▼

Rhodes had been hoping that he'd have time for lunch, but Hack's call had put an end to that idea. Now he'd have to go back to the jail and discuss his sex life.

A few years ago, someone had held a writing conference at an abandoned college in Obert. One of Clearview's former citizens who had gone on to become a model for romance novel covers had been murdered at the conference. Rhodes had investigated the crime and found the killer.

That was the good news. The bad news, at least as far as Rhodes was concerned, was that two women attending the conference had either learned something at it or had some natural talent for writing. They'd written a book about a Texas lawman named Sage Barton, a two-gun hero with .45 revolvers and the desire to use them. The book had sold well, and Sage Barton had returned in another volume. And another.

That was fine for the writers but not for Rhodes. Because the writers had known Rhodes and because Sage Barton bore a negligible physical resemblance to him, people in Clearview, where the books sold very well indeed, seemed to assume that Barton was based entirely on Rhodes.

Rhodes had enough trouble living down all the publicity he got on Jennifer Loam's Web site, and having people think of him as some kind of action hero had made matters considerably worse. At one time there had even been movie interest in the books, but that seemed to have faded for the moment, much to Rhodes's relief if not to the financial benefit of the authors.

Although Seepy Benton pointed out as often as possible that he and Sage Barton had the same initials, making it obvious who was really the model for Barton, no one took that argument seriously. Rhodes could understand why, but he wished they'd at least consider it. As it was, he was stuck with the identification and continued to feel that the less people heard about Sage Barton, the better.

If there was anything he didn't need, it was to have the authors of the books in his office asking about his sex life.

Maybe he could get them to ask about Seepy Benton's sex life. He'd try to persuade them to do that, except he hoped that since Seepy was dating Ruth Grady, he didn't have a sex life. If he did, Rhodes didn't want to know about it.

Rhodes parked the Tahoe in front of the jail and pulled the cap out of his jacket pocket. A man who was going to talk about his sex life shouldn't walk into a place with his hair blown all over everywhere by the wind. Rhodes whacked the cap against the seat to remove some of the remaining dirt and gravel. There was nothing he could to about the tire track.

He put the cap on, got out of the Tahoe, and went into the jail.

The authors, whose names were Claudia and Jan, sat by Hack's desk, laughing at something he'd said. All three of them looked at the door when Rhodes came inside.

Claudia had blond hair and startlingly blue eyes. Jan had dark hair, brown eyes, and dimples. She'd probably used those dimples to great effect in getting what she wanted from men in the past, but they wouldn't work on Rhodes. He was immune to that sort of thing.

"Took you long enough to get here," Hack said.

"County business," Rhodes told him. "That always comes first."

"We didn't mean to keep you from your work," Jan said with a smile that showed off her dimples.

Rhodes grinned, then changed the grin to a frown. He didn't want her to think the dimples were working.

"That's right," Claudia said. "We don't want to interfere with your job. I like the cap, by the way. You should wear one all the time."

"I might start doing that," Rhodes said.

"He's just tryin' to hide that thin spot in the hair at the back of his head," Hack said.

Rhodes ignored that remark. "Hack tells me you two have some questions for me."

Claudia laughed. "We heard what he said on the phone. He was just joking. That's not what we want to talk to you about at all."

"Well," Jan said, "it sort of is."

Rhodes pulled out his desk chair. "Why don't you bring your chairs over here so we can have a private conversation?"

Hack bristled. "You don't never want me to be in the loop."

"Don't start that," Rhodes said. "This isn't county business, and you don't need to hear it."

He knew that Hack would listen to the conversation and that

he'd hear it without any trouble. Their desks weren't that far apart, but Hack enjoyed complaining.

Jan and Claudia moved their chairs as Rhodes settled into his. When they were comfortable, Rhodes asked, "Now what's this about my sex life?"

The women laughed, and Claudia said, "I told you it wasn't really about that."

"But Jan said it sort of was, so what's going on?"

"It's about Sage Barton's sex life," Jan said.

Rhodes couldn't figure out what that had to do with him, and besides, Sage Barton didn't have a sex life as far as Rhodes knew. When he mentioned that, Claudia said, "That's the problem. Our publisher has noticed a little bit of a drop-off in sales, and our editor says that we might need to spice things up a little in the next book."

"By 'spice things up' you mean—"

"Sex," Jan said.

Rhodes noticed that she wasn't blushing. "I don't know what this has to do with me."

"Everybody knows you're the model for Sage Barton," Claudia told him.

Rhodes wished she hadn't said it. "Don't joke about that."

"She's not joking," Jan said.

Rhodes looked over at Hack, who was trying both to pretend that he wasn't listening and to hold in his laughter.

"Okay," Rhodes said, "even if that's true, and I don't believe it even for a second, I still don't know what it has to do with me."

"You're a lawman," Jan said. "Sage Barton is a lawman. So what we want to know is whether you have time for—"

"Sex," Claudia said.

Rhodes had had some strange conversations in this office, most of them with Hack and Lawton, but he'd never had a conversation quite like this one.

"You drove all the way down here from Dallas to ask me that?"

"It's not that far," Jan said, "and it's tax deductible."

"We like to check in now and then and see how you're doing, too," Claudia said. "You being our model and all. You never know what we might learn. We didn't know about the cap, for one thing. What do you think, Jan? Should we give Sage Barton a cap instead of that Western hat he wears?"

"I think Western hats are sexier," Jan said, "which brings us back to the point."

Rhodes was hoping they'd forgotten the point.

"So are you going to tell us?" Claudia asked. "About the sex, I mean."

This wasn't just the strangest conversation Rhodes had ever had in the office. It was the strangest he'd ever had anywhere, and it was also the most uncomfortable.

"Maybe we should've asked Ivy," Jan said. "She might be more forthcoming."

Claudia stood up. "That's a good idea. Does she still work at the insurance office?"

"Sit down," Rhodes said.

Claudia sat.

"I'm not Sage Barton," Rhodes said. "I'm married. He's not."

"Married people have sex," Claudia said. "I'm married. Jan's married. We have—"

Rhodes held up a hand. "I don't want to hear about it. What I'm trying to tell you is that what I do has nothing to do with Sage Barton. You can give him a rich and rewarding sex life with all those beautiful women he meets, and you don't have to worry about mine. I've read the books, and Sage Barton is the kind of man who'll make time for sex even if it's in the middle of one of those big gun battles he's always having."

Claudia looked at Jan, who pulled a ballpoint pen and a notepad from her purse.

"I knew we were right to come here," Jan said, bouncing a little in her chair. "This is the best idea ever. It will come as a big surprise and spice up our next book more than anybody could ever expect."

"What will?" Rhodes asked.

"Sex during a gun battle," Claudia said. "Can't you just see it?"

Rhodes didn't want to see it. "It doesn't sound . . . practical."

Jan looked up from the pad she was writing on. "Practical? Since when does sex have to be practical?"

"I didn't mean it like that," Rhodes said, wishing they'd quit twisting his words. "I meant that it's highly unlikely anybody's going to have time for sex during a gunfight."

"Don't worry about that," Claudia said. "We'll figure something out. Right, Jan?"

"Right." She closed the notebook and looked at Rhodes. "We'll be sure to mention you in the acknowledgments."

"Please don't," Rhodes said. "Really."

Both women stood up, and Rhodes did as well. Claudia said, "A mention in the acknowledgments is the least we can do after you've given us such a good idea. Something like 'And a special thanks to Blacklin County sheriff Dan Rhodes for the sex advice.'"

Rhodes heard something that sounded like choking coming from Hack's desk, but he didn't rush over to perform the Heimlich maneuver. He knew the sound was only smothered laughter.

"Thanks, Sheriff," Jan said. "You've been a huge help."

"Really," Claudia said. "We needed a little creative nudge, and you've given us one. Mentioning you in the acknowledgments is only right. Credit where credit is due."

"No," Rhodes said. "That's not necessary. Just knowing I've been able to help is all the thanks I need."

"We'll consider that," Claudia said, but Rhodes knew they wouldn't. They were going to put his name in the book as their sex adviser or something like that. He'd never live it down.

"Let's go, Jan," Claudia said. "We can get back to Dallas in time to write that gunfight scene if we don't dawdle."

They breezed out the door, laughing and talking. Rhodes thought about calling them back and trying to persuade them to forget about the acknowledgment, but knew it wouldn't do any good.

Hack was leaned over his desk, practically strangling with laughter. Rhodes sat back down and said, "Hack."

Hack sat up, but he couldn't answer. Rhodes gave him a couple of seconds to get control of himself, then said, "Hack," again.

Hack got control of himself and turned around. "Yeah, Sheriff?"

"If word of that conversation ever gets out, I'm going to lock you up in one of our cells for a week."

"You wouldn't do that."

"Yes, I would."

"What would the charges be?"

"I'd think of something. Mopery, maybe."

"There ain't no such a thing."

"There might be. I'll check the statutes."

Hack wasn't laughing now, but he didn't appear worried in the least. "That would be false imprisonment."

"You'd have to convince a judge of that. I don't think you could. I'm the sheriff, and you're the dispatcher."

"I'm the one does all the work around here, though. How about if I tell Lawton and nobody else?"

"You especially can't tell Lawton. You weren't supposed to be listening in the first place."

The telephone rang, ending the conversation, for which Rhodes was grateful, and Hack answered the call. Rhodes didn't try to listen in. He turned to his desk and started entering a report on Jake Marley's death into his computer.

Hack interrupted him. "Sheriff, we got trouble."

Rhodes thought of his suspicions about Jake's death. "You're right, but then we always have trouble."

"I'm not talkin' 'bout what you're workin' on. There's a fight at a yard sale over on Hick'ry Street. Corner of Vine. You're closer'n anybody."

Rhodes saved his work on the computer. Some times, and this was one of them, he wished he were like the big-city cops on TV, the ones who never had to work but one case at a time and didn't have to worry about fights at yard sales or women wanting to take revenge for a bad haircut by attacking a beauty shop with a sledgehammer or any of the other petty crimes that cropped up constantly in a small town.

On the other hand, there was really no reason to think that Marley's death was anything more than an accident except for one little abrasion, and dealing with all those petty problems did a lot to keep life interesting.

"Who's having the yard sale?" Rhodes asked.

"Robbie Atkins is the one who called. You know her, the one who claims she's related to Chet. Never claimed it till after he died, though. Mighty suspicious if you ask me. I bet she's not any more kin to Chet Atkins than I am."

Rhodes didn't want to get into a discussion of Robbie Atkins's ancestry.

"I'll go see what I can do about the fight," he said.

"Prob'ly be over before you get there," Hack said. He gave Rhodes a doubting look. "You gonna wear that cap?"

"What's wrong with the cap?"

"I don't think it's a good look for you, no matter what those women said."

"It's windy out there. I need a cap."

"Yeah, I guess it keeps that thin spot warm."

Rhodes stood up and tugged the bill of the cap. "It does, at that," he said.

Chapter 7

▼

Rhodes thought it was too cold for a yard sale, but the wind had calmed down a little, and the sun was shining, which helped. The temperature was probably nearer to fifty now than it was to forty, and even in the worst of circumstances people had a hard time resisting a yard sale. Weather like this wouldn't be a hindrance at all. Rhodes didn't need the cap anymore, but he decided to keep it on, anyway.

Robbie Atkins's house was an old white frame building with a hurricane-wire fence around the backyard. All the action was in the front, however, where several long tables were lined up along each side of the cracked concrete driveway. The tables were covered with sale items: clothes, glass and metal knickknacks, a couple of lamps, kitchen utensils, dishes, and other assorted castoffs.

The four or five people at the sale weren't looking at the tables, however. They were watching the two men off to the side in the yard. "Watching" wasn't the right word, really, since three of them were recording the events on their smartphone cameras. Rhodes knew that at least one of them would send the video to Jennifer Loam. Nothing was too trivial for *A Clear View of Clearview,* and a fight at a yard sale was sure to get some hits, especially if Jennifer came up with a clickbait headline. Rhodes knew she would.

Robbie Atkins ran over to the Tahoe as Rhodes got out. Robbie was tall, big-boned, and red-faced. She had a blue scarf tied around her head, and she was breathing hard.

"You need to stop them, Sheriff," she said. "I think Ted has a gun."

Ted Hensley was one of the men in the yard. The other man was Dick Blanchard. Rhodes knew who both men were. Ted owned a feed store that someone else managed for him. Blanchard was a retired postal worker. At the moment they were standing about ten feet apart, glaring at each other like two mean dogs trying to decide which one was going to make the first jump. Rhodes was surprised they weren't growling and their hair wasn't bristling.

"What's their problem?" Rhodes asked Robbie.

"It's that paper sack Ted's holding," Robbie said. "I don't know who picked it up first, but Dick claims he did and that Ted grabbed it from him. I'm afraid Ted's going to pull his gun."

Rhodes nodded and walked over to the men, careful not to get too close.

"You stay out of this, Sheriff," Ted said. He was at least a head taller than Blanchard. He was also heavier, and he was armed, too, if Robbie was right. "This is between me and Dick."

"You don't want to be fighting over a paper sack," Rhodes said.

"It's not the sack," Dick said. "It's what's in the sack. I saw it first, and he grabbed it away from me."

"That's not what happened," Ted said. "He put the sack down, and I picked it up. *That's* what happened. Now he wants me to give it back, and I'm not gonna do it."

"He told me he was going to shoot me if I didn't back off," Dick said. "You need to arrest him, Sheriff, and you need to make him give me that sack."

Rhodes looked at the sack. It was an ordinary brown paper bag, not a very big one, and Rhodes could see that someone had written "$1" on the side with a black marker.

"Are you armed, Ted?" Rhodes asked.

"I got a license."

"That's not what I asked."

"Yeah, I'm carrying. It's in a holster in the small of my back."

Ted wore a brown nylon jacket that zipped up the front. It hung several inches below his waist and easily concealed the weapon.

"I'm going to come take the sack," Rhodes said. "Don't reach for the pistol."

"What about him?" Ted asked, pointing at Dick with the hand that held the bag. "What if he's carrying?"

"You carrying, Dick?" Rhodes asked.

"I wouldn't need a gun for somebody like him," Dick said.

Rhodes wondered if Dick knew some secret martial arts moves, since Ted looked big enough to take on two men the size of Dick with his bare hands.

"That's not what I asked," Rhodes said.

"I'm not carrying," Dick told him. "I just want the sack."

"I'm taking it for now," Rhodes said, and he walked to Ted, who moved the sack away and tucked it under his arm. "I'll hold it until we get this settled."

"I picked this sack up off the table fair and square," Ted said. "Dick had it, sure, but he put it down. You ask him if he didn't."

70

"I put it down to get a dollar out of my billfold, and you grabbed it," Dick said.

"Fair and square," Ted said. "Possession is nine-tenths of the law, right, Sheriff?"

"Not necessarily. That's not written into the law, and every case is different."

"Well, I don't care what's written. I possess this sack, and I'm not giving it up."

Rhodes walked up to Ted. When he was within a yard or so, he said, "Hand me the sack."

"Nope. I'm keeping. I got it—"

"Fair and square," Rhodes said. "You told me. We're going to find a peaceful way to settle this, though, and until we do, I'll hold on to the sack." He stretched out his arm and wiggled his fingers. "Hand it over."

Ted hesitated, but only for a second. He drew the sack from under his arm and started to give it to Rhodes. As he did a fast-moving shape brushed past Rhodes, grabbed the paper sack, and kept right on running. It was Dick, his short legs pumping for all they were worth.

"Dad-blast that son of a bitch!" Ted yelled. He turned in the direction that Dick was headed, fumbling with his jacket and reaching behind his back.

Rhodes jumped forward and beat him to the pistol by a millimeter or two, jerking it out of the holster.

"No shooting," Rhodes said, sticking the pistol into the pocket of his jacket.

Ted didn't answer. He took off running instead.

Rhodes watched the two men as they hustled down the block. One of the other men in the yard who'd been watching the whole thing, the only one who hadn't been taking video, came over to Rhodes. He was a short little guy, and he hadn't shaved in a couple of days.

"How far you think they'll get 'fore they fall over?" he asked Rhodes.

"Maybe two blocks," Rhodes said.

"I don't know," the man said. "Ted looks like he's in pretty good shape, and Dick was a mail carrier for a long time. He walked his route, didn't ride like they do these days. They might last longer than that." He shaded his eyes and stared down the street. "They've already got a block's head start on you. You goin' after 'em?"

"That's my job," Rhodes said, and he started jogging in the direction Ted and Dick had gone. He wasn't going to run. He didn't think he needed to.

Sure enough, Dick seemed to be tiring. He was listing a bit to the left, and Ted was gaining on him. They got farther than Rhodes thought they would, however. Dick was in the middle of the third block before he tumbled to the side and landed under a big pecan tree, where he curled into the fetal position, wrapping himself into a ball around the paper sack. Ted was trying without success to uncurl him when Rhodes arrived on the scene.

For a little while Rhodes stood and watched Ted pull on Dick's arms, legs, and feet. Dick himself never budged. It was only when Ted drew back his foot for a kick that Rhodes spoke up.

"I wouldn't do that," he said. "If you do, it's assault. So far you're not in much trouble, but if you kick him, you will be."

Ted planted his foot back on the ground. Dick stayed right where he was.

"I'd like to know what's in that sack," Rhodes said.

Ted was panting a bit, but he managed to say, "Baseball cards."

Rhodes was disappointed. He'd hoped for a treasure map or a handful of gold coins.

"Mickey Mantle rookie card," Ted said, still a little breathless. "Topps, 1952."

"He only knows that because he saw me take it out of the sack," Dick said, his voice muffled because the side of his face was pressed to the ground. "That's why he stole the sack from me."

Rhodes wasn't up to date on the value of baseball cards, so he asked, "How much would a card like that be worth?"

"Depends on the condition," Ted said.

"That's not what I asked," Rhodes said.

He was getting tired of having to work so hard to extract information from people who refused to give him a simple answer. It was as if Hack and Lawton had turned the entire town into their clones. Or maybe nobody wanted to give him a straight answer because he was the sheriff.

"This one's not much better than a five," Dick said, still balled up on the ground. "Probably ten thousand dollars, though."

Rhodes whistled. He'd had no idea that a baseball card could be worth that much money.

"I take it that you weren't going to mention that to Ms. Atkins," he said.

"I was willing to pay what she was asking," Dick said.

Ted didn't say anything.

"She could use that money as much as either of you," Rhodes said. "Maybe more."

"I didn't ask her to sell it so cheap," Dick said. "That's why people go to garage sales, to get a bargain."

"I wish you'd stand up," Rhodes said. "Ted's not going to make a grab for the sack. Right, Ted?"

Ted nodded.

"He can't hear you," Rhodes said.

"I won't make a grab for it," Ted said.

"You hear that, Dick?" Rhodes asked. "Go on and get up."

Dick uncurled himself and got up, keeping a tight grip on the sack.

"Give me the sack," Rhodes said.

"I found it in the first place," Dick said, drawing back. He looked at Ted. "Possession is nine-tenths of the law."

"We'll talk that over with Ms. Atkins," Rhodes said. "She might have a different idea. Let me have the sack."

Dick looked as if he might take off running again, but he didn't. He waited a couple of seconds, looking first at Ted and then up the street to where the garage sale customers and Robbie Atkins stood looking back at him. He handed the sack to Rhodes.

"Who's going to get the card?" Ted asked.

"Not you," Rhodes said.

Chapter 8

▼

Robbie Atkins hadn't had any idea about the worth of the baseball cards, which had belonged to her grandfather. They'd been in a drawer in an old desk for years, and she hadn't given them any thought before she started looking for something to put in the garage sale. Several other cards in the sack were worth small sums, much smaller than the Mickey Mantle card, and after a bit of haggling Rhodes got Dick to agree to accept a percentage of whatever Robbie could sell the cards for.

"Sort of a finder's fee," Rhodes said. "Or you or Ted could buy the cards yourselves. Maybe Robbie would let you have them for the wholesale price."

Neither man expressed a desire to do that, but both of them felt free to express their opinions about Rhodes and the way he'd handled things. Rhodes didn't mind. He'd had much worse things said about him in his career as sheriff, and Robbie made up for it with her profuse thanks.

"What about my gun?" Ted asked when the argument was more or less settled.

"You can come by the jail and pick it up in a few days," Rhodes said. "I don't think it would be a good idea for you to have it right now."

"That's going against my Second Amendment rights," Ted said.

"I don't think so," Rhodes told him, "but you can sue me if it will make you feel any better."

Ted huffed off without saying more. Dick wasn't too happy with the situation, either, but at least he didn't make it any worse by trying to get smart with Rhodes. The thought of getting even a small amount of money might have been making him feel charitable.

After Dick left, Rhodes told Robbie to put the cards in a safe place, preferably a safety deposit box at the bank, and to think about how she'd like to sell them after she'd done a little research. Then he got in the Tahoe and left.

Most of Rhodes's afternoon was taken up with other petty problems and complaints. A chicken trying to cross the highway caused what passed for a traffic pileup in Blacklin County. A woman's grown son had sneaked into her house and stolen her credit cards. A man bumped another man's car with a shopping cart in the Walmart parking lot, starting a fight that involved four people.

It was a slow afternoon for crime in Blacklin County, for which Rhodes was grateful and which meant that he would be home in time for supper, but that would mean eating one of Ivy's healthy vegetable casseroles with tofu topping. Hoping to persuade her to eat something unhealthy and tasty instead, he called and asked if she'd like to have dinner at a restaurant.

"What did you have in mind?" Ivy asked.

Rhodes didn't want to say that he had something unhealthy and tasty in mind, so he said, "What about Max's barbecue?"

Rhodes didn't really want barbecue. It was Friday, and on Fridays Max's place had an all-you-can-eat buffet with fried catfish, hush puppies, french fries, cole slaw, corn, a salad bar, and a dessert, usually cobbler, with a choice of peach or apple. Rhodes figured he could skip the salad bar.

"Max's sounds fine," Ivy said. "I'll meet you at home. You need to feed the dogs before we go."

Ivy had regular hours at the insurance office, unlike Rhodes, who'd long ago given up the idea of being able to schedule his time.

"I'll try to be there by five thirty," he said. "I need to go by the jail first."

"Don't let Hack and Lawton keep you too long."

"I'll try not to," Rhodes said, "but you know how they are."

"I know how they are, but you're the sheriff. Pull rank on them."

Rhodes thought about how Hack and Lawton would react if he pulled rank on them, and tried not to laugh as he told Ivy good-bye.

As it turned out, he didn't have to worry about Hack and Lawton. Who he had to worry about was Bradley West, as Hack informed him on the radio almost as soon as he'd ended his call to Ivy.

"Bradley wants you to come by his office before he closes," Hack said. "He closes at five."

"It's nearly five now," Rhodes said.

"You got fifteen minutes. Maybe he won't keep you any longer than that."

"He's a lawyer," Rhodes said.

"Yeah, so maybe longer than fifteen minutes, 'specially if he wants to see you 'bout a client he's billing for his time. You're the sheriff, though. Gotta do your job."

Rhodes had a feeling he wasn't going to be able to meet Ivy at five thirty. "Did he say what he wanted?"

"Just that it was 'bout Jake Marley. You better get on to his office."

"I'm practically there already," Rhodes said.

Blacklin County had a number of lawyers. At the top of the heap was Randy Lawless, who occupied the Lawj Mahal in downtown Clearview. He was the one who got the clients who could afford him and were guilty enough to need him. He handled estates, too, and most of the town's wealthy citizens had him draw up their wills. Maybe not Jake Marley, however.

Bradley West was in the middle group of lawyers. He was known as a steady man in the courtroom, but the problem was that he'd been steady for fifty years and was considered over the hill by the younger folks, who wanted someone flashier. Some of the older people who'd known him for a long time weren't certain that his best days weren't behind him. He had one other problem as well. He had the worst toupee that Rhodes had ever seen, not that he'd seen a lot of them. It was an indeterminate color unlike the color of any real hair anywhere, and every time Rhodes had seen it, it could have used a good combing. A man with a toupee like that, well, it was hard for some people to trust him, the way it might be hard for them to trust a man they thought was trying to hide a thin spot in his hair under a baseball cap.

Rhodes took off the cap and tossed it on the seat beside him. It was uncomfortable, and it hadn't kept his head very warm anyway.

Unlike Randy Lawless's huge office building, Bradley's was unpretentious and out-of-the-way. It was in an old remodeled house on a residential street, and only a discreet sign in the front yard identified it as an attorney's office. In fact, the house wasn't just an office. It was where Bradley lived. His office was in what had been a couple of front rooms. Bradley had had the wall that separated the rooms removed, had some bookshelves built, and moved in a big wooden desk and a leather chair. It was a professional setup, but it wasn't fancy. Most of his clients weren't fancy, either.

Rhodes stopped the Tahoe at the curb and went up the concrete walk to the small wooden porch. He patted down his hair as best he could, rang the doorbell, and waited.

Bradley came to the door himself. He had a secretary, but she worked only part-time. Bradley's practice wasn't as big as it had been in earlier years.

"Come on in, Sheriff," Bradley said when he opened the door. "I appreciate your coming by on such short notice."

He was wearing the toupee, which sat slightly askew on his head. In the right light it appeared to be a reddish gray, like a squirrel, which had caused some people to joke, half seriously, that Bradley might have skinned a squirrel and made his own hairpiece. Rhodes couldn't criticize, considering the state of his own hair. Bradley also had on an old black suit, a white shirt, and a tie, all of them somewhat wrinkled but all of them clean and respectable.

"I'm always glad to help out the citizens of the county," Rhodes said.

"I know," Bradley said, "and we're all glad to have you looking out for us. Come on in the office."

The office was just off the little entranceway, and Rhodes followed Bradley in. The bookshelves were lined with law books, and the desk was cluttered with papers. On the wall behind the desk hung a couple of impressive diplomas with gold seals on them.

"Just hang your coat over there," Bradley said, pointing to a standing coat rack in the corner of the office.

Rhodes took off his jacket and hung it up while Bradley went behind the desk and sat in his big black leather chair. The desk had nothing on it other than a sheet of clear plate glass that covered it. Rhodes wondered if anyone else in Clearview had a glass-topped desk. It had been the fashion at one time, long ago.

Rhodes sat in the leather chair, a red one of the type Rhodes had once heard called a Giles chair. He didn't know who or what Giles was, nor did he care very much. As long as it was comfortable, it could have any name at all.

"I heard about Jake Marley," Bradley said, patting his toupee as if trying to get it back in place. "He was one of my clients, and I'd like to know more of the details about how he died."

Rhodes was glad Bradley had gotten right to the subject. Maybe they could finish this up quickly.

"Jake was climbing around in the grid at the old opera house," Rhodes said. "He must have fallen and broken his neck."

"Must have?" Bradley asked.

Rhodes had thought he could slip it by, but he should've known better. Anybody who thought Bradley had slowed down was wrong.

"That's what it looked like," Rhodes said. "You have any reason to think differently?"

"I'm Jake's lawyer," Bradley said, which, as seemed to be happening all the time lately, wasn't an answer to Rhodes's question.

This time Rhodes didn't take offense. He just said, "And?"

"I was his parents' lawyer, too. They both died fairly young, back when I was a much younger man myself. They left Jake quite well-to-do, but he never bothered to make a will until a few months ago."

Rhodes didn't see anything sinister in that. Lots of people put off making a will.

"He managed his own money," Bradley went on. "People wondered what he was doing out there in his house. Managing his money was part of it. He did it so well that he became even more well-to-do."

Rhodes settled back in the chair, or tried to. It wasn't as comfortable as it had seemed at first. He knew Bradley would get to the point eventually, but not as soon as he'd hoped. The chair would be an ordeal if Bradley took too long.

"Jake didn't have any heirs," Bradley said, "so he made me the executor of his will. Some of his money will be going to the continued restoration of the old opera house. I know people will be worried about that, but there's no need. He's left ample funds to take care of the complete job."

Rhodes was starting to feel a little uneasy. As far as he knew, Jake had been in good health.

"I know what you're wondering," Bradley said. "You're wondering why Jake would suddenly decide to make a will and to be sure he made provision for the theater restoration to be finished. I'll tell you, but first you should know about another provision. Jake also left money for the theater's continued preservation and use. He hoped it could become a part of a downtown renaissance."

Rhodes shifted in the chair. He still hadn't found a comfortable position. "That was thoughtful of him."

"Yes, it was. Except that there's a condition or two."

Here it comes, Rhodes thought. "What were the conditions?"

"Simple enough. The first play must be performed as scheduled, and it must be based on the ideas that Jake gave to Dr. Harris. You did know that Dr. Harris was writing a play, a version of a Dickens story, for the first performances at the theater?"

"I didn't know that Jake had given Dr. Harris his ideas for the play. Are those all the conditions?"

"No, there's another one. It's about you."

"Me?" Rhodes couldn't think of any reason Marley would make him a part of the conditions of the restoration of the theater. "Why me?"

Bradley patted his toupee again, shifting it slightly. "The reason isn't in the will, and Jake didn't tell me. The will just states that as a condition of the money being provided for upkeep and so on, you have to be at the first performance of the play."

Rhodes would have been at the performance anyway, since Ivy was involved in the theater's restoration, but why would Jake want to be so sure of it? What if there were complications?

"That's more than a year from now," Rhodes said. "Something could happen to me before then."

"You're a young man. You're in good health. What could happen to you?"

Rhodes wished the young part were true. "I have a dangerous job. I could have an accident. I could get sick."

"You seem good at surviving in your job, but I agree about accidents. They do happen, maybe even to Jake, and as far as a person's good health, one day isn't a guarantee of good health the next day. Jake did make allowance for all that, however. If for some reason you can't attend, he wants the current sheriff, whoever it is, to be there."

"Jake was of sound mind, I guess," Rhodes said.

"Very much so, and he wasn't nearly as curmudgeonly as people claimed. He wasn't what I would describe as jovial, but he was quite good-natured when we talked these things over. He laughed about them, but he wouldn't explain them. He just told me how he wanted the will to be written, and he expected me to follow through. So I did. He approved it and signed it, and now I have to see that the provisions are carried out."

Bradley was the second person to remark on Jake's near-joviality. Rhodes reminded himself to ask Ivy about that at dinner, assuming they ever got to have dinner.

"He must have had his reasons for those conditions."

"I'm sure he did," Bradley said, "but he didn't confide to me what they were. However, we haven't covered everything yet."

"There's more?"

"Just one more thing. The play has to be presented with the cast list that Jake has provided in the will. He may have given Dr. Harris a copy already, but I can make one if he hasn't."

Rhodes started to speak, but Bradley held up his hand. "I realize that the same things apply to the cast as to you. Someone could have an accident or severe illness. Jake didn't make any provisions for those things. He didn't seem worried about them."

Rhodes started to speak again, and once more Bradley held up his hand. "I know what you're thinking. We need to get to the heart of the matter."

Rhodes was ready to do that. "You're right. That's just what I was thinking. So what's the heart of the matter?"

"When a man comes to me and asks me to write his will with such specific provisions and then dies an accidental death only a few weeks later, I ask myself if there's any connection. Wouldn't you do the same?"

Rhodes had already asked himself about the accidental nature of

Jake's death, though he hadn't mentioned that to Bradley. "I sent word for Dr. White to perform an autopsy, if that's what you mean."

"That's what I mean," Bradley said. "I'm not usually of a suspicious nature, no more than most attorneys, anyway, but this time something just doesn't seem right."

Rhodes thought about his own hunch. "I know what you mean. Having the autopsy is a good idea."

Bradley used both hands on his toupee this time. He got it into place, and it didn't look quite so bad.

"Exactly," he said.

"I'd like to have a list of those cast members," Rhodes said. "Just in case I need it later."

He didn't mention what he might need the list for, and Bradley didn't ask. He opened the middle drawer of his desk and removed an ordinary white postal envelope. He closed the drawer and slid the envelope across the glass-topped desk. Rhodes stood up and got the envelope.

"There you go," Bradley said. "Just in case you need it."

"Thanks," Rhodes said.

"You going to open it?"

"Why don't you just tell me who's on the list."

"I'll let you see that for yourself. Except for one of them. I'll tell you that one. Jake was going to play himself."

"Himself?"

"How long has it been since you read *A Christmas Carol,* Sheriff?"

Rhodes didn't have to think about it. "I never read it. I've seen a couple of the movie versions."

"Then you should remember something about the characters. The ghosts, for example."

Ghosts. Rhodes wished that topic would quit coming up. "I remember them. Christmases Past, Present, and Future."

"There's another one," Bradley said. "The first one. People do forget him sometimes. Marley's ghost."

Rhodes remembered then. "Jacob Marley."

"That's right, and that's Jake's legal name. Maybe his parents had a sense of humor, or maybe they'd never read Dickens. I never asked. At any rate, Jake didn't make mention of who should take his place if he couldn't be in the play. Maybe he planned to be there, one way or another."

"There's only one way he could have been there," Rhodes said, "and that's not going to happen now."

"Maybe he'll be there anyway," Bradley said. "It would look good on the program. 'The ghost of Jacob Marley will be played by the ghost of Jacob Marley.' The play would be sold out every night."

"Not going to happen," Rhodes said.

Bradley smiled and leaned back in his chair. "You never can tell," he said.

Chapter 9

▼

Bradley West had given Rhodes several things to think about as he drove home, and the matter of the will was just one of them. He wasn't going to be more than five or ten minutes later than he'd told Ivy, so he didn't hurry.

The will was the most important thing Bradley had talked about, but another interesting point was Bradley's comment about Jake's joviality. Bradley was the second person that day to mention it, and while Jake might have been jovial around Aubrey Hamilton because he was interested in dating her, that wouldn't have been the case with Bradley. Aubrey had denied that Marley was interested in her anyway.

Rhodes didn't think that making a will was a time for happy conversations in most cases, yet Jake had impressed Bradley with his cheerfulness. What had happened to change Jake's personality? Had he always been Mr. Jolly, sitting alone in his house and cracking jokes to the wallpaper? Rhodes didn't believe that. Something had been going on. A man doesn't give up years of solitude and become a traveling ray of sunshine overnight. There had to be a reason for the difference in Jake's attitude.

It wasn't just a matter of a man making his will and being happy about it, either. It was the strange provisions of the will that mattered. Or did they? Rhodes didn't know why he was so suspicious about the cause of Jake's death. Other than one small bump on the head, there was nothing to indicate what Jennifer Loam had called foul play. The fact that Jake hadn't included a replacement for himself in the cast of characters in case of his death showed that he expected to be there, didn't it, Bradley's silly comment about his ghost notwithstanding?

Rhodes thought about Seepy Benton. Seepy would say the ghosts in the theater had communicated some message to Rhodes, one he was too dense to figure out, so that all he was left with was a hunch. Seepy would also be certain that Marley's ghost would be there for the performances, whether it manifested itself or not.

Since Rhodes didn't believe in ghosts, he could safely disregard that idea. What he needed was some fried catfish. He'd worry about Jake Marley and his nonexistent ghost some other time.

Ivy wasn't upset that Rhodes was a little bit late. "I never expect you to show up on time," she said. "Something always seems to come up. What was it this time?"

Rhodes was a little surprised she hadn't asked him sooner. Maybe she'd been waiting for him to apologize for being late, which he'd just done. Or maybe it was because on the drive to Max's Place, she'd wanted to know all about Jake Marley's death, and after filling her in on that, there hadn't been time for him to tell her where he'd been.

The air in Max's was thick with the smell of fried fish, and there was quite a crowd of diners. Rhodes wasn't the only one in Clearview who liked a good fried meal. He and Ivy found a table not too far from the buffet, which was Rhodes's preferred seating. He wanted to be able to get a refill plate without having to walk too far. The place was noisy with the chatter of the other customers, the clatter of silverware, and the folk music on the sound system, but Rhodes and Ivy could still talk to each other without having to yell. The noise gave them privacy in a way, since nobody at the other tables was likely to overhear them.

"I was at Bradley West's office," Rhodes said. "He was telling me about Jake Marley's will."

Ivy wanted to know all about that, too, so he told her in between bites of catfish and french fries and hush puppies.

"I like the part about Marley's ghost playing Marley's ghost," Ivy said when he was finished with his account.

"Don't start," Rhodes said, looking at his nearly bare plate. "I'm going back for seconds. Do you want anything?"

He knew he didn't have to ask. Ivy had stuck strictly to the salad bar, and she was still working on what she'd gathered up on her first trip.

"I'm fine," she said, and Rhodes went to get a clean plate and some more fish and french fries.

When he got back to the table, he asked Ivy how she and Jake Marley had gotten along.

"Just fine. He's worked well with all of us on the restoration committee."

"He wasn't sullen or withdrawn?"

"Not a bit. I'd expected him to be a little odd because of all the stories I'd heard about him, but he's been just like everybody else.

He gets upset about things now and then, but he's never rude or snappish. Most of the time he seems happy enough." Ivy paused. "I'm talking about him in the present tense. It's hard to believe he's dead. Anyway, he *was* fine. Upbeat, mostly."

"I guess all the stories about him were wrong," Rhodes said.

"If they were, why didn't he associate with people?" Ivy asked. "He was always in that house of his, year after year. No friends, no interaction with the town, nothing." She looked around the restaurant, at the people talking and eating, at the salad bar, at the loaded buffet table. "He never came out to a place like this to have a meal. Maybe he got something from the drive-through at the Dairy Queen or McDonald's, or maybe he just ate little frozen dinners that he bought at the grocery store late at night. The stories weren't wrong."

"Or maybe he had a secret life," Rhodes said. "Some of those stories had him sneaking off to bigger towns for fun."

"He didn't seem like the type," Ivy said, "but it's possible, I guess. You can never really know anybody, especially somebody who goes out of his way to keep his life a secret."

Rhodes ate his last hush puppy. "Until now. He didn't seem to be keeping it secret anymore."

Ivy pushed her salad plate away. "Oh, I wouldn't say that. He was more outgoing, but that didn't mean he talked about himself. He talked about the theater and how he hoped the restoration would be good for the town. Things like that. Never himself, though."

"Did he ever take an interest in anybody in particular?" Rhodes asked.

"Who do you mean?"

"Aubrey Hamilton. I wondered if he might have thought of asking her out."

"I wouldn't know anything about his love life, and I certainly wouldn't ask him. It didn't seem to me that he had that kind of interest in anybody, though. Why did you ask that?"

"He called her to come to the theater today, and I wondered why. I thought maybe they were an item."

"If they were, I didn't know it," Ivy said, "and nobody mentioned it at the Beauty Shack when I was there."

The Beauty Shack was a local center of information exchange, which was Ivy's preferred term for gossip. If Jake had been dating Aubrey, word would have reached the Beauty Shack by now, although maybe that simply hadn't been one of the topics discussed when Ivy was present.

Rhodes looked at his empty plate. He didn't really need a third trip to the buffet, although he wouldn't have minded another piece of fish and a few more hush puppies. He exercised his willpower instead and pushed his plate away, too. After all, he needed to leave room for some cobbler, preferably with a scoop of ice cream on top.

"Do you want cobbler?" he asked Ivy.

"I'll just take a bite of yours," she said, and Rhodes went off to serve himself some cobbler and ice cream. He'd be sure to get enough for Ivy to have a bite.

When he returned to the table, he discovered that Ivy had company. Seepy Benton and Harry Harris had joined her.

"The cobbler looks good," Seepy said. "Apple?"

"Yes," Rhodes said, looking at the large amount of cobbler and ice cream he'd managed to get into his bowl. "Ivy's sharing it with me. Are you here for dinner?"

"We are," Seepy said, "and Ivy invited us to join you. We'll just go to the buffet and come right back."

Rhodes started to say, "Take your time," but he refrained. He gave what he hoped was a noncommittal grunt instead and set his cobbler on the table. When Seepy and Harry stood up and headed to the buffet, Rhodes sat down.

"I had to ask them," Ivy said. "I could tell they wanted to sit with us."

"It's all right," Rhodes said. "I have some questions for them anyway, and Seepy will want to tell us all about his ghost hunting in the old theater."

"How much of that cobbler were you counting on me to eat?" Ivy asked, eyeing his bowl.

"As much as you want," Rhodes said, knowing that he was safe enough. One bite, two at most, would be all Ivy would take.

One was all she took, but it was a big bite by her standards. Rhodes didn't mind. There was still plenty left, and he was well into it when Harris and Seepy returned and sat down. Before they could start on their fried fish, Rhodes asked if they'd found any ghosts.

"We went back this afternoon," Seepy said. "The theater is full of them."

In what was becoming his standard routine, Rhodes said, "That doesn't answer my question."

"They're there, all right," Harry said, "although they haven't communicated with us yet."

Suspicions confirmed. "Then how do you know they're there?"

"We got several more convincing readings on the EMF meter," Seepy said. "If no other ghosts are there, Marley's must be. He'd have a good reason for hanging around. He'd want to see the way the work turned out."

Rhodes took a bite of the cobbler and ice cream. He wanted to finish it before the ice cream melted.

"I hope the theater restoration will continue," Harry said.

"You don't have to worry about the restoration," Rhodes said. He told Harry and Seepy what Bradley West had said about Jake's will, including the odd provisions.

"Did he tell you who the cast members were?" Harry asked.

"No," Rhodes said, "but he gave me a list of the names. I haven't had time to give them much thought."

"You're a busy man, all right," Seepy said. "The video of you disarming that man at the yard sale today was like something right out of a cop movie."

Rhodes had known the video would be on Jennifer's Web site, but he hadn't watched it. He didn't plan to, either.

Ivy looked at Rhodes. "You didn't tell me you'd disarmed anybody."

"It was great," Seepy said, and he launched into an exaggerated description of the episode with Ted Hensley, beginning with Jennifer's headline: SHERIFF PUTS NINJA MOVE ON ARMED MAN.

Rhodes didn't listen. He busied himself with his cobbler and ice cream. He'd just about finished when Seepy stopped talking.

Harry spoke up again. "You know, Sheriff, *A Christmas Carol* has ghosts in it."

"I know," Rhodes said. He wiped his mouth with his napkin and gave a regretful look at the empty cobbler bowl. "One of them is named Jacob Marley."

"Very good." Harris seemed a bit surprised at Rhodes's literary aptitude, and Rhodes wasn't going to tell him that he'd been reminded of the ghost in the play only that afternoon.

"I'm sorry Jake's dead," Harry continued. "Not just because it's such a loss to the community but because there was a lot I wanted to ask him before I wrote the play."

"For instance?"

"Well, for one thing, I wondered if he was aware of the resemblance between himself and *the* Jacob Marley."

"I didn't know there was one," Rhodes said. "Aside from the name, I mean."

"Well," Harry said, "I don't want to sound too much like an English teacher . . ."

"You don't mind a bit sounding like an English teacher," Seepy said. "I know you don't because I like to sound like a math teacher. Do you want to hear my lecture on linear regression?"

"Not right now," Harry said. "I'd rather tell the sheriff about Jacob Marley. You see, in Dickens's story, Marley doesn't appear in the flesh. He's dead to begin with, and his ghost appears to Scrooge."

"A ghost just like the one in the theater right now," Seepy said.

"Perhaps," Harry said, "but without the clanking chains that Dickens's Marley forged in life. Rather heavy-handed symbolism, and of course real ghosts don't go around clanking chairs."

"I'm glad to hear it," Rhodes said. "It would make it easier to find them, though."

"Yes, wouldn't it," Harry said. "But back to Jacob Marley. In the story he was a selfish man, one who didn't care about anyone else's hardships or sufferings. He cared only about himself and making money. Do you see the parallels with our own Marley?"

Rhodes thought about the real Jake, sitting there in his big house, not seeming to care a thing about the community or the people in it, doing nothing to help the town or the people who didn't have the resources that he had. Also, according to Bradley West, Jake had been making quite a bit of money along the way, piling it up for himself alone.

"I can see what you're getting at," Rhodes said, "but that doesn't mean Jake saw his life that way."

"Of course not, but there's more to it. Because of those bad qualities, Marley's ghost is doomed to wander forever, seeing the things he did nothing about and, now that he realizes the pain and suffering on the earth that he'd ignored before, not being able to do anything about them."

Rhodes thought it over, then said, "Jake was going to take the part of Jacob Marley in the play."

"Well," Harry said, "there you go."

"So," Ivy said, "do you think Jake came to realize his life was like Jacob Marley's and that's why he started doing things in the community?"

Rhodes realized that Ivy had hit on a possible answer to his own question about Jake, who could've been happy now because he'd finally found a purpose for his life beyond staying in his house and making money. If it wasn't *the* answer, it was *an* answer.

"I'm an English teacher," Harris said, "not a psychologist. I can't explain Jake's motives. I'm merely saying that he might have seen parallels between the character in the Dickens story and himself, and it's interesting that he was going to play that part."

"We can ask him about it if we get in touch with his ghost," Seepy said.

"That's not going to happen," Rhodes said.

Seepy smiled. "You can't be sure of that."

"I'm sure," Rhodes said, and then his cell phone rang.

Chapter 10

▼

The phone call was just a coincidence, Rhodes told himself later. It was inevitable that he'd get it as soon as Dr. White completed the autopsy, considering what he had to tell Rhodes.

Rhodes excused himself to Seepy and Harry by telling them that he had to do some county business. Ivy didn't ask what it was until they got to Rhodes's old truck.

"It's the autopsy report on Jake Marley," Rhodes said. "It looks like his death might not have been an accident." They got in the truck and clattered away from the restaurant. "I'll drop you at home and take the county car. I might need it."

Ivy didn't ask when he'd be home. She said, "Try not to stay out too late."

"I'm not expecting to be late," Rhodes said, "but you never know."

"I'll have a surprise for you when you get there," Ivy said.

"What kind of surprise?"

"That's for me to know and you to find out," Ivy told him.

Dr. White didn't usually stay around to discuss autopsy results with Rhodes. His reports spoke for him. This time, however, Dr. White was waiting with Clyde Ballinger, the funeral director, in the small brick house behind Ballinger's Funeral Home. Ballinger let the county use the funeral home for autopsies for a small fee.

Clyde always wore a dark suit and tie, and tonight was no different. Dr. White was dressed less formally in khaki pants and a blue shirt. He had a fringe of white hair and a few age spots on his bald head. He'd obviously cleaned up since doing the autopsy, and his hands and face looked freshly scrubbed.

On most occasions when Rhodes and Ballinger met, Rhodes made small talk with the funeral director about his habit of reading old paperback books with sensational covers, and the first thing Ballinger asked when Rhodes came through the door of his office was whether there had been any books at Ms. Atkins's yard sale.

"No books," Rhodes said.

He didn't ask how Ballinger knew about the yard sale, in the hopes that the funeral director would drop the subject.

"Baseball cards, though," Ballinger said.

"That's right."

Ballinger turned to Dr. White. "Did you know that some baseball cards were worth a lot of money?"

"I'd heard that," Dr. White said.

Ballinger shook his head. "I should've been buying baseball cards instead of books." He looked at Rhodes. "You didn't some here to talk about books and baseball cards, though."

"Nope," Rhodes said.

"You must have wanted a quick autopsy because you were suspicious about Jake Marley's death," Dr. White said.

Rhodes nodded. "I had a feeling something was off about it, and I did notice a contusion on the forehead that didn't seem likely to have been caused by the fall."

"I thought that might be it. The problem is that it's hard to tell which injuries on a person's body were inflicted in the few minutes before death and which ones happened shortly afterward or at about the same time. When someone's fallen from a height, there can be cuts and scrapes that are hard to pin down."

"I understand," Rhodes said.

"I'm sure you do," Dr. White said. "In this case, however, I believe that the contusion on the forehead was inflicted shortly antemortem."

"How can you tell?"

"It's as much a cut as a contusion, although the cut is hard to see without a close examination. It didn't bleed much because Jake Marley died so soon after being struck."

"You think somebody hit him?"

"Either that or he bumped his head against something."

Rhodes had been able to stand on the grid without having to worry about hitting his head, and Jake had been shorter than he was by a couple of inches. It wasn't likely that he'd bumped his head.

"Could hitting him with a bare hand have caused the contusion?" Rhodes asked.

"Doubtful. If someone were wearing a ring, that would be one thing that might have caused it. Jake's skull wasn't cracked, but he had a pretty hard blow. He died of a broken neck in a fall. That's certain. However, someone might have struck him and caused him to fall. It's a tricky situation, but I believe that's what happened."

"So someone murdered him," Ballinger said.

"That would be up to a jury to decide," Dr. White said. "He could've been hit accidentally. I do have a recommendation, however."

"The sheriff should investigate," Ballinger said.

"Exactly," Dr. White said.

When Rhodes got home, Yancey, the little Pomeranian, was as excited to see him as if he'd been gone for a month.

"Do they make tranquilizers for dogs?" Rhodes asked Ivy as Yancey danced around his feet.

Ivy ignored the comment. "Let's go in the kitchen and see about your surprise."

Rhodes had forgotten about the surprise. He followed Ivy into the kitchen, with Yancey threatening to trip him up at every step of the way.

"Have a seat," Ivy said when they arrived in the kitchen, and Rhodes sat at the little wooden table.

The two cats, Sam, the black one, and Jerry, the tuxedo cat, slept over by the refrigerator. Yancey's yipping and constant motion didn't bother them at all. Just looking at the cats made Rhodes think he needed to sneeze, but Ivy had almost convinced him that his cat allergy was all in his imagination.

"Do you want to know what I found out from Dr. White?" Rhodes asked.

"I know what he told you," Ivy said, opening the refrigerator.

"How do you know?"

Ivy took something out of the refrigerator and closed the door. "He wouldn't have called if there hadn't been something suspicious."

"That's right. It's not much, but it's something."

Yancey had gotten tired of bouncing around and gone over to sniff at the cats.

"Leave them alone," Rhodes said, although the cats didn't appear to be bothered. They didn't even wake up.

Yancey knew he was being addressed and turned back to Rhodes to give him a pitiful look.

"Go on to bed," Rhodes said. "The excitement's over."

Yancey hesitated. Sam woke up, yawned, stretched, and looked at Yancey, who didn't need any further encouragement. He ran out of the kitchen and headed for the spare bedroom where his doggie bed was. Sam stared after him for a couple of seconds, then closed his eyes and went back to sleep.

Rhodes looked at Ivy, who was holding something in her right hand. "What do you have there?"

"The surprise," Ivy said, sitting across from him at the table and setting a green-and-red can in the middle.

Rhodes looked at the can. It was a Dr Pepper can, but he'd never seen one like it before.

"Put on your glasses," Ivy said.

Rhodes put on his reading glasses to look at the can more closely, and then he saw the little red circle with the white words centered in it: MADE WITH REAL SUGAR.

"You need to give up your boycott," Ivy said. "It's time to enjoy life again."

Rhodes loved Dr Pepper, but for several years he'd been boycotting the drink because the company had shut down the bottling plant in Dublin, Texas, where Dr Pepper was still being made with sugar. Rhodes had been tempted to drink a Dr Pepper more than once since he'd begun his boycott. He'd even been tempted to try a Pibb Xtra, but so far he'd resisted either of those things. Now he was being tempted again. Severely tempted.

"I thought you only approved of healthy food," Rhodes said, speaking to Ivy but still looking at the can.

"That's right, but I hate to see you pining for something you enjoy. Now you can have the real thing."

"Unfortunate choice of words," Rhodes said.

"What?" Ivy looked puzzled. "Oh. I see what you mean. I'd forgotten that slogan. Are you going to try it or not?"

"For some reason I'm thinking of serpents and apples."

Ivy grinned. "I doubt the consequences of drinking a Dr Pepper will be as severe as the ones you're thinking of."

Rhodes removed his glasses, folded the earpieces, and slipped the glasses back into his shirt pocket. He reached out and took the can.

"It's nice and cold," he said.

"I know. Go ahead. Give it a try."

Rhodes popped the pull tab. "Maybe I should just forget it. I've probably lost weight since I stopped drinking these things."

"No, you haven't."

She was right. Rhodes hadn't lost any weight. That was a flimsy excuse. He lifted the can and took a swallow of the Dr Pepper. It was cold and sweet and fizzy, and if the taste wasn't exactly as he remembered, it was close enough. Drinking it was like hearing an old song and being reminded of a happy time in the past.

"Good?" Ivy said.

"Good," Rhodes said, setting the can back on the table. "There's something else I meant to mention to you."

"What's that?"

"Some people came by the jail today to ask about our sex life."

Ivy grinned. "I hope you didn't shock them."

"I tried not to."

"So who were these people?"

"Claudia and Jan. They needed some material for their next book."

"This is October, isn't it? Not April Fool's Day?"

Rhodes picked up the can and took another swallow of the Dr Pepper. It was just as satisfying as the first one had been.

"I'm not joking," he said. "They were serious about it."

"Was Hack listening in?" Ivy asked.

"Hack always listens in."

"I guess whatever you told them will be on the Internet by tomorrow, then, if it's not already."

"I didn't tell them anything," Rhodes said. "I like to keep a few secrets."

"So do I," Ivy said. "Did I mention that I might have another surprise for you tonight?"

"No, you didn't mention that."

"Well, I might."

"Can I finish my Dr Pepper first?"

"If you hurry," Ivy said.

Early the next morning Rhodes sat on the back steps, as he did on most days, and watched Yancey and Speedo, a border collie who lived outside, tussling over one of their squeaky toys. Ivy came through the back door and sat down beside him. She was wearing a gray wool sweater, and she wrapped her arms around herself.

"It's cold out here," Ivy said.

Rhodes nodded. It was cold, but the wind wasn't blowing, and when the sun was all the way up, it would be a nice day.

"The dogs like the cold," Rhodes said.

"I'm thrilled for the dogs," Ivy said, giving an exaggerated shiver. "What about Jake Marley?"

Speedo dropped the toy, a green rubber frog, and Yancey snatched it up. He ran as fast as he could, but his short legs were no match for Speedo's longer ones. The collie overtook Yancey and ran right over him. Speedo got the toy between his teeth and took off.

"Let's say someone killed him," Rhodes said. "It wouldn't be easy to find anyone with a motive. Hardly anyone knew him. He didn't have contact with anyone in town until recently. He was trying to do something for the community. Why would someone kill him?"

"Maybe it was an accident."

"Maybe," Rhodes said, though he didn't believe it for a second.

Across the yard, Speedo was stretched out beside the green Styrofoam igloo that he stayed inside of on cold nights. He had the frog between his front legs and bit it time after time, causing it to make its squeaky noise. Yancey hopped around nearby, occasionally making a grab for the frog but not having any luck.

"You thought he was killed all along," Ivy said. "You and Bradley West both. That's why he gave you that list of people that Jake wanted in the play. He thinks one of them might have killed Jake."

"What makes you say that?" Rhodes asked.

"For one thing, you told me that Jake wanted you to be at the play. That sounds to me as if he thought something might happen to him."

Rhodes was still puzzled about that part of the will. What good would it do for him to be at the play? Everybody already knew the story's basic outline, and Harry was just going to rewrite it with a Texas setting.

"There's something else," Ivy said. "Harry didn't quite get around to summarizing it last night, but the ghosts who visit

Scrooge show him his past, present, and future. Scrooge tells the last ghost that he's going to change, and he does. He becomes a happy man."

"Jake had already changed," Rhodes said. "He didn't need any visits from ghosts. He was happy. Or different, anyway."

Yancey trotted over and gave Rhodes a pleading stare while Speedo watched, head up, ears alert, feet still holding the frog to the ground.

"Are you going to help him?" Ivy asked.

"Nope. He has to do it on his own." Rhodes motioned with his hand. "Go on, Yancey. You can do it."

Yancey looked doubtful, but he took off to pester Speedo again.

"Maybe Jake was already happy because of something one of the people on that list did," Ivy said.

"Why would one of them kill him, then?"

"You're the sheriff," Ivy said. "That's what you're paid to find out."

Rhodes reached inside his jacket and pulled out the folded paper with the list of names Bradley had given him. He handed it to Ivy, who unfolded it and read off the names and their parts.

"Scrooge, Ed Hopkins. Ghost of Christmas Past, Glenda Tallent. Ghost of Christmas Present, Al Graham. Ghost of Christmas Future, Ron Gleason. I know all those people."

"Everybody in town knows all those people. They've lived here forever."

"That's true," Ivy said. "I wonder why there are only four of them."

"Jake was going to play Marley's ghost."

"That's still only five. There are a lot of other characters." Ivy handed the list back to Rhodes. "One of them's a woman. Why?"

"I've been wondering the same thing," Rhodes said. "Aren't all the ghosts in the story men?"

"Yes. That's going to be an odd change."

"Diversity," Rhodes said, although he was pretty sure Jake Marley didn't give two hoots for diversity.

"I wonder how the play will work with them wearing boots and cowboy hats," Ivy said.

"What I wonder is what those people have to do with Marley," Rhodes said. "Ed Hopkins has something to do with Aubrey Hamilton. She used to work for him, and she's the one who sold Marley the theater building. Ed would have liked to work that deal, so there's a connection. Al has the A+ Auto Repair. I doubt that he ever had to work on Marley's cars, since they were always new. Glenda sells insurance. She's your competitor."

"I'm not a salesperson," Ivy said. "I just work there."

"Right, so she's Thad Aiken's competitor. She sold Jake the insurance on the theater, so Thad might've been upset that he didn't get that contract."

"It wasn't that big a deal," Ivy said. "Surely you don't think Thad killed Jake."

"No. He's not even a suspect. On the other hand, there's Ron Gleason. He used to work for the city. Ran the water department, but he's retired now. I don't see any connection there."

"You'll think of one."

Rhodes put the list in his pocket and stood up. "We'll see."

Seeing Rhodes stand up, Yancey dashed across the yard.

"He knows you're about to leave," Ivy said.

Rhodes held out a hand, and Ivy took it, using it to pull herself up. Yancey started to yip. Speedo lost interest in the chew toy. He got up and went into his igloo. When Yancey saw that, he rushed back across the lawn and snatched the toy. Speedo came out of the igloo and chased him.

"Leave Yancey out here for a while," Rhodes said. "He needs the exercise."

Ivy laughed. "Sure he does. What are you going to do with those names?"

"Look into them," Rhodes said. "Let's go inside."

In the kitchen Rhodes asked Ivy if there'd been any problems between Jake and any of the people working on the theater restoration project.

"It's been mostly very friendly," Ivy said. "I told you he was happy."

"No personality clashes, no disagreements?"

"Not really. If you're looking for murder suspects, you'd better start with that list you have already."

"That's what I'll do, then," Rhodes said. "I wonder why he chose those particular people to be in the play. He can't be friends with them. As far as anybody knows, he doesn't have any friends in town."

"They're all about his age," Ivy said. "Maybe he knew them a long time ago."

"Old friends. That might be it. I'll be sure to ask them."

"There could be some other connection, though."

"They'll tell me if there is."

"You really believe people are that honest when a murder is involved?"

"Nope," Rhodes said, "but I keep hoping."

Chapter 11

▼

At the jail, Rhodes asked Hack what the crime report was, hoping that he'd get a straight answer.

"Ms. Tippet had her car stolen again last night," Hack said. "Third time this year."

"We know it wasn't stolen, though, right?" Rhodes said.

"We do, but she don't seem to be able to figure that out."

"Did you explain to her again that if she'd make the payments, they wouldn't keep repossessing it?"

"I gave it another try. I think she might've understood it this time, and if she gets the car out of hock again, maybe she'll do right from now on." Hack shook his head. "I wouldn't count on it, though."

Rhodes wouldn't count on it, either. "What else is going on?"

"You know about Odell Kinchloe's lawn mower?"

"The one he reported stolen last week?"

"Yeah, that's the one, and we ain't found it yet."

"I know, but we're working on it."

"Odell says he knows where it is."

Rhodes was glad to hear it. "Problem solved then. Where is it?"

"Tupelo, Mississippi."

Rhodes hadn't been expecting that. "Tupelo? Mississippi?"

"That's what I said."

"How does he know it's in Tupelo?"

Hack grinned. "It's a feelin', he says."

"A feeling? He doesn't have any proof?"

"Not a stitch. Just a feelin'. It's a powerful feelin', though, Odell says. He wants you to call the police in Tupelo and tell them to look for it."

"He have an address for us?"

"That ain't part of the feelin'."

"Then we'll keep looking for it around here," Rhodes said. "I don't think the Tupelo police would want to be bothered unless we have an address."

Hack picked up a piece of paper. "In case you change your mind, Odell gave me a complete description of the lawn mower. I wrote it down for you."

"I appreciate that," Rhodes said, tucking the paper away in a corner or the desk.

"I'll tell you what I'd appreciate," Hack said.

"What's that?"

"I'd appreciate it if I was kept in the loop. I know I'm just the dispatcher, but I need to know what's goin' on around here 'stead of bein' kept in the dark all the time."

"You mean about the autopsy on Jake Marley?"

"You know that's what I mean. You never tell me anything. If it wasn't for that Web site of Jennifer Loam's, I'd never find out what's goin' on in this place."

Rhodes started to argue, but thought better of it. He wouldn't be able to change Hack's mind, no matter what. It wasn't just Hack, either. Rhodes's experience had been that he'd never changed anybody's mind by arguing with them. He thought that when the rest of the world caught on to that important truth, things would change for the better.

"The autopsy shows that Jake's death was suspicious," Rhodes said.

"What's that mean?" Hack asked.

"You've been working here longer than I have. You know what it means."

Hack didn't bother to admit it. "Who you think killed him?"

"All I have is a place to start, a list of four people that might or might not have anything to do with it."

"You gonna tell me who they are?"

Rhodes told him.

"All of 'em are about Jake's age," Hack said.

"They were going to be in the play when the theater opened. So was Jake."

"Wonder if they knew him?"

Hardly anybody knew Jake, but Hack's question made sense. Rhodes had thought that Jake had picked people about his own age because they'd be appropriate for the parts, but maybe it was because he knew them. Rhodes would have to look for a connection.

"Who you gonna start with?" Hack asked.

"Jake."

"He's dead."

"Always the best place to start," Rhodes said, heading for the door.

"You're startin' to sound like—"

"Don't say it."

"—Seepy Benton," Hack said, but Rhodes was already outside and pulling the door closed behind him.

Rhodes wasn't really starting with Jake Marley. He was starting with Jake's house. First, however, he dropped by Bradley West's office to tell him about the suspicious nature of Jake's death. West wasn't surprised to learn that Jake had most likely been murdered.

"I knew there was something fishy about the play and the casting," Bradley told Rhodes. "I wish Jake had been more forthcoming about it, but when I asked him, he didn't want to say anything. I let it slide. He was the client, it was his will, and it was none of my business."

"If you think of anything that might help me, let me know," Rhodes said. "I'm going to check out Jake's house. Do you have a key?"

Jake, being dead, had no expectation of privacy, but Rhodes knew it was always best to keep everyone involved in an investigation apprised of what was going on, especially lawyers.

"No key," Bradley said. "Jake didn't expect me to need one. I'm sure you can find a way in."

"It won't be a problem," Rhodes said. "I know where I can get a key. Now about Jake's car—"

"It's still parked downtown," Bradley said. "I checked on it last night. It's fine, but it needs to be moved."

"I know where that key is, too," Rhodes said. "I'll have someone pick up the car and have a look at it."

"It's a Buick LaCrosse. Maroon. You can return it to Jake's house when you're finished."

"I'll take care of it."

"Don't break anything in the house."

"I'll be careful," Rhodes said.

Rhodes called Hack and told him to have Ruth Grady pick up the car key at Ballinger's, get the car, and give it a going-over. Then he drove to the funeral home himself and got the house key.

"You can call Bradley West and have him come by for the rest of Jake's possessions," Rhodes told Ballinger.

"You have any clues yet?" Ballinger asked.

Rhodes laughed. "Ask me that in a few days."

Jake Marley's house was outside the city limits of Clearview on the southeast side. For years there hadn't been any development in that direction, and the house had been all alone, surrounded by fields that had lain fallow and pastures that hadn't been grazed in years. There had once been woods along the roads, but the Marleys had cleared a lot of trees after the accident, not wanting to be reminded of the way their daughter had died, Rhodes supposed, or maybe they wanted revenge on the tree. Mesquite bushes had almost taken over the fields, but they'd been cleared away from some of them now that a bit of building had started along the narrow county road and new houses were creeping in the direction of the old Marley mansion. The houses were still a quarter of a mile away, but they'd eventually get closer.

Rhodes didn't know why the Marley family had decided to build outside the town. Maybe it had something to do with taxes, or maybe they'd thought a home of that size wouldn't fit into a small town. Rhodes had never been inside, but like everyone who'd lived in Clearview for any length of time, he'd seen the house from the outside.

Rhodes had been told that it resembled an English manor house, and he had no reason not to believe it. It was built of white stone and had two stories. Three wide windows on the ground floor took up most of its front. Three peaked dormer windows sat atop the second story. The garage was a semiattached building big enough for four cars. The wide lawn, still green even this late in the year, was perfectly trimmed, as were the hedges and bushes near the front door and the trees that grew near the house. Jake might have been a solitary sort, but he cared about appearances. He could afford to have a lawn service and landscapers who kept the place looking good.

Rhodes drove the Tahoe up the semicircular concrete driveway and parked in front of the door. The house itself looked immaculate, the white stone as spotless as if it had been power-washed only hours before. The key Rhodes had gotten at Ballinger's fit into the lock easily, and he turned it with hardly any effort.

Rhodes stepped into a stone-floored hallway and closed the door behind him. The house had the feeling that empty houses always have, a stillness and a quietness impossible when anyone is inside.

It had another feeling, too, a far creepier feeling. Seepy Benton might've called it a ghost, but that wasn't it. It was as if someone else had been in the place not so very long ago, maybe only minutes before. Rhodes didn't hesitate. He ran down the hall, past the stairway to the second floor, and into the kitchen. The back door was partially open, the frame shattered where someone had broken into the house. Rhodes opened the door and looked out.

The backyard was kept as neatly as the front. There was a lot of it, but within about a hundred yards there was a thick line of trees. Rhodes saw someone moving at a slow jog, about to enter the trees.

Rhodes didn't have time to call for backup. He ran past the swimming pool, now covered for the winter, and onto the clipped grass, his shadow running beside him. Neither he nor his shadow could catch up with the housebreaker, however. Before he'd gone thirty yards, the other runner had already moved into the trees.

A jackrabbit ran across the area just to Rhodes's left. He hadn't seen a jackrabbit in a while, just a few cottontails now and then. If he could run like the jackrabbit, he could catch his suspect, but there was no chance of that.

Rhodes didn't know how far the trees extended, and as he ran, he tried to remember the geography of that part of the county. If he was right, the woods didn't reach very far, maybe only a quarter of a mile, and they ended at an unpaved county road. However, the woods ran along the side of the county road for half a mile or so in both directions, so someone could easily hide in there and evade a search by one person. Or someone could have a car parked just about anywhere on the road and get away before Rhodes could get there.

Rhodes didn't have much choice, though. He had to keep going and try to catch up to whoever had broken into the house. Breaking and entering was a crime all by itself, and if something had been taken, burglary was part of the picture. Yet Rhodes wasn't as interested in the crime as he was in the reason for it. He'd like to know what anyone would want in Jake Marley's house. Was it an attempt to steal something valuable, or was it to remove something that might point to the person who'd killed Jake? Rhodes thought the latter possibility was more likely. It would be too bad if the break-in had been a success.

The air in among the trees was cooler and damper than out in the sun, and the ground was wet and springy underfoot. Rhodes had to be careful not to fall down as he dodged tree limbs and watched for holes. He was a little winded from his run and thought it best to slow down. In fact, it was best to stop completely for a second and listen in an attempt to pick up any sounds that the fleeing burglar might make.

Rhodes stopped. He heard his own breathing and the usual noises of the woods: birds calling, limbs moving in a slight breeze, a couple of squirrels scuffling through the tree branches. Nothing else.

A few half-dead leaves drifted down from the trees. Rhodes looked around to see if anyone was crouching nearby, ready to pounce on him, but he didn't see anything suspicious, just elm trees and a pecan tree or two and a persimmon tree with reddish orange fruit on it. Some of the fruit was on the ground, and Rhodes remembered a song his grandmother had sung when he was a boy:

Raccoon up the 'simmon tree
Possum on the ground,
Possum said to the raccoon,
"Throw them 'simmons down."

Rhodes wondered if a raccoon had tossed the persimmons down or if they'd simply fallen. He didn't see any raccoons or possums around to ask. He wasn't fond of persimmons himself, but he knew people who were. He'd heard a story about one of them, and a woman who might even have been too fond of the fruit. When she was in her early eighties, she'd had digestive problems, and a large mass had been found in her stomach. Ordinarily that would be very bad news, but not in this case. The mass had turned out to be undigested persimmon skins. It had been removed, and the woman had lived for a good many more years. Rhodes didn't know if she'd continued to eat persimmons.

After looking to the left and right and seeing no one, Rhodes decided that he might as well go straight ahead. It seemed reasonable that the burglar would have taken the most direct route to the house from the road.

Rhodes moved at a deliberate pace, stopping now and then to listen. The third time he stopped, he heard a car start. He sped up, still being careful. By the time he got to the road, the burglar was already gone. Rhodes got a glimpse of some kind of vehicle headed down the county road in the direction of town, but he couldn't tell enough about it even to know if it was a car or a pickup.

Across the road from the trees was a cleared pasture, fenced for cattle, and not far away was a turnoff from the road that allowed access to a gate. Rhodes walked down to the gate. That was where the burglar's vehicle had been parked, but the ground was too hard to have taken any impression from the tires. The road wasn't much used, and it was unlikely that anyone had passed by and noticed the vehicle. It wouldn't have aroused any suspicion if anyone had seen it anyway.

Rhodes called Hack on his cell phone and told him to send Ruth to the Marley house.

"She's lookin' into a report of a panhandler in the Walmart parkin' lot," Hack said. "Same guy's been reported two or three times."

"Tell her I need her worse than Walmart does right now. Somebody's broken into the Marley house, and we need to see what's missing."

"I'll get her out there," Hack said, "but the Walmart shoppers ain't gonna be happy if she don't run that fella off. We've had three calls about him already."

"We'll get to him later if he hasn't already left," Rhodes said. "I need her here."

"You're the boss," Hack said.

"Sometimes I wonder," Rhodes said.

Chapter 12

▼

What Rhodes and Ruth learned from their search of Jake Marley's house was that Jake was a good housekeeper who didn't leave clothes on the floor or dishes in the sink. He dusted regularly. He didn't have a lot of possessions, but he did have a library, an entire room of his house devoted to books, as well as an office, which was where he kept a desktop computer, a printer, and a scanner. And more books.

Rhodes didn't know much about rare books, but after looking through the library, he decided that one thing Jake had spent money on was books that were worth more than a few dollars. He had a great many volumes by Charles Dickens, which came as no surprise, and he even had a shelf devoted to magazines with Dickens's serials in them. There were some volumes of Shakespeare, but they didn't look old, and a lot of books by writers whose names Rhodes didn't recognize. Rhodes could check with someone about the value of those things if it became necessary. Maybe Harry Harris would know, or if he didn't, Willie Scott would. Rhodes had discussed rare books with Scott on an earlier case.

The books in the office were different and didn't appear valuable. Most of them looked fairly new, and they included a lot of crime novels by people like Harlan Coben and Alafair Burke and Joe R. Lansdale. Rhodes wondered if that was the same man Seepy Benton claimed to have studied martial arts with.

"If there was a burglar," Ruth Grady said after they'd searched the house thoroughly, "what did he take?"

Rhodes didn't have an answer. The bookshelves didn't look disturbed. The computer was still on the desk, and the two television sets in the house hadn't been touched.

Rhodes looked in the drawers of the computer desk. Papers relating to business dealings, bills, and a few other odds and ends that didn't look important. What might be more important was that the computer was on.

"Lots of people leave their computers on all the time," Ruth said when he mentioned it. "Some people think they should be turned off every night, but others say to leave them on."

"I think our burglar was using the computer," Rhodes said. "We'll have to check for fingerprints."

"We won't find any except for Jake's unless it was a pretty dumb burglar. Anybody who watches TV knows you have to wear gloves if you break into somebody's house."

"We have to go through the motions, though." Rhodes looked around the room. "We might get lucky."

"What are the odds?"

"Never ask me the odds," Rhodes said.

"That's not quite the right quote," Ruth said, and Rhodes wondered if Seepy had been making her watch Star Wars movies.

"Close enough," Rhodes said. "We need a computer expert to look at Jake's files."

"I know somebody," Ruth said.

Rhodes had been afraid of that. "I have a feeling I know who you're going to suggest."

"Seepy's really good with computers," Ruth said, "He could come right now."

"Fingerprints," Rhodes said.

"I'll tag and bag the mouse and keyboard. Seepy can bring his own to use. He has a few spares."

"Why am I not surprised?"

"You want me to call him?"

"Go ahead," Rhodes said. "Tell him to bring Harry Harris along. No ghost-hunting equipment, though."

"You think there might be ghosts here?"

"Absolutely not," Rhodes said.

Seepy and Harry arrived soon enough, but they hadn't entirely followed Rhodes's instructions. Maybe Ruth hadn't told them what he'd said. At any rate, they drove into the semicircular drive in their ghost hunters' van that was decorated with a gaudy sign on both sides. The signs were the same, each announcing that the van was owned by Clearview Paranormal Investigations. Since Seepy Benton had received his nickname from the fact that his initials were C. P., Rhodes had a feeling that the *C* and the *P* were supposed to have a double meaning. The two sheeted ghosts that floated at either end of the name didn't have captions, but Rhodes suspected they were Seepy and Harry in ghostly disguise, and he privately thought of them that way.

The good news was that Seepy and Harry didn't have any ghost-hunting equipment with them, or if they did, they didn't bring it into the house. Seepy had a wireless mouse, a wireless keyboard, and a small receiver that he plugged into the computer's USB port. Neither he nor Harry even mentioned ghosts.

"Windows 7?" Seepy said as he sat down at the computer. "Way out of date. Windows 8 was terrible, I'll admit, but Windows 10 isn't bad. At least the Bluetooth is working."

Rhodes didn't think that "isn't bad" was much of a recommendation. He told Seepy to stand back up.

"Why?" Seepy asked.

"I'm going to swear you and Harry in as temporary deputies. Unpaid. We want to make this investigation official."

"Did you ever unswear me from the last time?" Seepy asked.

"I'm sure I did."

"And I'm sure I wasn't paid."

"Just raise your hand. You, too, Harry."

"I'm honored," Harry said. "Did you know that T. S. Eliot was once made an honorary deputy of the Dallas County Sheriff's Department?"

"That's not true," Seepy said.

Harris had good posture, but he drew himself up even straighter. "Of course it's true. I wouldn't joke about a thing like that. He was an honorary citizen of Dallas, too."

"The guy who wrote that long, boring poem that nobody understands was a deputy?"

"Some of us like to think we understand the poem," Harris said, "and it's certainly no more boring than the binomial theorem."

"That's a matter of opinion," Seepy said.

"He also wrote *Cats,*" Harry said.

"The musical?"

"The poems that were made into songs for the musical."

"Maybe he wasn't so bad after all," Seepy said.

Rhodes thought the whole world was turning into Hack and Lawton, or maybe he was becoming too sensitive to silly arguments.

"I don't need to know anything else about T. S. Eliot," Rhodes said, "musical or otherwise."

"Sorry," Harris said. "Sometimes I get carried away."

"Don't let it happen again," Seepy said.

"That's enough," Rhodes said. He swore them in and left Seepy and Ruth to the computer while he and Harry went into the library. Harry took a deep breath when he saw the books and magazines that Jake had collected.

"I'm not an expert on book values by any means," Harry said, "but I can tell there's some pricey stuff here." He walked over to one shelf and pointed to the spine of a book. "This looks as if it might be a first edition of *A Christmas Carol*. I wouldn't touch it without cotton gloves on my hands. It's worth thousands. Tens of thousands."

He looked around the library and went to a small writing desk on one side of the room near a window. There was nothing on the desk. Harry opened a drawer and took something out.

"Gloves," he said, holding them up for Rhodes to see. "Jake was a true collector, a careful man."

Harry took the gloves and went back to the book he'd looked at. He put on the gloves, which were a little large for him, and carefully removed the book from the shelf. Rhodes walked over to take a look.

Harry opened the book. "Published by Chapman and Hall in 1843. First edition. Amazing. I've never seen one before." He shut the book and replaced it as carefully as he'd removed it. He waved a gloved hand to indicate the shelves. "The books in here are worth hundreds of thousands, I suspect. I've never seen a collection like it."

"Why would someone who broke into the house pass them up?" Rhodes asked.

"You might've interrupted them, or maybe they didn't know the values. Or they were looking for something else."

"I think that's it," Rhodes said, "but what else could it be?"

"That's your job," Harry said. "I'm an English teacher, not a detective."

"I wish Seepy had your attitude."

"He believes he's invaluable to your department, but then he believes he's good at everything."

"Tell me about it," Rhodes said. "Let's go see how good he is with computers."

"He's good," Harry said. "He's very good."

"I'll believe it when I see it," Rhodes said.

What Rhodes saw first was that Ruth was the one who'd found something important. She was standing by a bookshelf holding an oversized book bound in artificial leather.

"It's a Clearview Catamount yearbook," she told Rhodes. "Jake has three of them here from his high school years. That was a long time ago. It's hard to think of him being young."

It was especially hard in Jake's case, Rhodes thought, since he'd had only minimal contact with people in Clearview since that time. Rhodes wondered what the yearbooks were doing in the room with shelves full of crime novels and other fiction.

What was it that Ivy had said that morning? *Maybe he knew them a long time ago.*

"Let me have a look at that," Rhodes said, and Ruth handed him the yearbook. It was one from Jake's sophomore year, and Jake looked even younger than a sophomore. None of the people Rhodes was looking for were there, however. He flipped to the juniors. Still nobody, but he found them in the seniors: Ed Hopkins, Glenda Tallent, Al Graham, and Ron Gleason. Rhodes didn't know what high school was like when Jake had attended, but in Rhodes's day, the seniors hadn't hung out with the sophomores. Maybe it had been different when Jake was in school. It was at least a connection.

Rhodes was about to hand the book back to Ruth when a picture of a girl in Jake's class caught his eye. Elaine Garrett. She was a lot older now, and her hair wasn't cut in a classic bob, but Rhodes recognized her. He'd seen her earlier that morning. She was married now, and her last name was Tunstall. She'd showed up later than ex-pected at the Beauty Shack, and she'd been carrying an eight-pound sledgehammer. Rhodes flipped the page, and there was Harvey Tun-stall, looking bored.

Rhodes closed the yearbook and gave it to Ruth. "Keep this one and the others as evidence."

"Evidence of what?" Ruth asked, taking the book from him.

"I don't know yet," Rhodes said. "Let's see what Seepy's found for us."

"Nothing," Seepy said.

"You mean there's nothing on the computer?"

"No, I mean there's nothing here that will help you. He wasn't trying to hide anything. His e-mail account opens right up without a password, and it's mostly book orders from online dealers, rare books and new ones. He ordered a lot of books."

"I could've told you that," Rhodes said. "What else?"

"There are e-mails to Harry about the play, and e-mails to other people about the restoration of the theater. Nothing that looks like a clue to a murder."

"What about other things? Pictures, documents, that kind of stuff?"

"He didn't save pictures, and he wasn't a writer," Seepy said. "His browser history has been erased, but he has it set to erase every so often. It probably erased automatically. His home page has a news-feed on it, and that's about all. His bookmarks are mostly for book dealers. He doesn't have a Facebook page or a Twitter account."

Rhodes would've been very surprised if Jake had been on Face-book or Twitter or even known what they were. "Surely there's some-thing else."

"Not much," Seepy said, "and don't call me Shirley."

"I've seen that movie," Harry said. "It's hilarious."

"This isn't the time for movie reviews," Rhodes said. "We need to find something on that computer."

"What?" Seepy said. "I can't find it if it's not here. Maybe if I had my EMF meter."

"Never mind that," Rhodes said. "There aren't any ghosts here. What else is on there?"

"Nothing, really. He does have a couple of bookmarks for a news-paper archive, and he's looked through it occasionally."

"Looked for what?"

"The archive saves only the most recent searches. They're from the time the theater opened and then when it was a theater. He was researching it for the restoration, I think."

That was no help at all. "Can you tell if any files have been deleted recently?" Rhodes asked.

"I can check the Recycle Bin." Seepy moved the cursor and clicked the mouse button. "Don't see anything. Of course the Recycle Bin could've been emptied."

"Maybe whoever broke in was looking for something and didn't find it," Ruth said. "Either on the computer or in the house."

"That could be it," Rhodes said. "Or whatever was taken was so small that I didn't see the person carrying it, and it's not something we'd be likely to notice being missing. All right. We've done what we can for today. Ruth, I'll take the yearbooks with me and drop them off at the jail before I start interviewing people. You seal the place after we leave."

"What about me and Harry?" Seepy asked.

"You're now unsworn," Rhodes said.

"And unpaid."

"You knew that when you signed up."

"How about you just let me and Harry hang around for a while. Check the EMF meter and a few things like that. This old house has quite a history."

"No ghost hunting," Rhodes said. "We're leaving."

"Fine," Seepy said. "We'll go to the theater, then."

Rhodes wondered who was in charge of the theater now. Maybe no one was. Things were going to be disorganized for a while with Jake not being around to oversee them.

"Do you have your key, Harry?" Seepy asked.

Harry dug around in his pocket and brought out the key, holding it up for all to see.

"Good," Seepy said. "You want to come with us and make sure we don't break anything, Ruth?"

Ruth looked at Rhodes as if to say she wasn't responsible for Seepy. "Can't," she said. "I'm on duty, and I have an assignment."

"You'll be sorry if we find a ghost," Seepy said.

"I don't think I have a lot to worry about," Ruth said, and Rhodes smiled. Seepy wasn't going to put anything over on Ruth.

"You can't go to the theater now, even if you have a key," Rhodes said. "It's a crime scene. No trespassing."

"You sure do know how to spoil a guy's fun," Seepy said.

"All part of the job," Rhodes said.

Chapter 13

▼

The town of Obert, what was left of it, which wasn't much, sat on top of Obert's Hill. Down the hill and a couple of miles along the highway was the town of Wesley, where Harvey and Elaine Tunstall lived.

Driving down the hill from Obert, Rhodes looked out at the trees that covered the hillside. At the bottom of the hill the country flattened out. Cotton fields had once lined both sides of the road, but now the fields were barren or, like the hill, overgrown with trees. Every mile or so a house stood near the road. The people in the houses didn't have to worry about noisy neighbors. Or any kind of neighbors.

Within a few minutes, Rhodes reached Wesley, which had somehow managed to remain something that resembled a town, even though the population was under a thousand. Wesley still had a school and a post office. It even had a bank. That was about all it had, however. The buildings in what had been the downtown were in worse shape than the ones in Clearview. Several were just brick shells with grass and trees growing in the middle of them. One had collapsed, and bricks lay in heaps along what was left of the walls. A couple had false fronts that had been stuck on by hopeful entre- preneurs who'd lost their hope soon afterward. Now the windows were soaped or broken, and the buildings were vacant. There had been a cotton gin once, but cotton was grown on corporate farms now in the high plains and the Rio Grande valley, not in Blacklin County. Every little town had had a cotton gin once, but they had closed long ago. Hardly a trace of any of them was left.

All over the state little towns that had thrived for so long were dying or dead. The ones that were hanging on, like Wesley, would be gone soon, and even the somewhat larger ones like Clearview prob- ably wouldn't be around when the grandchildren of the people in the elementary school there now were grown.

It made Rhodes a little sad to think about it, and he was glad he wouldn't be around to see the end, when nobody remembered what it was like to shop in a little mom-and-pop grocery instead of Walmart or to have lunch in a little local restaurant instead of a glass- and-plastic national chain establishment. Or go to a movie in a little local theater like Clearview's old opera house.

That last thought reminded Rhodes of why he was in Wesley, and he turned off the highway onto a street paved with cracked asphalt. He drove a block to the Tunstall house. It was old and small but not run-down. It had belonged to Harvey's grandparents, and Harvey and Elaine had moved there years ago when the grandparents had died. Harvey was handy with tools, and he kept the place in good shape. He was in the front yard, working on his sidewalk.

Rhodes parked the Tahoe in the street and got out as Harvey picked up a piece of concrete and carried it to a flatbed trailer hitched to his pickup. The pickup was parked facing the street, and with the attached trailer it took up most of the driveway.

Harvey dropped the piece of concrete on the trailer, and it fell with a thud beside several other chunks, shaking the trailer a little.

"Looks like hard work," Rhodes said, walking across the lawn, which looked nothing at all like the one at Jake's house. The grass was mostly dead, and dirt showed through in several places.

"Sure is," Harvey said.

He was a large man, with wide shoulders and a big stomach. He had on a pair of overalls like the ones Elaine had been wearing the previous day and a long-sleeved shirt that had probably been dark blue once but was now faded to a lighter shade. He wore a pair of leather gloves but no hat, and Rhodes noted that his hair, while mostly gray, was still thick and wavy, with no thin spot in the back.

"What can I do for you, Sheriff?" Harvey asked. "I got a feeling you didn't come to help me bust up my sidewalk."

"Looks like you're about finished," Rhodes said, glancing at the broken pieces of concrete where the sidewalk had been. A sledge-hammer leaned against the side of the house, and Rhodes was sure it was the one Elaine had been carrying when she attacked the Beauty Shack.

"Just about," Harvey said. "Wanna help me pour a new one? I got another pair of gloves in the garage."

Rhodes grinned. "I'd like to help, but I came to talk to Elaine if she's feeling up to it today."

"She's okay," Harvey said. "She's in the house, watching some soap opera she recorded yesterday. She always records 'em, just in case she's not here. She was here yesterday, but she didn't feel like watching it. Too much excitement early in the morning."

Rhodes nodded. "She didn't do much damage at the Beauty Shack. You need to be sure she takes her medication, though."

"I try. She's pretty sneaky. She promises to do better, and she does for a while."

"Maybe she'll stick to the regimen this time."

"I hope so. What you want to talk to her about? Is she in trouble again?"

"Not as far as I know. This isn't about her. She went to school with Jake Marley, and I wanted to ask about him."

That wasn't entirely true, but Rhodes didn't want to go into his reasons with Harvey.

"Never liked Jake much myself," Harvey said. "Elaine, though, she dated him for a while." He grinned and got a faraway look in his eyes. "Turned out she liked me better."

Rhodes was never surprised to learn that high school experiences still mattered to people as they got older. Nobody ever seemed to forget certain things. People who'd known Rhodes in his high school years still sometimes called him Will o' the Wisp because of a story that had been in the local paper about a high school football game. He figured that if he lived to be a hundred, they'd still be doing it.

"Lucky for you," Rhodes said.

"Yeah." Harvey's grin disappeared. "You can go on in if you want to. Just knock on the door first to let her know you're there."

Rhodes went to the door, careful not to trip over any of the concrete, and tapped on the door. He opened it, went inside, and found himself in the living room. The venetian blinds were closed, and the only light came from the TV set. Elaine sat on an old couch with a coffee cup in her hand. She wasn't wearing overalls today. She had on jeans and a white blouse.

"Mrs. Tunstall?" Rhodes said.

Elaine looked away from the TV. "Hey, Sheriff."

She didn't seem surprised or upset to see him. Her medication must have taken effect.

"You ever watch *The Young and the Restless*?" she asked.

"I'm usually at work," Rhodes said.

"It's pretty complicated if you don't keep up with it," Elaine said. She picked up the remote control that lay beside her on the couch and turned the TV volume down. "There's these two families, see, the Newmans and the Abbotts, and they live in some town called Genoa City. I don't think it's a real town."

"Probably not," Rhodes said.

"You have a seat, Sheriff. This couch will hold both of us."

Rhodes sat on the couch, and Elaine continued to tell him about the soap opera, gesturing with the remote. "There's this man, Victor Newman, who has some kind of business, and he's been married to a lady named Nikki a few times. Seems like everybody on there's been married to everybody else at one time or another. Jack Abbott doesn't like Victor, and Victor doesn't like him. I don't much blame either one of them. They're both pretty mean sometimes. Anyway, he has this sister named Ashley. Jack does, I mean, he's the one that has the sister, not Victor."

Elaine stopped talking and looked at Rhodes. She set her coffee cup and the remote on the low table in front of the couch.

"I guess you didn't come to talk about a soap opera," she said. "I'm real sorry about what happened in town yesterday. Sometimes I get upset like that, but I don't mean to hurt anybody."

Rhodes wondered if she'd hurt anybody yesterday. If she had, it hadn't been at the Beauty Shack.

"You knew Jake Marley in high school, didn't you?" he asked.

"I sure did. I went out with him a few times. It was a real shame he died yesterday. He'd finally come out of his shell and started to do some good in his hometown."

"What was he like in high school?"

"He used to be just a normal boy, I guess you'd say. When I was going out with him, anyway. He liked the usual stuff, football, cars, things like that. That was before he got funny." She paused and looked at the TV, then back at Rhodes. "I don't mean funny ha-ha, you know?"

"I know," Rhodes said.

"What happened after a while was, he got all quiet and didn't talk to hardly anybody. He came to school most days, but sometimes he'd miss two or three days in a row. People said he wasn't sick but just staying at home. He managed to graduate, but just barely. Some of us thought maybe if his name had been Smith or Jones, he might not've, you know?"

"I guess that kind of thing can happen. Have you seen Jake since he's been working on the theater in Clearview?"

Elaine looked at the TV set. "I haven't talked to him or anything. I doubt he remembered me."

"You've never been by the theater to look it over?"

Elaine kept her eyes on the TV set. "I've driven by a time or two when I was in town. Just to see how it looked."

"But you didn't see Jake?"

"I think I saw him going inside once. I didn't stop to be sure."

"Did you drive by yesterday?"

"I don't remember. I'm real sorry about what I did, Sheriff." Elaine touched her hair. "I like this haircut just fine now. I hope Lonnie won't hold what I did against me."

"I'm sure he won't," Rhodes said, wondering if Elaine was telling the truth. It wouldn't have been easy for her to climb up that ladder with an eight-pound sledgehammer hanging from the loop on her overalls, but it could be done by a woman as strong as Elaine. "Did anybody know what it was that made Jake change?"

"Just one second, Sheriff," Elaine said. "I want to pause this DVR thing. This is Friday's show, and the last scene is about to come on. They always have a good last scene on Friday. I don't want to miss it."

She got the remote and pushed a button. The action on the TV set froze.

Elaine waited for a second, then set the remote back down. "I thought everybody knew what happened to Jake."

"It was before my time," Rhodes said. "I never heard the story."

"It was his sister," Elaine said. "She died in a car wreck."

"I did know about that, but I didn't know Jake changed afterward."

"Well, it wasn't like it happened in one day, you know? It was kind of slow. He just got more and more down and withdrawn till finally he was like I told you. He didn't associate with anybody even when he did show up at school, and then after he graduated, his parents died when he was pretty young. I guess that didn't help any. Maybe if he'd seen a doctor and gotten some meds . . ."

Rhodes didn't want to get into a discussion of Jake's medical condition. "What was his sister like?"

"She was a real pretty girl. Gwendolyn, that was her name, but everybody called her Gwen. Real pretty, and popular, too. She was a cheerleader one year. It was a real shame, what happened to her, that car wreck and all. People said she must've been drinking, but I never believed it. She wasn't that kind of a girl. She was real smart, had a lot of boyfriends."

"And Jake was sweet on you."

Elaine smiled. "I used to be real pretty myself. I wasn't ever a cheerleader or anything, but I went out with Jake a time or two. Did I tell you that already? For some reason he and I never hit if off, though. Harvey, now, he was really something in those days, good looker, football player, and once I started going with him, I wasn't interested in Jake anymore. Jake might've been richer, but Harvey's been real good to me, you know?"

"I know," Rhodes said. "You said Gwen had a lot of boyfriends. Do you remember who they were?"

"Oh, yes. They were the popular boys in her class. They all still live here in town. You probably know them. Ron Gleason was one. Al Graham. Ed Hopkins, too. She went out with all of them, played them against each other."

Rhodes wasn't a big believer in coincidences, though he knew they happened now and then, but the fact that the boys Gwen Marley had dated were the very men Jake had insisted on casting in the play Harry Harris was to write couldn't possibly be coincidental. Something was going on there, and maybe it was connected to Jake's murder.

"What about Glenda Tallent?"

"Oh, sure, I knew her. She was just as pretty as Gwen. They both ran with that same crowd, and they were good friends. Gwen and Glenda, the Two G's. When Gwen wasn't going with one of those boys, Glenda was."

"You're sure about those names?' Rhodes said.

"Sure I'm sure. I wouldn't forget a thing like that. They were all two years older than me, and that was a big difference in those days. I thought they were practically grown-ups. I thought they knew all about life and everything." Elaine paused. "I guess I was wrong. Nobody ever figures life and everything out, do they?"

"Not that I know of," Rhodes said. "It's not easy to do."

"Sure hasn't been easy for me and Harvey. We did all right for a while, but things happen, you know? I got sick, and sometimes I get off my meds. When you're young, who ever thinks something like that will come along?"

"Nobody," Rhodes said. He stood up. "Thanks for talking to me. I'm glad you're doing okay, and I appreciate what you told me about Jake."

"I'm sure sorry he's dead. He was funny for a long time, but he'd gotten a lot better."

"That's what everyone keeps telling me."

"It doesn't do him any good to be better when he's dead, though."

"Not a bit."

"It did before he died, though," Elaine said. "For a while."

"Yes," Rhodes said. "I guess it did."

Chapter 14

▼

Rhodes drove back to Clearview feeling that he'd learned something important. He didn't know exactly what it was yet, but the connections among Gwen Marley and the men Jake had insisted on casting in the play had to mean something. If Rhodes could figure out what the connections were, he might find the answer to why Jake was killed.

Or he might not, but it was a place to start. He thought about eating lunch before he talked to any of the men he wanted to see. They all had businesses in Clearview, so they might be at lunch themselves. Rhodes figured he could afford to take the time for a little bite. He didn't want to take too long, so he drove by the Dairy Queen and got a Jalitos Ranch Burger at the drive-through. He didn't order any fries, which he felt relieved him of any guilt incurred by having the burger.

He decided it would be a good idea to take the burger home to eat it. Ivy wouldn't be there, since she took a lunch and ate at her desk, which allowed her to take off early in the afternoon. She always offered to fix Rhodes a lunch, too, but the idea of eating a sandwich with turkey baloney and wilted lettuce didn't appeal to him. What appealed to him was the idea of having his burger with another of the Dr Peppers with real sugar.

Yancey was thrilled to see Rhodes come in, but he was thrilled to see anybody come in. It was as if he thought that everyone who left the house would be like poor Charlie on the MTA and never return, so he was overjoyed when someone did.

As for the cats, they were as indifferent as ever. Come, go, it didn't matter to them as long as they had food and water in their bowls. They hardly bothered to open their eyes when Rhodes came into the kitchen. They were disturbed enough to stretch and shift positions, but it was clear that Rhodes didn't matter to them at all.

Rhodes set his burger on the table and checked to be sure that they did have the essentials, and then he checked to be sure that Yancey did, too. All was well, so Rhodes got a Dr Pepper from the refrigerator and sat down to eat his burger, which had deep-fried jalapeños and pepper jack cheese among its ingredients. He'd need the Dr Pepper to cool his mouth.

It was a little difficult to eat at first because Yancey kept dancing around Rhodes's feet, but he got tired after a couple of minutes and lay down beside the chair for a little nap. Rhodes ate his burger, had an occasional swallow of Dr Pepper, and thought about his next step.

It occurred to him that he didn't know anything about Gwen Marley's death other than that she'd died in a one-car accident. It had happened nearly fifty years ago, but if there had been any serious talk about it at the time, it had all faded away, not even to be revived by Jake's sudden return to the world. That didn't mean nothing was suspicious about the wreck, however. It just meant that suspicions had been so few that they'd been forgotten. The sheriff's department would have done an investigation, but records that old might be hard to find. Some of the older files were kept in the court-house, where Rhodes had an office he seldom visited. He'd drop by there and see if he could find the reports of the accident. Then he could decide on how to proceed.

He disposed of the paper that had wrapped the burger by taking it to the outside trash bin. It wasn't that he didn't want Ivy to see it, he told himself. It was just to keep the smell out of the house.

When Rhodes went back inside, Yancey was awake and yipping as if he hoped Rhodes would stick around and give him a romp in the backyard.

"No time for fun," Rhodes told Yancey. "I have to go to work."

Yancey looked sad as Rhodes went out the door this time, even though Rhodes tried to reassure him.

"I'll be back," Rhodes said. "So will Ivy. Don't worry."

Yancey looked more than worried. He looked inconsolable, and Rhodes watched through the screen door as the little Pom-eranian slunk off to his bed in the guest room. The cats hadn't been disturbed by Yancey's excitement and had slept through the whole thing. At least Rhodes didn't have to worry that they'd miss him.

Rhodes walked by the Dr Pepper machine in the basement of the courthouse and looked at it with disdain. The soft drinks it held weren't made with sugar, so he couldn't be bothered with it.

He slipped into his office without running into anyone and went immediately to the door that opened into a storeroom that held boxes of dusty old documents from the sheriff's department. Everything now was stored electronically, which was fine, as long as the storage media didn't break down. Paper might be dusty, and it might turn yellow, but it didn't crumble to pieces for a long, long time if it was stored correctly. The courthouse was air-conditioned and sealed against the elements, so Rhodes was sure that the paper documents would be there until well after he was gone and some new sheriff was digging through them.

Rhodes didn't have to dig long this time. He found the box he wanted at the end of a row. It wasn't on top of the stack, but it wasn't on the bottom, either. It was right in the middle, so he had to move only two boxes to get to it. He flipped through the old file folders, all of them neatly fitted with typed labels, until he came to the one he wanted. When he took it out to his desk, Jennifer Loam was sitting in a chair, waiting for him.

"The door was open," she said, "so I made myself at home."

"I noticed," Rhodes said.

He knew the door hadn't been open. He never left it open. It hadn't been locked, however, and Jennifer was the kind of person who'd have tried the doorknob without even thinking about it.

"I checked by the jail," Jennifer said, "but you weren't there. Hack said he didn't know where you were. He sounded a little peeved about that."

Rhodes sat at his desk and laid the folder on it. He was surprised that a youngster like Jennifer would use a word like "peeved." "Hack gets that way a lot."

"He said you never kept him in the loop."

"He says that a lot, too."

Jennifer leaned forward. "You never keep me in the loop, either."

"You're not a member of the department."

"I'm a member of the press. I have an obligation to my readers to let them know what's going on in the county. I shouldn't have to track the sheriff down to find out what I need to know."

Rhodes laughed. "You've tracked me down often enough. You didn't have any trouble this time."

Jennifer laughed, too. "I've found you here before. I saw the Tahoe parked in your space outside and figured you'd be here."

"Good work. Maybe I should make you a deputy. What did you want to know?"

Jennifer turned serious. "The talk all over town is that Jake Marley was murdered, but I don't put gossip on my Web site. I'd like to know the truth."

Rhodes was surprised that Hack hadn't told her, but maybe she hadn't asked him. Too, she was dating one of the deputies, Andy Shelby. However, Andy hadn't been in on the investigation so far and might not have known anything about it. Or he'd kept his mouth shut, which Rhodes would've preferred.

"It's true that Jake's death is being investigated," Rhodes said. "I'm not sure that he was murdered, though. It might've been an accident, but we're investigating because the circumstances are suspicious."

"How are they suspicious?"

Rhodes wasn't going into the specifics because he didn't want to give too much away. He said, "Jake fell from a height. The question is whether somebody helped him fall. Right now, that's about all I can tell you."

"I can see why Hack gets peeved at you."

Rhodes spread his arms and turned his palms up. "I'm telling you all I can. We're just getting started with the investigation."

Jennifer looked at the file Rhodes had put on the desk. "Yet you came all the way over here. You must be working on something."

Rhodes put both hands palms down on the file. "It's just something I'm checking out. It might not mean a thing."

"So you're not going to tell me what it is."

"You know I can't."

"It never hurts to ask. Are you going to look at that file?"

Rhodes looked at it, then looked back at Jennifer.

"That's not what I meant," she said.

Rhodes opened the file, which, as he'd thought it would, contained the old forms used for investigations years ago. It also had several garish black-and-white photos of the accident scene.

"Okay," Rhodes said. "I've looked at it. I can't tell you what's in it, though, or even why I'm looking at it. It's part of an ongoing investigation."

"It must have been going on for a long time if the file was buried over here in the courthouse."

"I have to warn you against unwarranted speculation," Rhodes said.

Jennifer stood up. "I never speculate, but sometimes I conjecture."

"You have to be careful about that kind of thing."

"I know," Jennifer said. "I'll see you later, Sheriff."

"I don't have any doubt about that."

"Shall I close the door when I leave?"

"Good idea," Rhodes said. "You never know who might come in if it's open.

Jennifer laughed and closed the door behind her.

When Jennifer was gone, Rhodes read through everything in the file folder. The report was straightforward. Gwen Marley's car had been going too fast, missed a curve on a county road not too far from her home, and shot through a barbed-wire fence. The car had spun in a half circle, and the rear end had hit a tree. Gwen had been thrown from the car, hit her head on another tree, and died instantly.

Hardly anyone had worn seat belts in those days, so Rhodes wasn't surprised that Gwen had been thrown from the car. It happened often. She might have survived if her head hadn't hit the tree, but it did, so that was the end of the story.

Or it would have been had Rhodes believed everything he read in the report, which he didn't. He looked at the report again. It had been typed by a deputy named Goodman. Rhodes had never met him, and it wouldn't have mattered if he had.

The report said that there had been no one else on the scene when Goodman had arrived. Someone had called in the accident anonymously, and Goodman was the one sent to investigate. He apparently didn't see anything strange about the scene.

Rhodes did. He looked at the photographs of the scene again. They were brighter in the middle and darker toward the edges, thanks to the cheap flash attachment that someone had used, but everything was clear and sharp. The car was a four-door sedan, and both front doors were sprung open. The sheet-covered figure of Gwen Marley was on the wrong side of the car.

Goodman explained that oddity by saying that while both doors were open, Gwen had been thrown across the front seat and through the passenger door by the force of the impact and the fact that the car had been in a spin.

It was the kind of thing that could have happened, but it was only a bare possibility. Rhodes didn't believe it. He believed that there had been two people in the car and the second person had been driving.

Something was missing, too. There had been no autopsy, and

there were no toxicology results. Had alcohol been involved in the accident? All the sheriff's report said was that the driver had "apparently lost control of the car." Speculation about why that might have happened was missing.

Rhodes read the report again. Gwen had been seen in town earlier that night, and she hadn't been seen with anyone. When her parents were questioned, they said she'd been to a movie and that she'd been alone. Maybe she had at some point during the night, but when she hit the tree, she hadn't been alone. Rhodes would have bet on it. He felt sure that someone had walked away from the accident.

Rhodes thought about everything that had happened recently: Jake Marley coming out of his house and out of his shell and getting involved with the community, Jake's seeming personality change, his restoration of the theater, his insistence on a new version of *A Christmas Carol* being performed there, his will, his naming of the cast members of the play.

Besides that, there was what Rhodes had learned earlier from Elaine Tunstall about how Jake had changed after his sister's death.

Rhodes recalled what Harry Harris had said about Marley in the story of Scrooge and the ghosts. Marley had been thinking of all the things he'd seen and done nothing about. His ghost was there to remind Scrooge of his failings by having the ghosts show him his past.

Then something else popped into Rhodes's head, something else he hadn't thought of since high school. It was from his senior year when the class had to read *Hamlet*. Hamlet had put on a play to trick the king into confessing he'd killed Hamlet's father. Jake had a set of Shakespeare's plays on his library shelves. He'd have known about that. Was Jake trying to catch the conscience of one of the men he'd cast in the play? They'd all been in Gwen Marley's class, and she'd been friendly with all of them, according to Elaine Tunstall. Had one of them been at the movie with her and in the car afterward? If that was the case, had Jake just found out, or had he known all along? If he'd known all along, why wait until now to do something about it?

Another question, one that bothered Rhodes as much as the ones about his suspects, was why Jake had wanted him to be at the play. If he was indeed hoping that the play would reveal something about Gwen's death, did he hope that Rhodes would be able to make an arrest? That wouldn't be possible, of course, unless the accident had actually been a murder. There was no statute of limitations on that crime, but there was also no indication that Gwen had been murdered.

The questions didn't end there. Even more important was whether Jake's death was connected to the accident. It had been long ago, but the past was never dead in a small town. If Jake had planned to expose one of the men he'd cast in the play and the man had found out, it might be a motive for murder. It had been too long for any charges to be filed against anyone, but a ruined reputation could be just as disastrous as a jail sentence to some people.

Rhodes put everything back in the file folder and put the folder in the center drawer of his desk. He had a lot of people to see and a lot of questions to ask them. He might as well begin with Scrooge.

Like his former employee Aubrey Hamilton, Ed Hopkins was an independent real estate dealer, not affiliated with any of the nationally known firms. He'd been in business for as long as Rhodes could remember, and he and Aubrey were currently the only two Realtors in Clearview. He'd once had his office downtown, but now it was located out on the highway, which was where just about all the businesses in Clearview had moved, to get close to the big Walmart or at least to get out where somebody might drive past them on the way to Walmart. Unlike many of the businesses, however, Hopkins hadn't located in a strip center. He'd bought a building that had once been a pizza place and remodeled it into his offices. Rhodes parked in the ample parking lot and got out of the Tahoe.

He thought he smelled pizza, but that was probably just his imagination, like the smell of popcorn in the movie theater. He wondered why his imagination was always smelling food. Probably best not to think too hard about it.

Rhodes went into the building through a glass door that had HOPKINS REALTORS painted on it in gold, and a little bell rang over the door. The building had been divided into offices, although no one had an office there except for Ed. He didn't have an office manager or administrative assistant, and he hadn't taken on another agent since Aubrey had left. Business wasn't booming.

Ed's desk was in the big front room, but he wasn't sitting at it. Rhodes waited. He knew Ed was around. He would've locked the door if he'd been out with a client. Over in one corner stood a coat rack with a red jacket and a Western-style hat hanging from it. Ed wore the hat as kind of a trademark. Rhodes felt a momentary tinge of envy, but he suppressed it.

After a couple of seconds, Ed came down a short hall and into the office. He had on a sport coat but no tie. Rhodes could barely remember the time when businessmen wore ties to work.

"Hey, Sheriff," Ed said. "Good to see you. You in the market for some real estate today? A new house? Some acreage? Whatever you need, I have it."

Ed was almost as tall as Rhodes but thinner, with a narrow face and a prominent Adam's apple that bobbed up and down when he talked. His hair was thin all over, so thin on top that his scalp showed through. Rhodes wondered how long it would be before his own hair became like that.

"Business must be booming," Rhodes said.

The corners of Ed's mouth turned down. "I wish. I have plenty of properties. All kinds. What I don't have is plenty of buyers. Blacklin County isn't what you'd call a seller's market right now. I'd make you a good deal on some nice acreage or a fine house."

"I'm not in the market," Rhodes said. "I'm here about something else."

"Well," Ed said, looking disappointed, "have a seat and tell me all about it." He sat behind his desk and pushed a calendar and some kind of computer tablet aside. They were the only things on the desk aside from a little cardholder that contained some of Ed's business cards. "I don't have any appointments for a while."

Rhodes sat in one of the two chairs in front of Ed's desk. "You heard about Jake Marley."

"Sure did." Ed leaned forward and put both hands on his desk, palms down. "Worst news for the town in a long time. Jake had finally gotten his act together."

"How well did you know him?"

Ed leaned back in his chair. "I didn't. Nobody knew Jake."

"You went to school with him."

Ed brushed that off. "Yeah, but that was a long time ago. Haven't been in touch since then."

"He went to Aubrey to make the deal for the theater."

"Yeah." Ed sighed. "I didn't even hear from him. Kind of hurt my feelings. I could've used the business."

Rhodes wondered just how badly Ed's feelings had been hurt. He said, "He must've been happy about the deal. He seemed to like her."

"I wouldn't know about that," Ed said.

He didn't seem to want to talk about Aubrey, so Rhodes said, "How much did he like her?"

"I'm sure I don't know. It's none of my business how she got him to do a deal. I don't discuss my competitors."

Rhodes changed the subject. "Jake's death might not have been an accident. You know anybody who might've had something against him?"

"Not an accident?" Ed didn't look as surprised as Rhodes had thought he might. "Who'd want to hurt Jake, now that he was doing some good around here?

"That's what I'm trying to find out. You have any ideas?"

"Not a one."

Rhodes saw that he wasn't going to get very far with that line of questioning. "I guess you knew Jake's sister. You must've been about the same age."

Ed looked up over Rhodes's shoulder, as if he saw something interesting in the parking lot. Rhodes almost turned to look, but he didn't. He was sure there was nothing out there other than the Tahoe.

"That was a long time ago," Ed said. "High school days. Ancient history now."

"She died in some kind of accident, I think."

Ed continued to look at something over Rhodes's shoulder. Maybe it was something only he could see.

"Yeah, she did. Sad story. Car went off the road. Hit a tree. Killed her instantly. So I heard."

"She was alone in the car?"

"What I heard." Ed finally looked back at Rhodes. "I wasn't there."

"Do you know if she'd been drinking?"

"I just told you I wasn't there. Why are you asking about Gwen?"

"Someone mentioned her today. Said Jake changed after she died."

Ed looked back out at the parking lot. "That's true, I guess. I don't remember all that well, but it seems like he wasn't ever the same. Well, until here lately. He's getting out of the house now and showing himself in town."

"He hasn't been in touch with you at all?"

"Nope. He wouldn't have any reason to be, now would he? He got Aubrey to help with the theater deal, not me, as we've said."

"I wonder why he didn't come to you."

"Don't know. His business who he deals with."

"He thought about you at least once," Rhodes said. "You know about the play that's planned for the grand opening of the theater?"

"I've heard a little. That's a year or more away, though."

"It's based on *A Christmas Carol*. Jake specified in his will that he wanted you to play a part in it."

For the first time Ed looked disconcerted. "Me? A part in a play? What are you talking about?"

"You'd be Scrooge," Rhodes said. "He gets visits from the Ghosts of Christmas Past, Present, and Future. He's reminded of a lot of things he'd rather forget."

"That's just crazy. I don't believe in ghosts. I don't know anything about the play. I'm not an actor, and I'm not going to be in any play. I don't know what Jake was thinking. I haven't seen him in years. Nobody told me about this."

"He wanted you, Ron Gleason, Glenda Tallent, and Al Graham to be in it." Rhodes said. He didn't mention that the will said that Jake wanted him to be in the audience. "Maybe it was supposed to be a surprise."

"Well, it damn sure is." Ed looked at his watch. "Too bad I can't do it. I have an appointment in ten minutes. Got to show the old Logan house to somebody from Houston who wants to get out of the big city and retire to a nice, quiet little town. That is, if you don't have any more questions for me about Jake."

Rhodes didn't believe that Ed had an appointment, considering what had been said earlier, but he didn't think he was going to get anything else from him. He stood up.

"I don't want to keep you from making money. Those folks from Houston will love the old Logan place, I'm sure."

"I hope so," Ed said. He'd regained his composure. "I've been trying to find a buyer for months. Nearly a year. Not a lot of houses moving these days."

"Good luck, then," Rhodes said.

Ed got up and fetched his hat from the coat rack. He curled the brim, then settled it on his head. He walked over to Rhodes and said, "I hope you're wrong about Jake's death not being an accident. I'd sure hate to think somebody killed him."

"Me, too," Rhodes said.

Chapter 15

▼

Ron Gleason wasn't at home. His wife was, however. Genie Gleason was a slim woman who looked years younger than Ron because she was. Ron had been a bachelor for a long time and gotten married when he was in his forties to a young woman who worked in his office at the city hall. People around town had said it would never last, but it had, and it seemed to be a solid union.

"Ron's at the cabin," Genie told Rhodes when she answered the door. "He always has a big fish fry for his friends at his office this time of year. Not that he has an office anymore. He started doing it when he was with the water department, and he's kept on doing it. He invites the people who used to work there with him."

"You're not going?" Rhodes said.

"I'm going," Genie said. "I'm just letting Ron do all the work to get ready. I'll be leaving in an hour or so. What do you want with him? I hope he's not going to jail for frying fish."

Rhodes grinned. "I'm not going to spoil his fish fry. I just wanted to talk to him about someone he knew a long time ago. Jake Marley."

"Poor Jake. It's so sad, what happened to him."

"It is," Rhodes said. "Did Ron hear from him lately?"

"I think they talked on the phone a time or two. Not for long, though. Ron hadn't seen Jake in years and years."

"Jake liked to keep to himself, all right. Where's this cabin of yours?"

"It's on some acreage we own outside of town," Genie said. "Ron built it when he retired."

She gave Rhodes directions on how to get there, and Rhodes realized that the cabin was located along the same county road that ran behind Jake Marley's property, about a mile away.

"Thanks," Rhodes said. "I'll drive out that way. Maybe I can give him some help."

"The cabin's set back off the road," Genie said, "kind of back in the woods. The gate to the road will be open, so you can just drive in. You shouldn't have any trouble finding it. Just follow the ruts."

"I can do that," Rhodes said.

The cabin was set well back off the road in a little clearing in the woods, which weren't as thick here as they were in the southeastern part of the county but which were thick enough to get lost in.

Rhodes parked well out of the ruts and away from the house so that if any of Ron's guests arrived, they could park easily and wouldn't block the Tahoe. He got out of the Tahoe and looked over the cabin. It wasn't anything Abe Lincoln would've recognized. It appeared to have only one room, but the outside was shielded by weather-resistant siding, and the roof was covered with high-quality shingles. The windows were small, but they had double panes.

In front of the house were two long wooden picnic tables with benches. Not too far away sat an old black washpot on an iron grate. Several large rocks helped balance it there. Rhodes walked over and looked into the pot. It was about half full of cooking oil. Pieces of dried wood lay under the pot.

Ron Gleason came out of the house and saw Rhodes. "Hey, Sheriff. Did you come for some catfish and hush puppies? I'm about to get the fire started, and you're welcome to stay. There'll be plenty."

Ron wasn't slim like his wife, but he was taller and carried his weight well. He had on a black trucker's cap with a bill that shadowed his face, faded jeans, and a green shirt. He also wore a stained apron that had once been white but was now a sort of off-gray color. He had big hands and wore a large Masonic ring on his right ring finger.

"Caught the catfish myself," Ron said. "Cleaned 'em, filleted 'em, and froze the filets in water. They'll be just like fresh. I got 'em inside now, all thawed and soaking in buttermilk. I'll put the meal on 'em in a few minutes and cook 'em. The meat'll be so tender it'll melt in your mouth."

Rhodes thought about the offer and was tempted. Fried fish right out of the grease and onto the plate would be hard to beat, especially with hush puppies on the side. If Ivy had been with him, he'd have accepted, but she wasn't, so he didn't.

"I wish I could stay," he said, "but I just came by to ask you a few questions about Jake Marley."

"That was a hell of a thing, him falling like that," Ron said. "Let me get us a couple of lawn chairs and we can sit down."

He went inside and came back out with two folded lawn chairs, a butane lighter, and some newspaper. He stopped and gave Rhodes the chairs.

"Unfold those things while I light the fire," Ron said. "I need to get it started so the oil can come to a nice boil."

Rhodes unfolded the chairs and sat in one of them while Ron started the fire and got it going. It was getting late, and the sun had started to go down. Standing close to the fire might feel good later on.

"I got lights on in the cabin," Ron said, coming to sit beside Rhodes. "What'd you want to ask me about Jake? I haven't seen him for years, so I doubt I can help you much."

Funny how Jake had started appearing in public, yet nobody admitted having seen him, Rhodes thought. "He hasn't been in touch with you about anything?"

"Not me. I don't work for the city anymore, so I couldn't help him with the water in that old building even if he asked me to."

"But he didn't ask you," Rhodes said.

Ron leaned back in his chair. "Nope. Some of those old buildings, the pipes are bad. Some of 'em, maybe the pipes are okay. I don't know about that one."

"You knew Jake in high school, didn't you?"

"Sure. His family was mighty big in those days."

"What about his sister?"

"Gwen? Yeah, I knew her. Sad story."

"Sad?"

"You bet," Ron said. "Died in a car wreck all alone. I'd call that sad."

"I was talking to Ed Hopkins this afternoon," Rhodes said. "He told me you dated her."

Ron didn't say anything for a second or two. When he spoke his voice was tight.

"I went out with her a couple of times, maybe. Ed went out with her more than I did."

"He didn't mention that. He said he thought he saw someone with her in the car in town the night she was killed in the accident."

Ed had said no such thing, but Rhodes didn't mind misleading Ron a little.

"It wasn't me," Ron said. "I heard nobody was with her. She was by herself when they found her."

"That's what the police report says, but I wonder if it's right. Do you know if she'd been drinking?"

Gleason crossed his arms over his chest. "How would I know that? I wasn't around her. We were all underage then, though, so we didn't drink."

Rhodes thought that if nobody underage ever drank, the alcohol-related industries would take a big hit, but Ron wasn't going to admit anything, not even this many years later.

"Jake was a lot different after the accident happened," Rhodes said, "or so Ed tells me."

Ron relaxed a little at the change of subject. "That's true. He wasn't the same. We could all see that. A real shame. 'Course, lately he was getting out and about, taking an interest in things again. Took him a long time, but that's understandable."

"Why?" Rhodes asked.

Again Ron hesitated. "He and Gwen were really close, I guess. Living out of town like that. You know how it is."

They hadn't been too far out of town, and Rhodes didn't know how it was, but he didn't mention it. He said, "Somebody broke into Jake's house today."

"Really? People sure are worthless. Who'd do a thing like that?"

"Maybe you saw whoever it was," Rhodes said. "He came in

through the back way, parked his car on the road that runs by your place here."

"Nope. I was out here this morning, though."

Rhodes found that interesting. "Getting ready for the fish fry."

"Nope. You ever seen a cougar?"

Rhodes had to think about that one for a second. He knew that the word "cougar" had taken on new meanings over the years.

"You mean the cat kind of cougar?" Rhodes asked.

Ron laughed. "That's the kind, all right. Ever seen one?"

"Just bobcats," Rhodes said. "I don't think there are any cougar in these woods. They've all moved out to far West Texas."

"That's what I thought, but I swear I heard one the other night. Not a roar exactly, but mighty close, so I've been coming out here and looking around for signs that maybe there's a cougar."

It was possible that Ron was telling the truth, or maybe he was just making an excuse in case someone had seen his pickup on the road that morning.

"Found any signs?" Rhodes asked.

"Not yet, but I'm gonna keep looking. I think it's out there."

Rhodes didn't think so. If there were any cougars in East Texas, they'd be over in the Big Thicket, not in Blacklin County.

"You know," Rhodes said, "sometimes a feral hog makes sounds that aren't too different from a cougar's roar. It's not easy to tell the difference. You see any signs of feral hogs?"

Ron frowned. "Yeah, there's plenty of those."

That was an understatement. Rhodes had been battling feral hogs off and on for years, but there wasn't much he could do. He was almost ready to bow down to the state's new porcine overlords. Although hunters and landowners around the state were reducing the population of the animals by 30 percent a year, it was a losing fight. At the rate the hogs were currently reproducing, it would be necessary to reduce the population by 70 percent a year just to maintain the current population, and that population had already overrun the state.

"I'm not saying it was feral hogs that made the sound," Rhodes said, although that's what he believed, "but that would be a lot more likely than a cougar."

"You're probably right." Ron's disappointment was plain. He brightened. "I'm gonna keep looking, though. You never know."

Rhodes thought he knew, but it wouldn't do any good to continue the discussion. Ron wanted to believe in the cougar, so why not let him? There was no harm in it.

"While you're at it," Rhodes said, "try to get rid of some hogs. One more thing. Did you know that Jake mentioned you in his will?"

Ron was plainly startled. "He what?"

"He specifically named you as one of the people he wanted to have a part in the first play presented at the theater when it reopened. You'd be the Ghost of Christmas Future."

"Not me." Ron shook his head. "I'm not an actor. I'm a retired water department guy."

"It was Jake's last wish. You, Ed Hopkins, Al Graham, and Glenda Tallent all had parts."

"Yeah, well, Jake's not here to see me turn it down, so he won't be bothered."

Rhodes heard a car driving up the rutted path to the cabin and turned to look.

"That's Doug Wilkinson," Ron said. "He'll have a carload. I need to check on that oil. It's probably boiling, and I need to turn on the outside lights and start frying fish. You can forget about me being in that play."

"I will, but I don't know about Jake's lawyer."

"To heck with his lawyer. Now I really do need to get started here."

Rhodes took that as his cue to leave. He thanked Ron and got in the Tahoe while Doug was parking his car. Rhodes didn't want to have to explain himself to anybody at the moment. He had a lot to think about.

Driving back to town, Rhodes considered what he'd learned, or guessed at, from his conversations with Ron and Ed. It was clear to him that neither of them wanted to talk about Jake, and neither of them would admit to having talked to him in recent years or even having seen him. They didn't want to talk about Gwen, either. Rhodes was sure they had something to hide.

Ron could easily have been the one who broke into Jake's house, but there was no way to prove it, and he wasn't going to admit it. Rhodes decided he wouldn't think too much about it. He didn't want to start drawing unwarranted conclusions. Maybe what he needed was a different perspective, and Harry Harris was the one who could provide it, unless Rhodes wanted to read *A Christmas Carol* again. Harris seemed like the lesser of two evils, and Rhodes decided to call him as soon as he got home and talked it over with Ivy.

"Good idea," Ivy said when Rhodes told her that he was going to ask Harris for more information on *A Christmas Carol*. "I remember a little about the story, but not much. Of course, you could always just watch the movie. Or movies."

"I like the old one in black-and-white," Rhodes said, "but I didn't see any DVDs of any of the movie versions in Jake's house today. The movies are probably a lot different from the book anyway. Aren't they always?"

"Usually. Give Harry a call, then."

It turned out that Harry was at the theater with Seepy Benton. This didn't make Rhodes happy, but it wasn't his theater, Jake was dead and wouldn't care, and Harry had a key to the place. Maybe Jake's ghost would object. Rhodes supposed he'd go to the theater and find out.

Ivy wanted to go along. That was fine with Rhodes. She might pick up on something he missed.

"You can take me to dinner afterward," Ivy said.

"Sounds like a good idea to me," Rhodes said. He didn't plan to mention that he'd had a burger for lunch. Not that there was anything wrong with that.

Chapter 16

▼

When Rhodes and Ivy got downtown, the area was entirely deserted except for the CPI van parked in front of the theater. The theater was dark, like all the other buildings on that side, but across the street, Randy Lawless's office building shone white in the lights the lawyer had installed.

"I wonder if all that light will interfere with the ghost hunting," Ivy said.

"I don't think the ghosts will be bothered," Rhodes said, "since the lights are outside and the ghosts are inside, or they would be if there were any ghosts, which there aren't."

They'd driven to the theater in their Edsel, an antique car Rhodes had picked up in the course of an investigation, which was the way he'd picked up the dogs and cats that lived with them. Unlike most people, Rhodes didn't think the Edsel was an ugly car. The fish-mouth grille had a kind of odd charm, and it was certainly different from any other car that Detroit had made in the 1950s.

Rhodes kept a flashlight in the glove compartment, and he reached across and got it out. The Edsel had a wide front seat, so it was a long reach. The flashlight was a powerful LED tactical flashlight, and it would provide plenty of illumination. It was also rechargeable, and Rhodes wasn't sure when he'd last hooked it up. It was supposed to hold a charge for quite a long time, however, so he wasn't worried.

"You think you'll need that?" Ivy asked.

"I'm betting that the only light in there is the ghost light," Rhodes said. "I want to be prepared."

It was a good thing he had the flashlight, because when they went inside, they found that the lobby was in total darkness. Rhodes turned on the flashlight. Its beam was as bright as advertised, and they went to the door into the theater.

"Are you going to turn off the light now?" Ivy whispered.

"Why?" Rhodes asked. He didn't whisper.

"You might disturb the proceedings."

Rhodes didn't care if he did disturb the proceedings, but what he said was "I don't think so."

He pushed open the door. Sure enough, the ghost light was on, not giving much illumination at all and throwing shadows all around the auditorium. Rhodes pointed the flashlight beam along the aisle so that he and Ivy could see where they were putting their feet.

It had gotten chilly outside as the sun went down, and the inside of the theater seemed even colder than the outdoors. Rhodes didn't believe that the difference was significant, however, at least not in a supernatural way.

Harry and Seepy sat in the front row, both of them bent over and looking down at something. Rhodes and Ivy walked forward, Ivy quietly and Rhodes not attempting to subdue the sound of his footsteps. When they got to the front row, Rhodes saw what the two men were looking at. It was a Ouija board that lay on Seepy's lap, and Seepy had his fingers on the planchette, which wasn't moving at all.

"Spirits not cooperating?" Rhodes asked, his voice echoing faintly in the nearly deserted theater.

Seepy and Harris looked up, and Seepy said, "Maybe they sense the presence of nonbelievers in the building."

"I believe," Ivy said. "It's the sheriff here who's a skeptic."

"They weren't cooperating even before you came," Harry said. "This is the first time we've tried this method, though. We might not be skilled enough yet."

"It's only seven o'clock," Rhodes said. "I thought ghosts came out at midnight."

"Ah, yes," Harry said, " 'the very witching time of night, when churchyards yawn and hell itself breathes out contagion to this world.' That's from *Hamlet,* you know."

Rhodes was tempted to say that he knew, but the truth was he'd forgotten that part of the play. For all he knew, Harris might be making it up.

"Ghosts are always around," Seepy said. "Even during the day. It's just that they seem to prefer darkness."

He gave Rhodes's flashlight a pointed look, and Rhodes turned the flashlight off.

"We're not here for ghosts," Rhodes said, "not the kind you're looking for, anyway. I want to talk about the ghosts in *A Christmas Carol.* I thought you might be able to give me some help, Harry, since you're writing the play."

"A Texan-ized version," Harry said. "It will be set in a little Texas town like Clearview, except in the last century. Scrooge will be a wealthy saloon owner who runs the town and is the leading employer. He mistreats everyone who works for him, and—"

Rhodes interrupted him. "I'm sure it'll be great, but I want to know about the original version. Tell me about the Ghost of Christmas Past."

"He's the first one who appears, of course," Harry said, seeming a little miffed that Rhodes had cut him off. "After Marley's ghost, that is. He's the one that reminds Scrooge of a time when he was a different and better person. Scrooge had a sister, Fan, whom he loved, and there was Belle, a woman to whom he was engaged. She could never marry him because she realized he loved money more than he loved her."

"What happened to the sister?" Rhodes asked.

"She died in childbirth. Very sad."

A beloved sister who'd died. The parallel to Jake was obvious, but this was Scrooge, not Marley. Rhodes wondered if it mattered. Jake could've been attracted to the similarity without having it connected to Marley's ghost. The part about Belle didn't fit, but even if Jake hadn't become engaged to Elaine Tunstall, they'd at least dated when they were in school, and she'd chosen someone else.

"What about the Ghost of Christmas Future?"

"Technically speaking," Harris said, "that would be the Ghost of Christmas Yet to Come."

"Okay," Rhodes said. "What about that one?"

"He shows Scrooge that when he dies, nobody cares or mourns him. Nobody even wants to attend his funeral unless there's going to be free food. People steal from his house. The only people who show any emotion at his death are happy that he's died."

People stealing from his house. Rhodes thought about the episode at Jake's place earlier that day. Somebody had taken something, all right. Rhodes was convinced of that, but he didn't know yet what it was. A book, maybe, or a flash drive for the computer, but something. In this case, too, the event was more applicable to Scrooge than to Jake Marley. Rhodes didn't know if anyone was happy about Jake's death, but someone had surely killed him.

"Tell me about the Ghost of Christmas Present," Rhodes said.

"Ah," Harry said. "He's the one who introduces Tiny Tim. You know how important Tiny Tim is to the story, I suppose. In my version of the story—"

"I know about Tiny Tim," Rhodes said, "but I don't think he applies to what I'm looking for. What else happens?"

"The ghost shows Scrooge some happy parties where people are having fine Christmases. One celebration is at the home of Scrooge's nephew Fred, who invited Scrooge to be there. Scrooge isn't there, though. He's never been interested in being happy, and he hates Christmas."

" 'Humbug,' " Rhodes said.

"Correct," Harry said. "The people at Fred's party talk about Scrooge. They all feel sorry for him because he hurts nobody but himself by his actions. In the play I'm writing—"

"We'll get to that another time," Rhodes said, thinking that this ghost's revelations fit with Jake. He'd hidden himself away from the town, but the town wasn't hurt by it. Jake had withdrawn and made himself into something like a hermit, limiting his human contact. He'd been the only one to suffer for that.

Now that he had the information he wanted about the ghosts, Rhodes didn't know what to do with it. There was more thinking to be done, or maybe Ivy would have some ideas.

"Is there anything else you want to know?" Harry asked.

"That'll have to do for now," Rhodes said. "I'll let you two get back to your ghost hunting."

Seepy set the Ouija board and planchette on the floor. "Maybe they don't want to talk to us tonight."

Almost as soon as he said it, a creaking noise came from high above the stage. It sounded as if someone might have stepped on the catwalk in the grid.

"On the other hand, maybe they do want to talk to us," Seepy said. "That must be Jake walking around up there."

Rhodes didn't think so. "These old buildings always make noises. That's just something shifting around."

Seepy was already out of his seat and headed for the stairs to the stage. "Jake, are you there? Jake, do you have something to say to us?"

At the same time, Harry picked up the Ouija board and planchette. He put the board in his lap, put the planchette on it, and laid his fingers on the planchette.

"Jake," Harry said, "do you have a message for us?"

The planchette didn't move, and Rhodes turned to Ivy. "You ready to go?"

"Sure. Where shall we eat?"

The creaking noise from above the stage got louder before Rhodes could answer. Rhodes looked to see where Seepy had gotten to and was surprised to see that he was already at the ladder to the grid. Rhodes hadn't known Seepy could move that fast.

"Hold on," Rhodes called to Seepy. "You can't go up there. You're not deputized."

Seepy stopped and turned around. "I'm not a deputy, but I don't have to be. I'm a ghost hunter. I'm trained to deal with these situations."

"Stay where you are," Rhodes said, and climbed the stairs to the stage. When he got up on the boards, he walked back to Seepy. "Who trained you?"

"I learned on the Internet."

"If that doesn't qualify you," Rhodes said, "nothing does."

The creaking above them started again, although it wasn't as loud as it had been.

"I'm the sheriff," Rhodes said, "and if there's anybody up there, I'm the one to go. This is a murder investigation now, not a ghost-hunting expedition."

Seepy moved aside. He didn't look overly disappointed. "All right, you go ahead then."

Rhodes didn't really like the idea of going up into the grid, but he thought he should at least take a look to see if there was a Phantom of the Opera House up there.

"Take this," Rhodes said, handing Seepy the flashlight. "Go turn on the big lights so I can see up there."

Seepy took the light, and Rhodes started up the ladder. The creaking stopped, but Rhodes kept going. He was about a fourth of the way up when Seepy said, "The lights won't turn on."

Rhodes was pretty sure Seepy was smart enough to know how to turn on the lights, but he climbed back down the ladder and walked over to where Seepy stood flicking the switch from ON to OFF and back again.

"See?" Seepy said.

The creaking started again.

"That's Jake for sure," Harry said.

Rhodes held out his hand. "Give me the flashlight."

Seepy complied, and Rhodes stuck the flashlight in his hip pocket. He could see well enough to climb the ladder, thanks to the ghost light. When he got to the grid, he'd turn on the flashlight, which would make it practically like daylight up there. What could possibly go wrong?

Best not to answer that question. Rhodes started up the ladder again, the flashlight heavy in his back pocket. He climbed the ladder without too much trouble, and when he'd planted his feet firmly on the grid, he pulled out the flashlight and turned it on. The beam was wide and white and strong. Rhodes saw nothing in front of him that didn't belong there. The creaking sound had stopped.

"You should turn off the light," Seepy called up from the stage. "Ghosts prefer the dark."

"You told me that," Rhodes said.

"Because it's true," Seepy said.

Rhodes had no intention of turning off the light. He flashed the beam to the left and right. As far as he could tell, nobody was on the grid but him.

"That noise was just the wind," he said.

" 'Let me see, then,' " Harry intoned in a theatrical voice from his seat, " 'what thereat is, and this mystery explore. Let my heart be still a moment and this mystery explore. 'Tis the wind and nothing more!' "

Rhodes knew that quotation. It was from "The Raven," and if it hadn't been the wind in the fly loft, it had been nothing more than a bird. Rhodes wasn't afraid of birds, Alfred Hitchcock's movie notwithstanding. However, while it was possible that a bird had gotten into the theater and was flapping around in the fly loft, it wouldn't be making the sound that Rhodes had heard, and it wouldn't be flying around at night. A bat might be up there, too, but Rhodes hadn't heard of any bats being in the theater.

Rhodes was about to turn and go back to the ladder when he

thought he saw movement in the far right corner of the fly loft, and then he heard the creaking noise again. He turned the flashlight in that direction and thought he saw something that might have been dust move through the beam. He took several steps along the grid and found the spot where the catwalk turned to the right. He made the turn and took a step, keeping the light pointed at the spot. He saw nothing there now, but he could still hear something. He took another step forward.

That's when the flashlight went out.

Rhodes stood still and waited for a few seconds so his eyes could get adjusted to the sudden absence of light. The ghost light was below him, and its light was so faint that Rhodes felt for a short time as if he were in complete darkness. He'd thought his flashlight had a good charge, but he must've been wrong. The lights down below wouldn't work, either, but that was just a coincidence.

When he could see about as well as he was going to be able to, Rhodes clicked the button on the flashlight a few times. It didn't respond, so he turned around and started back.

At his first step, the board broke under his feet. His foot went through the board, and the flashlight flew out of his hand. He thought he heard someone yell, but he couldn't be sure because of the roaring in his ears.

Rhodes didn't fall far. Only one board had broken, and while his leg was jammed into the gap between two boards, he wasn't in any danger of falling.

Until several other boards broke.

Rhodes plunged through the hole in the catwalk, pieces of board falling with him. For a fraction of a second he thought of how Jake Marley's body had looked as it lay on the stage. He wondered how it would feel when he landed, or if he'd feel anything at all.

Chapter 17

▼

Rhodes decided not to find out how it would feel to hit the stage, not if he could help it. He reached out with both hands and caught hold of the board just in front of him. His arms were almost pulled out of their sockets as they took his full weight, and he swung forward, then back.

He swung a couple of times, not far, then steadied. He didn't look down. He looked up at the grid and at the board he was holding on to. He knew he couldn't hang on for long.

"I'm calling the fire department," someone shouted. Seepy.

"This is going to be the most-watched thing ever," someone said.

Jennifer Loam? Where had she come from? It didn't matter. All that mattered was holding on to the board.

How could she be recording anything? It was then that Rhodes realized the lights on the stage had come on.

"Don't let go," Ivy called. "We're getting help."

Rhodes didn't plan to let go, not voluntarily, but he couldn't maintain his grip for long. The fire department wasn't going to do him any good. It wasn't like he was a cat stranded at the top of a telephone pole. By the time a ladder could be brought, he'd be down on the stage. Maybe he'd break only his legs or his back and not his neck.

Or maybe he could pull himself back up onto the catwalk. It wasn't as if the other option had any appeal at all.

Rhodes wondered how long it had been since he'd done a pull-up. Years. Decades. But that was all right. He wasn't going to try to set a record and do seven thousand of them. He only had to pull himself up once. How hard could it be?

Really hard, as it happened, since his fingers were holding on to a board, not a bar that they could curl around for good gripping. That didn't matter. He had to stop thinking about it and give it a try.

Swing forward, back, and up. That was how to do it. Give himself a little momentum, time it just right, give one final push with his arms if he got any height on the backswing, and he'd be fine.

Either that, or he'd be down on the stage, which was where he'd wind up anyway if he didn't do something quickly.

Rhodes took a deep breath, then swung himself forward, back, and up. Scooting his hands in the moment of the backswing, he pushed up with his arms and threw himself forward as hard as he could. He landed on the catwalk, not quite as far forward as he'd hoped, but he jammed his fingers between two boards and pulled himself a few more inches toward safety. He felt his center of gravity shift, and he knew he wasn't going to fall now, even though his entire length wasn't up on the grid. He took a couple of gasping breaths, reached out, took hold of the edge of another board, and pulled himself forward again.

He lay still and breathed rapidly, and he could feel his heart beating against the catwalk. He wasn't in a hurry to go anywhere, and he hoped that if he didn't move for a while, his heartbeat and breathing would slow down. If they didn't he might be in as much trouble as if he'd fallen.

"Are you all right?" Ivy asked from somewhere below.

"Sure," he said. "Dandy-rootie."

"He's not all right," Ivy said to someone. "He's never said 'dandy-rootie' before in his life."

Rhodes didn't bother to respond to that. He tried to regulate his breathing and was glad to find that it was returning to normal and that his heartbeat had slowed. In another week or two, he might even be able to stand up.

"This is disappointing," Jennifer Loam said. "Sage Barton would have jumped up by now and tossed off an amusing joke."

"Dandy-rootie," Rhodes said, but so softly that he wasn't sure anyone could hear him.

"Jake Marley must want you to stop asking questions, Sheriff," Harry said. "He didn't mean for you to get down from there in one piece."

Rhodes didn't think that was strictly true. No matter how bad the fall might've been, he'd still be in one piece. It would be a pleasure to correct Harry, but why waste the breath to do it?

Besides, he didn't think Jake Marley had had anything to do with his fall. Rotten boards had been the problem, even though they hadn't seemed rotten earlier in the day.

Why had the lights come on, though? Some kind of short in the switch, probably. That had to be it.

Rhodes thought he might be able to sit up. His arms were still trembly, but he pushed himself up and twisted around into a sitting position. Standing wouldn't be too hard if he took it slow. His legs felt like rubber bands, but after a couple of seconds he was okay. He started toward the ladder.

"Stay there," Ivy said. "The fire department will be here in a minute."

"I'm fine," Rhodes said. "Dandy-rootie." And it was true. The closer he got to the ladder, the steadier he became. His heartbeat and breathing were fine, and descending the ladder didn't seem intimidating in the least.

He gripped the rung in front of him, put a foot on another rung slightly below the catwalk, and went right on down. When he got to the bottom, Ivy was waiting for him. She put her arms around him and hugged. He hugged her back.

"Great," Jennifer said. "Just hold that pose."

Rhodes didn't need any encouragement, but he couldn't stay in one spot forever. He released Ivy and looked at her. "I'm fine. Just a little shaken up, but nothing's broken. I'm hardly even bruised."

"Good," Ivy said, "but don't you ever scare me like that again."

"I'll try not to," Rhodes said, looking around the stage at the pieces of boards that lay around. He saw his flashlight. The beam was strong and straight. The fall must have jarred it on.

He heard a commotion in the lobby, and a couple of men burst through the door into the theater.

"Everything's fine," Rhodes said, glad his voice was steady and strong enough to reach the back of the auditorium. "I got down by myself."

The two men stopped.

"Are you sure you're okay?" one of them said.

"I'm sure. Thanks for coming, but I'm fine."

The two men looked at each other.

"I have video," Jennifer Loam said. "Would you like to see it?"

"Darn right," one of them said, and they both walked down the aisle and came up on the stage.

"Where did she come from?" Rhodes asked Ivy.

"She was driving by and saw the CPI van and the Edsel out front. She thought something newsworthy might be going on."

"She was right," Seepy said. "I'm trying to come up with a clickbait headline now. I'm still doing a little work for her, you know."

Rhodes didn't say anything. He went over and picked up his flashlight. The heavy aluminum casing wasn't even dented. He clicked the switch, and the light went off. He stuck the flashlight in his back pocket.

"How about this," Seepy said. " 'Catwalk Collapse—You Won't Believe What Happens Next!' "

"The alliteration at the beginning is nice," Harry said, "but it kind of falls apart after that."

"I'll work on it," Seepy said.

The two firemen finished watching the video and were suitably impressed.

"You gotta get that online," one of them said.

Rhodes recognized him now. His name was Phil Binks.

"Oh, I will," Jennifer told him. "I'll do it tonight."

"Good," Phil said. "I'll tell my wife about it." He looked at Rhodes. "She's a big fan of yours, Sheriff. She thinks you're great."

Rhodes didn't know what to say to that. For a second he was afraid Phil would ask for his autograph, but the awkward moment passed, and Phil and the other fireman left.

"I should put you on salary, Sheriff," Jennifer said. "You're the star of my Web site."

"She doesn't pay much," Seepy said.

"I could always use the extra income," Rhodes said, "even a small amount, but I don't think the county would like the idea."

"I deserve a raise," Seepy said. "You know those great clickbait headlines I write? They're what makes you a star."

"The sheriff was a star before you started writing headlines," Jennifer said. "I have to go home and get this edited and ready to go. Thanks for another great show, Sheriff."

Rhodes didn't tell her she was welcome, but she didn't seem to care. She told everyone good-bye and left.

"What happened up there?" Ivy asked. "I know you fell through the catwalk, but how?"

"Maybe I need to go on a diet," Rhodes said. "Let's have a look at those boards."

He picked up two pieces of board, one in each hand, and looked at the breaks. They were jagged, and Rhodes flicked bits off with his finger.

"They just broke," Rhodes said. "They look to be a little bit rotten."

"Ha," Seepy said. "Those boards aren't rotten. It was Jake Marley, for sure. Did you see him up there?"

"No," Rhodes said. "I didn't see Jake Marley or anybody else. There wasn't any ghost. There wasn't anything."

"What about the lights?" Harry asked. "They all came on at once, and nobody was even near them."

"Seepy had been messing with them earlier," Rhodes said. "Some kind of problem with the switch, probably."

"Ha," Seepy said. "You just don't want to admit that there's a ghost in here."

"I'll tell you what," Rhodes said. "If you catch a ghost and keep him around for me to see or talk to, I'll believe he's here. Otherwise, I don't think so."

"Are you still thinking about eating somewhere?" Ivy asked.

Rhodes realized that he was hungry. Almost falling to his death had given him an appetite.

"Let's go to the Jolly Tamale," he said. "I could use a chile relleno."

"I've heard they have spinach enchiladas now," Ivy said.

"You can have those," Rhodes said. "I'm having a chile relleno." He looked up at the hole in the catwalk. "Or two."

"I guess you deserve them."

"Darn right I do."

"Wait a second," Seepy said. "What about that noise we heard? It's stopped now. Jake's through for the night."

Rhodes looked at Harry. "It was just the wind and nothing more."

"Right," Seepy said, "and if you believe that—"

"Don't try to sell me a ghost-busting kit," Rhodes said, "or a bridge in Brooklyn, either. I didn't see anything up in the fly loft, and everything that happened has a perfectly logical explanation."

"Logic isn't truth."

" 'Beauty is truth,' " Harris said.

"I know that one," Ivy said. "John Keats."

"You get an A," Harry said. "Can you name the poem?"

"Do I get extra credit?"

"I'll pay for dinner at the Jolly Tamale if you'll invite me to go with you."

Seepy nudged him with an elbow.

"And of course if you allow Seepy to come along, I'll pay for his dinner, too."

"And Dan's?

"Of course. That's understood."

Ivy turned to Rhodes. "Want to invite them?"

"Why not? I can use a free meal," Rhodes said, knowing for sure he'd be ordering two chile rellenos.

"Okay, then," Ivy said. " It's a deal. 'Ode on a Grecian Urn' is the poem."

"Right you are," Harry said. "A lot of people think it's 'Ode *to* a Grecian Urn,' but it's not."

"I knew that," Seepy said.

"I'll take your word for it, but it doesn't matter. You're getting a free dinner anyway."

"Can I give a math quiz while we eat?"

"No," Harry and Rhodes said together.

"You can't mention ghosts, either," Rhodes said. "Is everybody ready to leave? We need to turn off the lights first."

"Not the ghost light," Seepy said. "Doing that might cause problems."

"I wouldn't think of it," Rhodes said. "Get your stuff gathered up, and let's go eat."

"Dandy-rootie," Ivy said.

Chapter 18

▼

The next morning was a Sunday, and Rhodes hoped it would be a quiet day. He was sure it hadn't been a quiet Saturday night, however, because Saturday nights were never quiet, even in a rural county. Rhodes went to the jail to catch up on what had gone on, but of course Hack didn't want to talk about that. He wanted to talk about what had happened in the theater.

"Out of the loop," Hack said. "You never keep me in the loop, ain't that right, Lawton."

Lawton, who was standing over by the door into the cellblock, nodded. "I'm not in the loop, either, but I'm just the jailer, so I guess I don't matter. You'd think the dispatcher ought to know what's goin' on, though, know where the sheriff is, and stuff like that. It might be important in case of some emergency."

"Sheriff was the one havin' the emergency," Hack said. "Not that we'd know about it if it wasn't for the Internet. That's the only way to find out anything around here."

"Sheriff hangin' up there and pullin' a Burt Lancaster," Lawton said. "Never saw anything like it." He paused. "Well, except back when Burt Lancaster did stuff like that. You ever see Burt Lancaster, Sheriff? In the movies, I mean."

"I've seen his old movies on TV," Rhodes said. "I was nothing like Burt Lancaster. Trust me. He was an acrobat. I'm just a sheriff."

"Looked like Burt Lancaster to me. A real death-defyin' act, that's what it was."

"You gonna tell us how it happened?" Hack asked. "Says on the Internet it was a ghost."

"It wasn't a ghost," Rhodes said, and he gave them the short version of what had gone on in the theater.

"Sounds like a ghost to me," Hack said. "How 'bout you, Lawton?"

"Bound to be a ghost. Boards don't break themselves." He gave Rhodes a critical look. "'Course it wouldn't hurt some of us to shed a pound or two."

"Never mind that," Rhodes said. "Tell me what was going on in town last night."

Hack went through a litany of the usual sort of happenings, a broken-down car abandoned on the side of a county road, a couple of domestic disturbances, an incident of road rage that resulted in a fistfight, a home invasion . . .

"Hold it," Rhodes said when Hack came to the home invasion. "You'd better tell me about that one. Sounds serious."

"Well," Hack said, "it wasn't the usual kind of home invasion."

If Rhodes had possessed an extra leg in the proper place, he'd have kicked himself because he realized he'd fallen into Hack's trap. There was nothing he could do now, however, except carry on.

"What kind was it, then?"

"Started with a call from Cassie Winston. You know Cassie? Married to Lester? Lives out toward Obert?"

"I've heard of Cassie and Lester. What about them?"

"We got a call from Cassie. Prob'ly came in about the time you was hanging from those boards. That about right, Lawton?"

"Sounds right to me," Lawton said. "See, Cassie and Lester—"

Hack swiveled his chair the better to glower at Lawton. "I'm the one tellin' this."

"Well, you asked me—"

"I asked you if the time was about right, and you just kept on goin'."

"Don't start," Rhodes said. "Just tell me, Hack."

"See?" Hack said to Lawton. "The sheriff said 'Just tell me, Hack.' Wasn't no Lawton mentioned or even hinted at."

"Hack," Rhodes said.

"Okay, okay. Where was I?"

"Cassie called," Lawton said.

"Who asked you?"

"You didn't ask anybody in partic'lar, so I thought—"

Rhodes sighed. There were times, and this was one of them, when he wondered if Hack and Lawton rehearsed their dialogue when he was out of the office. He wouldn't have put it past them.

"You two are going to be the death of me," he said. "Tell the story, Hack. You keep quiet, Lawton."

Lawton looked hurt. Hack looked smug.

"Like I was sayin'," Hack continued, "Cassie called and said somebody was trying to break into the house. Poundin' on the door, yellin', takin' on. She was there by herself, 'cause Lester was in town pickin' up a couple of frozen dinners at the Walmart. They like those organic enchiladas that they get there. I don't know whether organic food's any better than any other kind myself, but ever'body has a different taste, I guess."

"Hack," Rhodes said.

"All right, all right, you don't have to rush me. I told her to keep calm and asked if she had a gun in the house, which she did, like just about ever'body who lives in the country. Said she already had it out and pointed at the door, so I told her I'd send out a deputy."

"You told her not to shoot anybody, I hope."

"Sure did. Told her, 'Don't you pull the trigger 'less you just have to. You don't want it on your conscience if you kill a man.'"

Lawton couldn't hold back. "'Specially if it's your husband, 'cause that's who it was. See—"

"That does it," Hack said, pushing back his chair and standing up. "You're always takin' over, and this time you've broke the camel's back."

"Sit down, Hack," Rhodes said.

Hack sat down. Rhodes didn't think he'd have done anything, but it was good to make sure.

"Now let me get this straight," Rhodes said. "Cassie Winston called in a home invasion report, but it was really just Lester coming back from Walmart. She got her gun but didn't shoot him. Is that about it?"

"Yep," Hack said, "but if it hadn'ta been for me, she mighta shot Lester right through that door. I'm the one told her not to shoot, but do I ever get on the Internet? Heck, no, not me. I'm just the dispatcher, good old Hack, doin' his job and savin' lives instead of fightin' ghosts and actin' like Burt Lancaster."

"Lester forgot his key," Lawton said, and Hack didn't even bother to shush him.

"He'll remember next time," Rhodes said.

"I bet he will," Hack said. "Cassie finally figgered out who was bangin' on the door, so she let Lester in. Still had the pistol in her hand. She said he dropped those frozen dinners right there on the floor."

"She's the one who told you all this?"

"Nope, Andy told me. He's the deputy I sent out there. He got there just about the time Lester and Cassie were gettin' it all straightened out. They even offered him a bite of enchilada if he wanted to stay, but he had to get back on patrol."

Rhodes thought briefly about the chile relleno he'd eaten the previous night. He'd decided against two after all, which had been a good decision. One had been plenty, and it had been delicious, far better than some frozen dinner would've been, organic or not.

"That's all you have to tell me?" Rhodes asked. "No serious accidents, no injuries, no break-ins?"

"Nope," Hack said. "The big excitement was the home invasion."

"'Cept it wasn't a real home invasion," Lawton said. "It was just—"

Rhodes held up a hand to stop him. "I've heard enough about that. I'm going to interview someone this morning, and maybe even two. I'll check in again later."

"You gonna tell me who you're gonna interview?" Hack asked. "Or do you want me to guess?"

"Glenda Tallent and Al Graham."

"Where you gonna find 'em? Might be at church."

"Not this early," Rhodes said.

Glenda Tallent lived on a shady street that had once been in a nice part of town. Most of the houses were run-down now, but not Glenda's. She and her husband had kept the house in good repair through the years, and after her husband's death, Glenda had continued to do so. The other houses had cracked walks in front, and one or two of them sat a little off the level, but the walks in front of Glenda's house were almost new, and the house was as level as a pool table. The paint was fresh, and the flower beds were weeded. Glenda's car, a red Cadillac, was parked in the driveway under a big pecan tree that had shed leaves all over it.

The car was a sure sign that Glenda was at home, so Rhodes parked the Tahoe in the street and got out. He looked at the Caddy as he went up the walk to the front porch. He hoped Glenda didn't leave the car there all the time. It wouldn't be long until the pecans started falling, if they hadn't already begun.

The cold weather had all blown on through, and the day was warm and sunny. The temperature would probably get into the seventies later. That was one thing Rhodes liked about living in Texas, not just the changes in the weather but the changes for the better, particularly later in the year.

Rhodes took the three steps up to the covered concrete porch and went to the door. Glenda didn't have a doorbell, so Rhodes rapped on the frame. After a couple of seconds, Glenda Tallent opened the door.

Glenda was a slight woman who had once had red hair, but it was now fading to blond. Her green eyes still had a bit of sparkle, however.

Younger people these days, and a lot of the older ones, too, dressed comfortably and casually for church. Not Glenda. She wore a lime green skirt and jacket with white shoes that had a short heel.

"Good morning, Sheriff," she said when she saw who was standing on her porch. "Did you come to proselytize me for the Baptists on this nice Sunday morning? It wouldn't do you any good if you did. I'm a Methodist born, sprinkled, and raised, and there's no way I'm changing now. I'm too old to be dunked."

"I didn't come here to proselytize for the Baptists," Rhodes said. "Just to talk for a minute or two."

"Well, in that case you can come in," Glenda said, stepping aside and allowing Rhodes in the house. "Come on back to the kitchen and have a cup of coffee."

"Thanks, but I don't drink coffee."

"Don't drink coffee? What kind of sheriff are you?"

"The kind that doesn't drink coffee."

"I didn't know there was that kind. How about a doughnut? I have an extra."

Rhodes hadn't had a doughnut in years. "That sounds good."

"Come along, then."

Glenda led the way across the hardwood floor of her living room, through a short hall, and into the kitchen, where there was a small round Formica-topped table and two chairs that might have been in the house for fifty years or so. On the table sat a coffee cup beside a saucer with a glazed doughnut in it. A fork lay on a cloth napkin beside the saucer.

"You sit down," Glenda said. "I'll get your doughnut. It's just a plain glazed one."

"That would be fine," Rhodes said.

Glenda brought him the doughnut in a saucer like hers. She put the saucer on the table and laid a napkin and fork beside it.

"I don't like to eat with my fingers," she said, "but you can if you want to."

"I'll use the fork."

"Fine. You go ahead and take a bite while I get you a glass of water. It's just tap water, but you need something to wash down that doughnut."

She ran water from the sink faucet into a glass, set the glass in front of Rhodes, and took her seat at the table.

"You haven't taken a bite yet," she said.

Rhodes took a bite. The doughnut was fresh, and the sugar glaze melted in his mouth.

"Good," he said. "Very good."

"I got it at the Daybreak Doughnut Shop," Glenda said. "You should get you some there. They have all kinds."

Rhodes was sorely tempted, but he knew the last thing he needed was doughnuts.

Glenda took a sip of her coffee. "Coffee's cold. I need to freshen it."

She got up and brought a glass carafe to the table. She poured coffee into the cup and put the carafe back on the counter.

"You're quite the athlete, Sheriff," she said when she returned to the table. "I saw the video of you swinging around above the stage last night. I don't believe many people could've done what you did."

"I was lucky," Rhodes said. "Scared, too. Being scared helps."

"Pooh. I don't believe you were one bit scared. You just swung up on that platform like an acrobat."

"Burt Lancaster," Rhodes said.

Glenda brightened. "Exactly! My, he was something in the old days. I saw him in a movie called *Trapeze* when I was a girl. And that Tony Curtis wasn't bad, either." She considered Rhodes. "Not that you're too bad yourself."

"These are mighty good doughnuts," Rhodes said, turning aside the compliment.

"They are indeed," Glenda said, smiling.

She and Rhodes ate their doughnuts without any further comments about athletes or appearances. When he'd finished, Rhodes drank some of the water, wiped his mouth with his napkin, and told Glenda why he was there.

"I thought that was probably it," she said. "I was really sorry to hear about Jake. We used to be friends, back in high school, but you must know that already."

"I'd heard you were," Rhodes said. "What happened to change that?"

"I expect you know that already, too. Jake wasn't the same after his sister died in that car accident. He stopped seeing all his friends and started to withdraw. After a while, he withdrew completely. Nobody could reach him. He might as well have been dead himself."

"Did he get in touch once he decided to come back to life?"

"Yes, he did," Glenda said.

Rhodes was surprised. He'd been prepared for her to say she hadn't heard from Jake, the same as everyone else had done.

"He called me about insurance on the building he bought, the old theater," Glenda said. "I didn't even have to use my feminine wiles, which was a good thing."

"Why was it good?"

"Because at my age it wouldn't work. I don't have any feminine wiles left."

She paused and looked at Rhodes as if waiting for him to contradict her, so he obliged.

"I wouldn't be too sure of that," he said.

Glenda smiled. "Thank you, Sheriff, for saying so. Feminine wiles might work for some people, though, if not for me."

"Anybody in particular?"

"That was purely hypothetical. I was happy to help Jake out. I told him that on a building that old, I'd have to have someone look at it, but he told me he'd had it inspected before he bought it. Once he provided me with the paperwork, I wrote up a policy for him."

"Who did the inspection?"

"Rick Shepherd. I've used him before. He's good at the job. Jake brought the report over to the office, and I looked it over. I did a policy for him. He was happy with it, and we had a deal."

"Did you talk about the past, about high school? The old gang?"

"No, it was strictly business. I'd never bring up that accident. He'd grieved for years about that. Why remind him, now that he'd finally gotten better?"

"Someone was out at his house yesterday," Rhodes said. "Was that you?"

Glenda looked puzzled. "Why would I be at his house?"

"Maybe to pick up something you'd left there."

"I didn't leave anything. All our business was over and done with."

"Maybe it wasn't business."

"Then it wasn't me."

Rhodes didn't think he'd get any further with that line of questioning, so he shifted directions. "Did Jake ever tell you about the play he'd commissioned for the theater?"

"No, we didn't get into that. As I said, strictly business. I knew about the play, of course, but that was because I read about it on the Internet."

Everybody read things on the Internet. Rhodes was going to have to start keeping up better.

"On *A Clear View of Clearview*?" Rhodes asked.

"Yes, there, and of course on the 'Talk of Clearview' Facebook page."

Rhodes knew that the city had a Facebook page, but it was devoted to civic facts and meetings and such. He didn't know anything about a talk page.

"It's gossip," Glenda said, "and more. You can ask about getting a lawn mowed or a house cleaned, and people will give suggestions. That kind of thing."

Rhodes had a feeling that was one more thing he'd need to look into when he had time. Seepy Benton probably knew all about it.

"Was there any gossip back when Gwen Marley had her accident?" Rhodes asked.

Glenda looked at the ceiling. "I don't remember. It's been so long."

"I wondered if there was anyone with her in the car when she had the wreck."

"She was alone. Everybody knows that. I remember reading about it in the paper. We were all very sad."

"Not as sad as Jake."

"No. When Gwen died, a little of Jake died, too, I think. It was so nice to see him when we talked about the policy on the theater. He was almost like himself again."

Rhodes had more to ask, but Glenda stood up and took his saucer, glass, napkin, and fork. She carried them to the counter and then came back for her own dishes.

"Was Jake's death an accident?" she asked after putting them on the counter. "I read on the Internet that it was suspicious."

"It was. Do you know anybody who'd want to hurt Jake?"

"Of course not. Who even knew him?"

"Hardly anybody," Rhodes said.

"That's right. I hate to chase you out, Sheriff, but you know we Methodists start church a half hour earlier than everyone else. We like to get out in time to beat the Baptists to the restaurants."

Rhodes stood up. "Did you know you had a part in the Christmas play?"

"Yes, I'd heard that. I won't be doing it, though. I'm not an actress. I just sell insurance. I'm going to have to show you out now. I don't mean to be rude, but I really do need to get ready for church."

She looked ready to go to Rhodes, but he didn't argue. He let her lead him to the front door.

"Thanks for the doughnut," he said. "It was very good."

"I'm glad you enjoyed it. I hope you catch whoever killed Jake. If it wasn't just an accident, that is."

"I'll do what I can," Rhodes said.

Rhodes knew that Al Graham wouldn't be going to church. He kept the A+ Auto Repair shop open seven days a week, and while he sometimes turned things over to his son and took a break for a day or two, he was the one who worked on Sundays so his son and his family could go to church. As for Al, he wasn't a churchgoing man.

Al's business was located not far from the south edge of town in a big tin building that had a tall, wide opening in front and a concrete floor. Beside the opening was a regular door, and behind it was Al's office.

The parking lot was hard-packed dirt, and there were five cars and two pickups parked there. One of the pickups belonged to Al, and Rhodes figured the other one and the cars were waiting for repairs. Rhodes stopped beside the cars and got out of the Tahoe. He didn't see anyone working inside the building, but he did see a car with the hood up. Beside it was a large red piece of equipment on rollers. Rhodes figured it was a diagnostic computer, but he couldn't tell. It might've been a toolbox. The interior of the building wasn't well lit.

Al used trouble lights for his work, and Rhodes saw one dangling from the hood of the car. The light wasn't turned on, though.

Rhodes walked across the lot to the door to the office and went inside. Al sat at an old desk that was covered with papers. The walls were hung with calendars that advertised auto parts. Some of the calendars were flyspecked and dated back decades. The office smelled of auto grease.

Al put down his papers, and Rhodes noticed grease under his fingernails. He looked up at Rhodes. "Whatcha need, Sheriff? Time to get the county vehicles overhauled? Need new spark plugs for that Edsel of yours? An oil change? How about a ring job?"

Al was a short, compact man with a pale, wrinkled face that hadn't seen much sunshine. His short gray hair curled out from beneath his black A+Auto Repair baseball cap. The words in front were red. He wore a pair of half-glasses and peered at Rhodes over the tops of the lenses.

"Edsel's fine," Rhodes said. He sat in a heavy wooden chair and squirmed a little to get comfortable. "Runs like a new one."

"The new ones didn't run all that good," Al said. "So I'm told, anyway. Good cars to work on, though, like all those old hoopies. Plenty of room under the hood so a man could get to things easy. Today it's so crammed under there, you can't find a crevice big enough to slip a penny in. You don't have to know what you're doing, either. You just hook 'em up to a computer and let it tell you what to do. Makes things easier, but it takes the fun out of knowing what's wrong and how to fix it." He leaned back in his chair. "I miss the old days."

"The old days are what I came here to talk about," Rhodes said. "I want to ask you a few things about Jake Marley."

"Old Jake." Al took off his half-glasses and laid them on a stack of papers. "Damn shame about him. Sure was sorry to hear it."

Everybody said the same thing. It made Rhodes wonder why none of them had ever reached out to Jake while he was brooding his life away.

"You knew his sister, Gwen, too," I guess.

"Sure. Pretty girl. Bad way to die. Sometimes I wonder if her car was taken care of the way it should've been. I was interested in cars even back then, liked to work on 'em, take an engine apart and see what made it run. The Marleys could afford to keep their cars up, though, so I guess there was nothing wrong with it. It's just something I think about."

Rhodes wondered how much Al thought about it.

"Seems like that kind of accident might be more related to drinking than car trouble," Rhodes said. "You ever hear anything like that?"

Al looked at his fingernails as if he were inspecting the grease beneath them. "Gwen didn't drink, far as I know. Too young."

"What if there was somebody else in the car with her? Would that've made a difference?"

"Don't see how. Probably would've been two people dead instead of one. Anyway, there wasn't anybody else. Everybody knows that."

"Everybody knows a lot of things that aren't true."

"Sure, like how you should warm up a car on a cold morning, which is baloney now with these new cars. It was true in the old days but not anymore."

Rhodes noted the quick change of subject. "Did you see Gwen that night?"

"By herself, driving around town. Another sad story, just like Jake's, except I hear somebody might've killed him."

"Might've," Rhodes said. "I'd like to find out who."

Al leaned forward. "Good luck."

"You know anybody who had a reason to kill him?"

"Money's always the motive, right? I've seen enough TV shows to know that. Jake had plenty of money. Find out who inherits it, and you'll find out who might've killed him."

"I've seen his will," Rhodes said. "You're mentioned in it."

Al's eyebrows went up so high that they almost disappeared under the brim of his cap. "Me? He's leaving money to me?"

"I didn't say that. I said you were mentioned in his will. He wanted you to take a part in the play that will be given in the theater next year."

"That's a good one," Al said. "Me in a play. I'm about as much an actor as I am a rodeo cowboy or a rocket scientist. I work on cars. I don't get up on a stage."

"Jake wanted you to play the Ghost of Christmas Present."

"I don't know about any ghosts. I don't know much about that story they're going to be doing except about Tiny Tim and 'Bah, humbug.' That's what I say about me being in it. Bah, humbug." Al looked down at all the papers on his desk. "I'm not gonna be in any play. We about done with this, Sheriff? I got to get to work on that Ford out there."

"One other thing," Rhodes said. "Someone was out at Jake's house yesterday. Looking for something, I think. You know anything about that?"

"I haven't been out that way in a long time," Al said, "and there's nothing out there I want. Now, then. I really do need to get to work. The ox is in the ditch."

Rhodes stood up. "Maybe I'll bring the Edsel in one day, let you look it over just to see what an old car looks like again."

"You do that," Al said, but Rhodes could tell he didn't mean it.

Chapter 19

▼

Rhodes knew he wasn't Sherlock Holmes, and he knew that *CSI: Blacklin County* was never likely to become a hit TV series. Or any kind of TV series. Rhodes relied mainly on talking to people and waiting for someone to lie to him or make a mistake that would lead him to the answers he was looking for.

Talking to the Tunstalls and the others who'd known Jake, Rhodes had been told so many half-truths and heard so many misleading statements that he wasn't sure what to believe or disbelieve. He needed to go somewhere and think things over, and what better place than home, where Ivy might be able to help him sort things out? He called Hack on the radio to let him know where he was going.

"Nope," Hack said. "You'll be going somewhere else. I was just about to call you. We got a little emergency you need to handle first."

"A 'little' emergency?"

"Yeah. That means nobody's hurt. Yet."

Sundays were usually slow days for the sheriff's department.

Rhodes couldn't imagine what kind of emergency there could be, but Hack would get to it eventually.

"Where's the emergency?"

"Out at the Walmart parkin' lot."

Rhodes turned a corner and headed in the direction of Walmart. It wouldn't take long to get there.

"What's the trouble? Shoplifting? Somebody making meth in a car trunk? In a restroom?"

"Nothin' like that. It's a road rage thing."

Road rage incidents could be serious. Rhodes wondered why this one wasn't.

"Tell me about it," Rhodes said.

"It's a couple of guys must've had a fender-bender. They're standin' around jawin' at each other. No guns in sight yet. Got a crowd watching. You might wanna get on out there."

"I'm practically there already," Rhodes said. "Send me some backup."

"Duke's on his way, but he was out toward Thurston. Might take him a little longer than you. Don't get shot before he gets there."

"I thought you said there weren't any guns."

"*Yet.* I said no guns *yet.* You never know what might happen."

"That's the truth," Rhodes said. "If I get shot, you be sure I get a nice obituary that mentions there were no guns pulled until I got there."

"You ain't gonna get there if you don't get goin'."

"I'll be there by the time you sign off."

Driving toward the Walmart, Rhodes once again wished he had the luxury to work on one thing at a time. Instead of trying to figure out who was lying to him about Jake's death, he was going to have to break up a fistfight. He hoped he wouldn't forget any important things he'd heard. He'd written down a few points last night that he remembered from his conversations with Ron and Ed, but he hadn't had time for note-taking this morning. It would be a shame if a road rage incident made him forget something important.

It took Rhodes two minutes to get to the Walmart parking lot. Walmart on Sunday was like Walmart on any other day, which meant that it was busy. Rhodes wasn't sure there were days of the week as far as Walmart was concerned. Every day was as busy as any other, and on the inside, it was like being in a Las Vegas casino in one way: no clocks. Time didn't exist once you entered. When you came out, maybe you were ready for a little excitement, like watching two men fight over some kind of silly driving incident.

Rhodes saw a small crowd gathered near the highway, so he parked the Tahoe nearby and went over to see what was going on. The crowd was orderly, but there was a bit of yelling. Rhodes could make out a few words that sounded like "Come on, Pert, give it to him" and "Don't just stand there, Latham, slug him!"

A man at the edge of the crowd turned and saw Rhodes. He recognized him and yelled, "Sheriff's here! Let him through."

People moved out of the way, and Rhodes walked past them to the front of the group. He saw two men standing practically nose to nose, not saying anything. The crowd had quieted, and nobody was egging them on now that Rhodes was there.

Rhodes didn't know the two men, but he'd heard their names. He said, "Which one of you is Pert?"

The man on Rhodes's left turned his head. He was short and squatty, at least six inches shorter than the other man. His head was shaved, which Rhodes figured solved the problem of any thin spots, and his eyes were set close together. His nose was a bit crooked, as if it might've been broken at least once before.

Rhodes barely had time to take in any details, because almost as soon as Pert turned his head, Latham slugged him hard in the left ear.

Pert staggered, whirled, and flailed at Latham with his right fist, but Latham was rangy and had a much longer reach. He hardly had to move backward to avoid the blow.

The crowd got excited again, and people started calling encouragement to their favorites.

"Way to go, Latham! Take his head off!"

"C'mon, Pert! Don't let a little stinger on the ear slow you down!"

Rhodes had hoped to stop the fight by talking to the two men and getting them to settle down. Obviously that wasn't going to work, thanks to Latham's sneak attack. Rhodes was about to step between the two men when Duke touched his shoulder.

"Need some help, Sheriff?"

Duke was as tall as Rhodes, and wider. Since he was able to wear a Western hat without looking silly, he always wore one, and it made him appear even bigger than he was. Rhodes often thought Duke's nickname had been given to him because of his slight resemblance to John Wayne, a resemblance that didn't hurt one bit when it came to dealing with rowdy Blacklin County residents. He was the perfect ally to have when it was time to stop a fight.

"You take the short one," Rhodes said. "I'll take the tall one."

"You got it," Duke said.

He stepped forward and grasped the still slightly dazed Pert in a bear hug, pinning his arms to his sides with no trouble at all, while Rhodes advanced on Latham.

"We need to talk about this little incident," Rhodes said to Latham. "Get everything settled."

"He started it," Latham said, backing away. "I was coming over the hill into town, minding my own business, and he zoomed past me and cut me off. Nearly scared me to death. I followed him in here and told him he needed to learn how to drive, and he started cussing me and making remarks about my appearance. He said I looked like a snake with legs. I don't let anybody talk to me like that."

Rhodes loved the "he started it" phrase. It sounded like something a four-year-old would say, and it always amused Rhodes when someone who was supposedly adult tried it. It happened more often than people might guess.

"He might not see it the same way you do," Rhodes said. "You come along with me, and we'll all talk it over."

"I'm not going to jail," Latham said.

He ran forward, giving Rhodes a hard shove and surprising him. Rhodes stumbled back several paces, and Latham made a run for his car. Rhodes went after him, but Latham's long legs covered the ground quickly. He was into the car and behind the wheel by the time Rhodes got there. The door slammed before Rhodes could make a grab for him.

"Open the door, Latham," Rhodes said, tapping on the window, but Latham ignored him and started the car. He peeled away, and his front tires screamed as they laid rubber on the parking lot.

Duke had put Pert in the county car and was coming back to help Rhodes. Latham nearly ran over him, but Duke was able to jump out of the way.

"He's sure in a hurry," Duke said as Rhodes passed him on the way to the Tahoe. It took a lot to get Duke excited.

"You take Pert to the jail," Rhodes said. "I'll get there when I can."

He jumped into the Tahoe and took off after Latham, who'd made a rookie mistake. The county line was only a couple of miles to the east, but Latham had headed west. He'd be in Blacklin County for a while, and Rhodes thought he could catch him.

The problem was that Rhodes didn't like car chases. They put others at risk. Luckily it was Sunday and church was still in session, so the streets would be practically deserted after they got out of the vicinity of Walmart.

They got out of that vicinity quickly, and Latham tried to elude Rhodes with a few quick rights and lefts through a residential section of the town. It was a good plan, since the Tahoe wasn't the most maneuverable vehicle Rhodes had ever driven. However, he was familiar with all the streets and didn't have much trouble keeping up with Latham. In only a couple of minutes, they were headed down a street Rhodes knew even better than the others. It was the street his house was on.

A couple of large pecan trees grew in Rhodes's front yard, and the local squirrels, of which there were many, liked to climb around in them or to look for pecans under and around them. As Latham approached Rhodes's block, a squirrel tried to make a jump from a tree branch to a telephone line. It missed and fell into the street almost directly in front of Latham's onrushing auto.

Rhodes watched as Latham jerked the wheel hard to the right in an attempt to avoid the squirrel. He succeeded in that, but he didn't miss the pecan tree. The car smashed into it. The sound was like an explosion in the still Sunday morning air. The car's airbag inflated, and the driver's door sprang open. Latham, a little dazed from the impact of the airbag, stumbled out of the car. Leaves and pecans were still raining down from the pecan tree.

Rhodes stopped the Tahoe and jumped out. Latham saw him and ran across Rhodes's front yard. He turned down the driveway and headed to the back of the house. Rhodes glanced at Latham's car as he passed it. It was probably totaled.

As he jogged after Latham, Rhodes thought that at least Jennifer Loam wasn't there to be getting everything on camera. Maybe this time, he'd escape without any publicity.

Rhodes had nearly caught up with Latham when Latham pushed open the gate in the back fence and ran into the yard. Rhodes slowed to a walk. He didn't think Latham could climb the fence to escape, and there was no other gate.

Speedo must have thought that Rhodes had brought a new friend over for a playdate, because as soon as he saw Latham, he grabbed his squeaky toy and ran toward him. Latham stopped and turned toward the back door of the house just as Ivy opened it and Yancey streaked out into the yard.

Yancey appeared to have the same idea as Speedo, and he headed straight for Latham, who must have been more surprised than frightened to see the little fuzzball bouncing toward him. He turned and ran toward the back fence with both dogs at his heels, Yancey yipping as loudly as he could, which wasn't very loud, and Speedo with his jaws clamped down on the squeaky toy.

Rhodes stopped walking and looked at Ivy.

"Somebody you know?" she asked.

"He's the guy who hit our pecan tree."

"I heard the crash," Ivy said. "I was glad to see the tree was still standing. Who is he? The dogs seem to like him."

"They like everybody."

Ivy pointed. "He's trying to climb the fence."

Rhodes turned back to see what was happening. Latham had a grip on the top of the board fence and was trying to climb over, but Speedo had dropped his squeaky toy and had a firm grip on

Latham's right pants leg. Yancey danced around trying to bite the other pants leg.

Rhodes laughed. Latham wasn't going anywhere.

"I'm glad you enjoy your work," Ivy told Rhodes, "but I wish you wouldn't bring it home with you."

Rhodes walked over to the fence, where Latham stood with his hands still gripping the top of it. He turned his head and gave Rhodes a dejected look. Speedo still had hold of one pants leg, and now Yancey had hold of the other one. Speedo was quiet, but Yancey shook his head and emitted his version of a fierce growl.

"You should consider deputizing those dogs," Ivy said.

"I might do that," Rhodes said. "They're almost as helpful as Seepy Benton, and he's been a deputy before."

"Damn dogs," Latham said.

"Don't insult my animal companions," Rhodes said. "Just face the fence and put your hands behind your back."

Latham didn't resist. He lowered his hands and put them behind him. Rhodes pulled a pair of zip-tie handcuffs from his back pocket and put them on him.

"We're going to walk over and sit on the steps," Rhodes told Latham. "My wife is going to call for someone to come get you. Now turn around."

Latham turned around, but it wasn't easy with a dog hanging on each pants leg. He had to drag a dog along with each step, although Speedo helped out by walking a bit. Yancey just got carried. On the way, Rhodes bent down and picked up the squeaky toy.

"Did you say something about me?" Ivy asked as they approached the steps.

"I thought you might call Hack and have him send a wrecker. Tell him to send Duke out here for the prisoner. I think I'll stay for lunch."

"Prisoner?" Latham said. "I'm not a prisoner."

"Do you like 'arrestee' better?" Rhodes asked. "I'm going to give you your Miranda warning now."

"I'll go make that call," Ivy said, as Rhodes reeled off Latham's rights.

Latham shook his left leg. "Can you get these dogs off me?"

"Sure," Rhodes said, and he tossed the squeaky toy across the yard.

Speedo and Yancey let go of Latham's pants at the same time and went tearing across the yard after the toy.

"Let's sit down and rest," Rhodes said. "Do you know whose house this is?"

"I might be dumb enough to try to get away from you, but I'm not so dumb I can't figure out this is your house."

"I kind of liked that pecan tree."

"I kind of liked my car."

"Your insurance will take care of that. My pecan tree's not insured."

Latham didn't respond.

Rhodes knew that while Texas drivers had to show proof of insurance to get their state inspections and license renewals, too many people would buy insurance on a monthly payment plan during the month that inspections and renewals were due, then not make any more payments until they needed proof of insurance again.

"You're not one of those, are you?" Rhodes asked.

"One of what?" Latham asked.

"One of those people who don't have insurance."

Latham didn't answer.

"I guess you are. Is that why you ran?"

Latham didn't answer that one, either.

"Maybe it's not just insurance," Rhodes said. "Maybe there's more to this than you've told me. I noticed a dash cam in your car. If it's not damaged, and if it was on when you had your little trouble with Pert, it might tell us something."

Latham must have been taking his right to remain silent seriously, as he just sat there, mouth shut.

Rhodes didn't push him. He watched Speedo and Yancey tussle for the squeaky toy, which by either stealth or guile Yancey had managed to get hold of. Speedo rolled Yancey over in the grass twice, but Yancey wasn't giving up the squeaky toy.

Finally Latham said, "Okay, Pert didn't cut me off. I chased him down because he's been sneaking around behind my back with my girlfriend. I found out about it this morning. He did say I looked like a snake, though. I couldn't let him get by with that, not and sneak around with my girlfriend, too."

Duke walked through the gate at that point. He looked at the dogs, then at Rhodes and Latham.

Duke hitched his pants up and said, "Which one'a you two am I supposed to take to the hoosegow?"

Rhodes had heard better imitations of John Wayne, but Duke's was passable. Rhodes stood up, pulling Latham along with him.

"This one," Rhodes said. "Book him for destruction of private property, evading arrest, speeding, simple assault, and endangerment to start with. No proof of insurance. We'll probably think of some other things, too. Maybe there's a law on the books about damaging pecan trees."

"Well," Duke said, "it is the state tree of Texas. Don't mess with Texas."

"You two kill me," Latham said.

Duke walked over and took Latham's arm. "Come along, Pilgrim. Let's go."

"Who're you supposed to be, anyway?" Latham asked. "Clint Eastwood?"

Duke looked at Rhodes. "What's our departmental policy on police brutality?"

"We're against it," Rhodes said. "Latham's been in a car wreck, though, so he might've gotten marked up in the accident."

"Now just a damn minute," Latham said.

"Abusive language," Duke said. "I'll add that to the charges instead of roughing him up. That be okay, Sheriff?"

"Sure thing, Pilgrim," Rhodes said.

Chapter 20

It took Rhodes a few minutes to get Yancey separated from the squeaky toy and back in the house. Once inside and released, Yancey didn't linger in the kitchen. He went straight to the spare bedroom and his doggie bed.

"Tired out," Rhodes said.

"You or Yancey?"

"Not me," Rhodes said. "I'm a bundle of energy." He looked at the cats, asleep by the refrigerator. "Just like those cats."

"I didn't have anything fixed for lunch," Ivy said. "I wasn't expecting you to drop in."

Rhodes heard a noise out front. "The wrecker's here."

"Probably didn't bring us lunch, though."

"What were you going to have if I hadn't shown up?"

"I made up some pimento cheese, so I was going to toast some wheat bread and have a sandwich."

Rhodes was pretty sure the pimento cheese would be made with low-fat cheese and reduced-calorie mayonnaise. Real cheese and real mayo were about a hundred times better, but he could make the sacrifice since he planned to wash the sandwich down with one of the Dr Peppers with real sugar.

One of the cats got up and stretched, putting its front legs straight out and raising its rear into the air. Then it lay down on the floor and went back to sleep.

"Would you mind making me a sandwich, too?" Rhodes asked. "I'm plumb tuckered out from chasing criminals."

"Your John Wayne is worse than Duke's, Pilgrim. He did sound a little like Clint Eastwood, you know.

"You were listening?"

"Of course I was. I don't get a lot of entertainment around here. I'll make you that sandwich now. You can get your own Dr Pepper if you want one. Too much sugar's not good for you, though."

Rhodes got the Dr Pepper, not feeling guilty in the least. He sat at the table and popped the tab. After taking a satisfying swallow he said, "I want to talk something over with you."

Ivy put two slices of whole wheat bread in the toaster. "What would that be?"

"Jake Marley's death. I could use a little help in sorting things out."

"We could be just like Nick and Nora Charles."

"Except that William Powell didn't play a sheriff and that you're better-looking than Myrna Loy."

"You silver-tongued devil, you. You're just hoping I spread the pimento cheese thick, the way you like it, and put butter on the toast."

"That would be nice," Rhodes said, and he took another swallow of Dr Pepper.

Ivy said, " 'No, Sheriff. No, I'm not going to do that. You see . . . that's what I'd do if I were the kind of girl that you think I am.' "

She was doing Angie Dickinson's character, Feathers, from *Rio Bravo.*

"Not bad," Rhodes said. "How many times have we seen that movie?"

"Probably not enough."

"You're right," Rhodes said. "You can't see that one too often, even if you do have the dialogue memorized."

The toast popped up. Ivy took it, put it on a plate, and spread on the pimento cheese. No butter. When she was finished, she cut the sandwich in two and put it on a plate that she set in front of Rhodes.

"You go ahead and start," she said. "After I make mine, we can talk."

Rhodes had practically finished his sandwich before Ivy sat down. It hadn't been bad, considering its low-fat contents. He drank his Dr Pepper while Ivy ate, and when they were both finished, Ivy took the plates and utensils to the counter and set them there.

"We can wash up later," she said when she returned to the table. "Now let's have that discussion."

Rhodes started with Gwen's death in the automobile accident. He explained about the crime-scene photographs and how it was possible but very unlikely that Gwen would have been ejected from the passenger side of the car. To Rhodes's way of thinking, that meant someone else was in the car with her, probably driving.

Ivy said, "So you think that Jake had either known all along who it was or that he was putting on that play to get the other person to confess."

Rhodes thought it made sense, what with all the ghosts of the past and present and the way the character of Marley's ghost fit the present Jake Marley. Marley's emergence from his isolation could be attributed to his finally getting revenge on the one who caused his sister's death.

"I think there was a cover-up after the accident," he said. "Maybe Jake didn't even know the whole story." He told Ivy about the lack of an autopsy and toxicology report. "The Marleys had the power and the money to buy a cover-up. It might have taken only one of those things, but I'm pretty sure that's what happened."

"You'd never cover up anything like that," Ivy said.

Rhodes grinned. "I appreciate your faith in me, but the truth is, I've never been tested. If someone offered me enough money or made the right threat, I might cave."

Ivy shook her head. "I know you better than that."

"I hope you're right. Anyway, I think Jake finally realized that something was wrong about the night Gwen had the accident, and he was going to use the play somehow to find out what really happened."

Ivy wasn't so sure. "So you think one of the four people he wanted to be in the play had something to do with the accident. Why?"

"Because he asked for them specifically to be actors in his play. They all hung around together in high school. They all told the same story about the night Gwen died, and it all adds up to 'I wasn't with her, so she must've been alone.' They all said alcohol couldn't have been involved, though it seems as if it might've been. It would've been a good excuse at the very least. Something is off somewhere. Besides, I think they've been talking to each other about my little visits to them."

"What makes you think that?" Ivy asked.

"This morning I asked Glenda Tallent if she knew Jake had wanted her to be in the play. She said she'd heard about that. There's no way she could've known unless Ron Gleason or Ed Hopkins told her. I haven't told anyone but those two."

"I knew," Ivy said. "I didn't tell, but I can think of two other people who knew, too. Bradley West would be one of them."

"And the other one?"

"Jake Marley."

Rhodes thought about it. Glenda had said she didn't use her feminine wiles on Marley, which might well have been true. It might also have been false. A little flirtation with an old friend, or the brother of an old friend, and Jake might've become talkative. It was something Rhodes hadn't considered. If Marley had told Glenda about the play, and if she knew much about the story, she might very well have figured out what his motive was in presenting it. He moved her up on the list of suspects.

"What do you think about Elaine Tunstall?" Rhodes asked.

"She's all right when she's on her meds," Ivy said.

"That's not what I meant."

Rhodes explained that Jake and Elaine had dated in high school and that Elaine hadn't arrived at the Beauty Shack as soon as she should have if she'd left home when Harvey said she had.

"She might've been at the theater," Rhodes said. "She could've been the one who killed Jake."

Ivy looked skeptical. "What would've been her motive? She's been married to Harvey almost forever, and she gave up Jake for him. It wasn't as if Jake ran out on her or anything."

"Elaine and Harvey have had a hard life," Rhodes said. "All during that time, Jake's been sitting in his big house with plenty of money. He never stepped in to help out any of his old friends."

"I don't think either of them did it," Ivy said, "but I guess it could've happened that way."

Rhodes thought about Ed Hopkins and his real estate business that wasn't doing well. Jake hadn't helped him any, hadn't even asked him to look into the theater ownership. Jake hadn't helped Al Graham, either, a man who worked seven days a week to keep his auto repair business going. He'd helped Glenda Tallent, though. Rhodes moved her down a notch on the list of suspects.

"Part of the problem," Rhodes said, "is that nobody saw anybody else in the theater. Downtown Clearview's not what it once was, I know, but surely somebody who parked at the theater would've been noticed. Somebody would've driven by or been in one of the other buildings."

"Nobody would see if someone went in the back door," Ivy said.

"It was locked. Some of the people working on the play or on the building have a key to the front, but not to the back."

"Jake could've let someone in."

She was right. Jake had known his killer, because they'd been up on the grid together. No way would Jake have been up there with a stranger.

"I should've thought of that," Rhodes said. "Maybe you should be the sheriff."

"No thanks," Ivy said. "I don't want to wind up hanging by a board up above a stage. I'm not sure I could save myself like you and Sage Barton."

"Let's leave Sage Barton out of this. We need to figure out who killed Jake."

"Maybe the ghosts got him."

Rhodes didn't laugh. "You know better than that."

"Something nearly got you," Ivy said.

"Rotten boards, that's what nearly got me. No ghosts were involved."

"Maybe."

"For sure."

"Have it your way," Ivy said. "I'm more on Seepy's side of things."

Rhodes grimaced. "I'm not sure that's a good thing. What I need is information, not talk about ghosts."

"I'm going to the beauty shop tomorrow," Ivy said. "Maybe I can pick up some information there."

"That might help. I'm not sure what I should do, though. I'm still sorting through everything, but I don't have a solid suspect. Just four people who might've done it."

"You might try talking to some people who were around at the time," Ivy said. "They might remember things that weren't in the paper. They might even know some gossip from around then. You never know where that might lead you."

"Good idea. I happen to know somebody who was around, and he loves to gossip. If he'll give me a straight answer, it could be a big help. I'll talk to Aubrey Hamilton again, too. Maybe she's remembered something that will give me a tip. I could use one about now."

Ivy stood up. "We can do the dishes before you leave. That will help clear your head."

Rhodes didn't think so, but since there weren't many dishes to do, he didn't mind helping. He would have, too, if his cell phone hadn't rung.

The caller was Hack, who said, "Duke tells me you're lollygaggin' around at your house, havin' a nice lunch while crime runs wild."

"I had a pimento cheese sandwich," Rhodes said. "What crime are you calling about?"

"Did I say I was callin' about a crime?"

"I thought you implied it."

"Don't get fancy with me. I didn't call about any crime, but I did call about some trouble."

"Fine. I just inferred that you'd called about a crime."

"Did I say not to get fancy with me?"

"I think I remember that. What kind of trouble?"

"Mayor trouble," Hack said.

"Uh-oh," Rhodes said.

Since Clearview didn't have its own police force, the sheriff's department provided law enforcement under a contract with the city. Rhodes therefore answered to the county commissioners, not to the mayor of Clearview, but that didn't stop Clifford Clement from having his say and trying to boss Rhodes around. Rhodes had to pay attention to him, but he didn't have to follow his orders if he gave any. Mostly he just wanted to let Rhodes know that the mayorship was an important job even if nobody other than Clement thought so and that Rhodes was at least in a small way an employee of the city. Clement also liked to let the voters know how hard he was working for them, and this required him to appear to be pushing the sheriff to do his job the way Clement wanted him to do it. If Rhodes found Jake's killer, Clement would find a way to get some of the credit.

Rhodes didn't mind, as long as Clement didn't get carried away, and he couldn't really avoid the man without offending him and causing political problems between the city and the county. Problems like that could affect funding and salaries and even hamper Rhodes and his deputies when they were doing their jobs, so Rhodes always met with Clement when the mayor asked.

Today, Clement was having lunch at the Jolly Tamale, and he

wanted Rhodes to meet him there. Rhodes regretted having eaten the pimento cheese sandwich. If he hadn't, he might've treated himself to a chile relleno. He wouldn't be doing that now, however.

When Rhodes arrived at the restaurant, there were only a couple of cars in the parking lot. Most of the diners had already finished their lunches and gone home to watch football or take a nap. Rhodes followed football, but he hadn't seen a game in a long time. He hadn't had a nap in an even longer time.

He parked the Tahoe and went inside the restaurant. The mariachi music coming from the speakers was muted, which meant it would be possible to have a conversation, and there were only two tables with people sitting at them. Clement was in a booth at the back of the restaurant, and when a server came up to Rhodes to ask where he wanted to sit, he told her that he wouldn't be ordering and that he'd join the mayor.

Clement didn't look happy to see Rhodes. His fringe of gray hair and his gray, well-trimmed beard gave him a distinguished look, and he capitalized on that with the voters. The way he was frowning now, however, wouldn't have won him any fans.

"Have a seat, Sheriff," Clement said, without rising or offering to shake hands. "We need to talk."

Rhodes was tempted to say, "What do you mean *we*?" He resisted and sat down.

The chips and dip were still on the table. Rhodes resisted partaking of those, too. He was proud of his resistance so far, but he didn't know how long it would last. Clement's plate had been cleared away, so Rhodes didn't know what the mayor had eaten, but he supposed it was tasty.

"Have a good meal?" he asked.

"It was fine," Clement said, "but I didn't ask you to come here to talk about food."

"I didn't think you did."

"Of course not. What we need to talk about is Jake Marley."

"What about him?" Rhodes asked, trying to assume a look of innocent concern.

"He's dead, to begin with."

Rhodes didn't say anything.

"Look," Clement said, "here's how it is. I've been out of town for a couple of days. My wife's father is sick, and we spent a few days helping out. She's still there, and I'm not happy about the situation. So I have enough aggravation as it is. Then I get back last night and go to church this morning. The first thing I hear when I get there is that Jake Marley is dead, that he fell off something in the theater, and that it probably wasn't an accident. Why wasn't I informed about this?"

The arrival of a server cut off the mayor's little tirade as she set a glass of water on the table.

"I know you said you weren't going to eat, Sheriff," she said, "but I thought you might like to have a glass of water."

Rhodes thanked her and decided he'd have a chip after all. Resistance was futile. He took a chip out of the bowl and held it up for Clement to see. "Do you mind?"

"No, I don't mind. Take all you want. What I want to know is—"

Rhodes bit into the chip. It made a satisfactory crackle and momentarily halted the mayor again. Rhodes chewed slowly.

"Are you through yet?" Clement asked after Rhodes had taken a sip of water.

"How's the salsa?" Rhodes asked.

Clement sighed. "It's good, always is. Have some."

Rhodes got another chip, dipped it in the salsa, and ate it.

"You're right," he said. "Very good." He took another swallow of water.

"I don't think you're taking me seriously, Sheriff," Clement said.

"I am, though," Rhodes said. "You weren't informed about Jake Marley because it's not my job to inform you about anything. You have to inform yourself. I investigate, but I don't inform."

"Well, I don't like finding things out so long after they've happened."

"It's hard to keep up when you're out of town," Rhodes said, "but you could check *A Clear View of Clearview* on the Internet. Everybody else does."

"My father-in-law doesn't have a computer, much less Wi-Fi, but never mind that. Tell me about Jake Marley."

Rhodes told him, not going into much detail.

"So the theater restoration will continue?" Clement said.

Rhodes finally understood why Clement had called him. He hadn't been concerned about Jake's death. He'd been worried that the theater project would fall through and that people might blame him.

"Jake fixed his will that way," Rhodes said. "You don't have to worry about the theater project. You might need to find someone to take charge of it, though, unless Jake mentioned that in the will, too."

Clement sat up a little straighter on his side of the booth, and Rhodes thought he knew who the mayor might have in mind to take over the supervision of the work on the theater.

"What's really important," Clement said, "is that you find the killer. The murder of a prominent citizen can give the town a black eye."

Jake's promotion to prominent citizen was probably justified. He hadn't been involved in the community for fifty years, but when he'd emerged from his self-imposed exile, he'd gotten involved in a big way. It appeared that Clement was more worried about the town's reputation than about Jake's death, and Rhodes supposed that was natural, too. Nobody knew Jake, except those who'd gone to school with him.

"We wouldn't want the town to have a black eye," Rhodes said.

"No, indeed. Have another chip, Sheriff."

Rhodes didn't want another chip. He was ready to get out of there, so he asked if Clement wanted anything else.

"No, not a thing," the mayor said. "I'll trust you to get the job done in your usual efficient manner."

Rhodes had no difficulty in detecting the slight sarcasm in the remark, but it didn't bother him.

"You can count on me, Mr. Mayor," Rhodes said, and if there was any sarcasm intended it went right over Clements's head.

"I'm sure I can," Clements said.

Chapter 21

▼

On his way back to the jail, Rhodes drove through what remained of downtown Clearview and tried to imagine it when it had been not just a busy small town but had been booming with the influx of thousands of people because oil had been discovered. That had been nearly a hundred years ago, and the town had gone from a sleepy little backwater to a city of thousands almost overnight. Rhodes had heard the stories from his grandparents, who had been alive but too young to remember for themselves. They were repeating what they'd heard from their parents and others who had been there.

Within days of the discovery of oil, con men and gangsters, card-sharps and criminals, hustlers and entrepreneurs, had all arrived together, along with roughnecks and preachers and doctors and prostitutes. Bootleggers thrived. Hundreds of people swarmed every block of the muddy streets. A tent city sprang up, and buildings followed quickly. Within only a few weeks certain sections of the city had such bad reputations that people avoided them at night. Gunfights weren't uncommon, and more than one man had been shot down in the street for reasons now long forgotten.

It had been an exciting and lawless time, and although nobody currently alive remembered it, people still referred to the boom days now and then, almost as if they hoped the good times would come again. Or the bad times, depending on your point of view. More exciting times, for sure.

A stranger seeing the downtown now, or what was left of it, would have a hard time believing that it had once been so full of life and licentiousness. On a Sunday afternoon, it was completely dead. Not a soul walked the streets. Not a car was parked anywhere. There was no traffic moving through the area except for Rhodes's Tahoe. Rhodes thought that if he stopped and got out, he wouldn't hear a sound, unless a freight train happened to pass through on the tracks a few blocks away.

He wondered what life had been like for the lawmen in those days. If the stories he'd heard were true, more than a few of them were happy to look away from any wrongdoing as long as they got a substantial payment in return. Rhodes didn't think he'd have fared too well. It was too hard for him to look the other way.

He drove on to the jail and went inside. Hack and Lawton were talking about the Houston Texans and how everybody thought they'd be playing better than they were, so Rhodes didn't interrupt them. He sat at his desk and did some paperwork until they decided to notice him.

"Mayor give you any trouble?" Hack asked after a while.

"No more than usual," Rhodes said, swiveling his chair around to face Hack. "I told him what I knew about Jake Marley's death, and he was satisfied."

214

"That man's never satisfied," Lawton said from the doorway to the cellblock. "Not that I've ever heard about."

"He's all right," Rhodes said. "You just have to understand him."

"Which you do," Hack said.

"I like to think so."

"Well, you just keep thinkin' that," Hack said. "You gonna tell *us* what you know about Jake's death?"

"I'd put you in the loop if I could, but I don't know any more than I've already told you. Fact is, I was going to ask you for some help. You and Lawton, both."

Lawton walked over to stand by Hack's desk. "You want us to help you find out who killed Jake?"

"That'd be a first," Hack said, not looking at Lawton, "considerin' we ain't usually even in the loop. Nobody even tells us what's goin' on, much less asks us to do any crime-bustin'."

"Crime-bustin's not exactly what I had in mind," Rhodes said.

"Well, what is it you did have in mind, then?"

"You two have lived in Clearview all your lives. You probably remember the days when Jake Marley was a youngster and his sister was killed in a car wreck. Rolled the car and got thrown out. Died on the spot."

"Sure, I remember that," Hack said. "Lawton prob'ly remembers better'n I do, seein' how he's a good bit older."

"Six weeks," Lawton said. "I wouldn't call that a good bit."

"More like seven," Hack said, "but who's countin'?"

"Sounds to me like you're countin'."

"Nope. Not sure I can even count that high. Just makin' a remark about you bein' a good bit older'n me."

"Six weeks. You know it's just six weeks. That ain't nothin'."

Rhodes wondered if there'd ever been a sheriff who had to break up a fistfight between a jailer and a dispatcher or if he was going to be the first. One of these days it was bound to happen. Not today, though. He wanted the two men to help him out, not beat each other senseless.

"It doesn't matter who's the oldest," Rhodes said. "I just need somebody with a good memory."

"Well, that'd be me," Hack said. "We younger fellas got a lot better recall than some old geezers I could name."

"You better not be callin' me a geezer," Lawton said, "'cause I ain't one. I'll match my mem'ry up against yours any day of the week."

"I'm glad to hear it," Rhodes said, "because now's your chance. This was fifty years ago, though, so you'll have to be sharp."

"I'm sharp as a Gillette Blue Blade," Hack said.

"Ain't been such a thing as Gillette Blue Blades in so long, the sheriff don't even know what you're talkin' about."

"You do, though, you old geezer."

Lawton looked over at Rhodes. "I know a little bit about the law, Sheriff. There's such a thing as a justifiable homicide, ain't there?"

"Not in this case, and as happy as I'd be to testify on your behalf, I don't think you'd get off without a sentence. Maybe just manslaughter, but I'd a whole lot rather you'd tell me what you know or heard about that car wreck."

"Okay," Lawton said, with a glare at Hack. "I'll tell you how it was, since I got such a clear mem'ry of it and some others might not have."

"'It was a dark an' stormy night,'" Hack said.

"All right," Rhodes said, "that's enough of that. Let Lawton tell it. If he gets anything wrong, you can let me know. Not until after he's finished, though. Until then, you keep quiet."

Instead of looking cowed or ashamed, Hack looked pleased with himself, and once again Rhodes wondered if the byplay between him and Lawton was really a well-orchestrated plot to drive him crazy. He'd have to worry about that another time. He told Lawton to get on with his story.

"It wasn't a dark an' stormy night," Lawton said. "It was a pretty nice night, as I remember, what with it bein' about this time of year. Big harvest moon at night, a little cool, but not bad, kinda like the nights around here lately. You wouldn't think about anybody gettin' killed on that kinda night, but that's what happened."

"Thanks for the weather report," Hack said.

Lawton ignored him. "The way I heard it, Gwen Marley was going too fast as she come to that curve out near the Marley place. Lost control of the car. It went into the bar ditch, flipped, rolled, and hit a tree. Threw her out, and she hit another tree. Killed her dead as a hammer."

It occurred to Rhodes that maybe he'd been overthinking things in looking for a motive for Jake's murder. A driver who was bouncing around in an old car that was rolling over might wind up on the passenger side. He still didn't regard it as likely. He thought anybody in that situation would've been hanging on to the steering wheel with both hands.

"What about later on?" Rhodes asked. "Was there any gossip about the accident? Did anybody have any doubts about how it happened?"

"I guess there's always some talk after somethin' like that. I heard she was seen around town with some of her friends, but they all said they weren't with her. The talk died down after a while. The Marleys likely put the kibosh on it."

"How?" Rhodes asked.

"Well, I remember there was just one little article in the paper about the wreck. Nothin' like you'd expect when somebody from a big rich family dies. Wasn't a lot of talk about it, either. Maybe word got out that the Marleys didn't want any big article or any talk about the wreck. They wanted to forget all about it. Cut down all the trees where it happened."

"What about drinking? Any of that going on that night?"

"Coulda been if Gwen was out with her friends. Those were some wild kids back then, got in a good bit of trouble, but you wouldn't know it now. They're all sober and quiet as far as I know. Good citizens, all got good jobs, except Ron Gleason, and he had one till he retired. Come to think of it, ever'body's a little wild when they're kids. That's the best time for it." Lawton looked at Hack. "Too late for some of us now."

"Yeah, you," Hack said. "Let me tell you, Sheriff, those kids had a reputation. They might all be respectable now, like Lawton says, but back in those days, they'd hell around the town in their cars on Saturday nights, and more'n once they'd be having somethin' to drink while they was doin' it. You oughta look into the old arrest records. I bet you'd find somethin' on that bunch."

"I'll do that," he said. "Anything else you can remember?"

"Nope," Lawton said. "Not me."

"Not me, either," Hack said, surprising Rhodes by not trying to top Lawton. "Seems like all that was just a little while ago, not fifty years or more, though."

"Time goes faster for folks as old as you are," Lawton said.

"Goes fast for me, too," Rhodes said, standing up and getting ready for a fast exit, "and I'm not half as old as you two."

They were still sputtering when he got out the door.

Rhodes hadn't been to the courthouse on Sunday in years. It was closed, locked, and completely deserted. He had a key to a basement door and let himself inside, locking the door behind him. His rubber-soled shoes squeaked on the floor as he walked along the marble-floored hallway. He ignored the Dr Pepper machine again and went straight to his office, thinking that for once Jennifer Loam wasn't going to be able to track him down, not unless she had a key to the courthouse. Come to think of it, he wouldn't be surprised if she did.

One reason Rhodes hadn't looked into the old records for Gwen's friends was that fifty years ago they might not have been eighteen. If they'd been juveniles, they probably wouldn't have been arrested, and if they had been there would be no record.

Driving was different, however, and teenagers could get in even more trouble than adults for reckless driving or for driving under the influence. If Gwen's friends had been helling around in cars, as Hack had put it, they might have had an accident themselves or they might've been stopped for DUI. It was worth a look.

Since Rhodes had already found the box from the year of Gwen's death, he didn't have to search for it. He located it again easily, carried it out into his office, set it on the desk, and started to go through it.

It took Rhodes a while to find what he was looking for, but when he did, he wasn't shocked at his discovery. One of Gwen's friends had been cited, all right. The one who'd received the citation was Al Graham, who'd been driving over a hundred miles an hour just outside the city limits after a short chase that had begun in town. Al had been seventeen at the time, and since it was a second offense, he'd had his license suspended. Two other passengers in the car were Ed Hopkins and Ron Gleason, both of whom showed signs of intoxication. Al, however, did not, which was lucky for him. Glenda Tallent and Gwen Marley were also in the car, but there was no mention of their being under the influence.

Five passengers, probably all seated comfortably. Cars had more room in those days. Rhodes checked the date of the incident. It had been one week before Gwen's death.

None of the old records had been computerized, and Rhodes wasn't going to go through the boxes year by year to find out any more about Al Graham. What he had was enough to convince him that he was on the right track. Since Al had at least two citations for reckless driving, and since he was a friend of Gwen's, wasn't it possible that he'd been driving the car on the night she died? His friends would cover for him, then and now. Rhodes wondered how he could get them to talk. So far he hadn't been very successful, but it was worth another try. He didn't need all of them to talk. Just one of them would do the trick. Today wasn't the day to try, however.

Rhodes returned the records to the box and put the box back in the storage room. He'd check with Hack to see if he was needed for anything, and if not he'd go home. He wanted to check on his pecan tree.

Rhodes called Hack from the old-fashioned landline phone on his desk. Although Rhodes could tell that it pained Hack to admit it, there were no lawbreakers running loose in the county and wreaking havoc on the citizens. So Rhodes told the dispatcher that he'd be at home if he was needed.

"I'd prefer not to be needed," he added.

"That'll depend on what happens," Hack said.

"I know that, but make sure it's a real emergency if you call me."

"Like if somebody kidnaps the mayor."

"That might qualify, but let somebody else handle it. Call me if World War III starts, though."

"Got it," Hack said. "World War III."

"Right," Rhodes said, and he hung up and went home.

Rhodes parked the Tahoe in the driveway and went to look at the pecan tree. It would survive, he decided, but it looked bad. A large chunk of the trunk was badly damaged, and the whole tree looked as if it had been knocked a little off plumb. While he stood there looking at the tree, Rhodes thought about Gwen Marley. If cars had been required to have airbags fifty years ago, she might have survived the crash that killed her, but in those days very few cars even had seat belts. And the ones that did have belts had only the kind that locked across the driver's lap. Those might've saved some lives, but they'd also cut a few people almost in two. The harnesses being used now, along with the airbags, were a lot safer. Or they were supposed to be. The recent scandal involving a recall of over forty million vehicles with possibly defective airbags, airbags that could be more dangerous than any accident, had shaken a lot of people's faith in the devices.

Rhodes was still a believer, however, in the airbags and the seat belt harnesses. Latham was able to get out of his car and run away after he hit the pecan tree thanks to his airbag. He might have gone through the windshield otherwise.

Ivy came out of the house and joined Rhodes. He could hear Yancey yipping behind the closed door.

"Your dog is feeling left out of things," Rhodes said.

"I don't want him to come out here and get run down by some crazy driver," Ivy said. She pointed at the tree. "Like the one that did that."

"He did it to avoid hitting a squirrel," Rhodes told her.

"Maybe there's some good in everybody, but was that really the smart thing to do?"

"Happens all the time," Rhodes said. "People don't think about what's going to happen to them in a situation like that. There's not time for them to think. They react instead, and the natural reaction is to try to avoid hitting the squirrel."

"Sometimes you wind up hitting the tree, though. It might be sad to hit a squirrel, but it's sadder to injure yourself and tear up your car."

"The squirrel doesn't think so."

Ivy shook her head. "I'm not so sure squirrels think. Maybe what they do is reacting, too."

Rhodes didn't respond. He looked at the damaged pecan tree.

"I can almost see the wheels turning in your head," Ivy said. "Is that tree really that important to you?"

"It's not the tree," Rhodes said.

"What, then?"

"Just thinking."

"That's always a good thing."

"Nope," Rhodes said. "Not always."

Chapter 22

▼

No emergencies worthy of Rhodes's attention occurred for the rest of Sunday, so he was able to spend some time with Ivy, the dogs, and the cats. Ivy and the dogs seemed glad to have him around. The cats were indifferent, which Rhodes knew was only to be expected. Cats, or at least these two, were always indifferent.

He got an early start on Monday after a romp with Speedo and Yancey. Both dogs were perky because it had gotten cooler again overnight, although there was no wind this time, just a crisp fall day with bright sun and low humidity. If every day were like that, Rhodes wouldn't mind. Some people said they'd get bored with the sameness, but Rhodes didn't think he would.

When Rhodes got to the jail, Hack didn't even have any exciting incidents to tell him about or any stories to draw out at great length. After the car chase with Latham, things had calmed down considerably. Pert and Latham had both been booked and then bonded out. Rhodes hoped they'd settle their differences in a gentlemanly manner, though he didn't really hold out much hope for it. Latham would probably blame the wrecked car on Pert, and that could be the beginning of a whole new feud.

"Only thing that happened was late yesterday afternoon," Hack said. "We got a call about Old Man Everett again."

Everybody in town referred to Russell Everett as Old Man Everett. He was a couple of years younger than Hack, but Rhodes chose not to point that out. He was glad that Lawton was working back in the cellblock, for Lawton surely would have pointed it out, and that would've started another argument that might've gone on endlessly.

"What's Mr. Everett done this time?" Rhodes asked, hoping for a straight answer.

"Put chocolate chips in his yard."

Rhodes wasn't sure he'd heard that right, and he didn't consider it a straight answer. "Chocolate chips?"

"Chocolate chips is what I said. Your hearin' startin' to get bad?"

"I was just surprised. I don't think we've ever had a case of somebody putting chocolate chips in his yard, and I'm pretty sure there's no law against it."

"Might be in this case. It was Charlotte Chandler that called. She's always walkin' her dog down the sidewalk in front of Old Man Everett's house. Old Man Everett don't like that dog."

"He doesn't like any dogs," Rhodes said.

They'd had calls about Everett more than once because he'd be standing on his lawn with a water hose when people walked their dogs by his house. He'd never squirted anybody, but it was clear that he was threatening to do so. His complaint was that people allowed their dogs to use his lawn as a restroom and then didn't pick up the results. He was tired of it, so he brought out the water hose.

The implied threat hadn't worked, though, because nobody took him seriously except Charlotte Chandler. She'd called the sheriff's department and said that if Old Man Everett squirted her or her dog, she was going to file charges against him for assault. Rhodes had gone out for a little talk with Everett, who'd said he'd stop standing there with the hose but that he'd "by God find another way to stop those damn dogs from messing up my lawn."

Everett took good care of his lawn. It was one of the greenest in town, if not *the* greenest. Everett fertilized every spring, and if it didn't rain, he watered. He cut his own grass and did his own edging. Someone had once told Rhodes that he'd seen Everett out in the yard edging his driveway with a pair of scissors, but Rhodes didn't believe that. It might've been true, however. Everett was mighty proud of that grass, and his threat about finding another way to stop the dogs had been a serious one.

Apparently the other way was chocolate.

"Charlotte says dogs like chocolate," Hack said.

"So do I," Rhodes said, who wouldn't have minded a bit of it at that very moment.

"Yeah, ever'body likes it, but it's bad for dogs, accordin' to Charlotte. She says it'll kill 'em."

Being the owner of two dogs, Rhodes had read about the effects of chocolate on creatures of the canine persuasion, so he knew a little about the subject.

"It depends on the size of the dog and the kind of chocolate," he said. "Ms. Chandler has a Shih Tzu, so it wouldn't take much, not nearly as much as it would take for Ms. Bettinger's Great Pyrenees, for example."

"That Bettinger dog's the size of a Shetland pony."

"At least. Can't Ms. Chandler keep her Shih Tzu under control? It's not any bigger than Yancey."

"Name's Horace," Hack said.

"Whose name?"

"That dog's name. Horace. Mighty funny name for a dog."

"Wasn't that the name of Ms. Chandler's first husband?"

"Believe it was. Name makes more sense now. Anyway, she ain't got no more control of that dog than she had of the original Horace, and she's worried about other dogs, too. She ain't the only one goes by Old Man Everett's place."

"Is the problem solved?" Rhodes asked, hoping he wasn't going to have to deal with it.

"For now it is," Hack said. "Duke went out and talked to Old Man Everett, and he cleaned up the chocolate chips. Duke made him run the lawn mower over the yard, too, and that chopped up whatever was left pretty good. Dog'd be hard-pressed to find any of it. Who knows what Old Man Everett'll come up with next, though."

"Not me," Rhodes said, "but we'll worry about that when it happens."

"Be easier if folks would clean up after their dogs," Hack said.

"Most do."

"That ain't what Old Man Everett says."

"He's a little bit biased."

"A lot biased, I'd say. You gonna hang around here today, or you got somethin' in mind?"

"I'm going to try to get a handle on Jake Marley's death," Rhodes said.

"You got any good ideas?"

"I have some ideas, but I don't know how good they are. I have to talk to everybody again. I followed up on that suggestion you made about looking for the old arrest records. I found out that Al Graham had a couple of arrests for reckless driving. Might be something to look further at."

"Am I gonna get a raise?"

"I'll be sure to mention to the commissioners what a great job you're doing."

"That'll do the trick, all right," Hack said.

"Sure it will," Rhodes said.

Aubrey Hamilton's real estate office was out on the highway in a small four-building strip center located practically in the Walmart parking lot. It was a good location, Rhodes supposed, since if there was one place everybody in town went, it was Walmart. To get there from just about anywhere in town, you had to drive past the little strip center, and the business with the biggest sign was Aubrey's. It was white with red letters that said:

AUBREY HAMILTON REAL ESTATE
BUY SELL TRADE
WHATEVER YOU WANT, WE HAVE IT

Besides the real estate office, the center contained a fabric shop, a computer repair shop, and a vacancy where there had once been a TV repair shop. Even the location hadn't saved that business. Nobody in Clearview repaired TV sets anymore, or much of anything else. When one stopped working, people just bought a new one. Rhodes supposed that was easier than the old way of doing things, but it seemed wasteful to him.

Two cars were parked in the lot of the strip center, including Aubrey's Chevy Malibu with the magnetic signs on the doors advertising her business. The lack of cars wasn't unusual since it was early, and people who worked in the center also had a parking area in back.

Rhodes pulled the Tahoe into a spot in front of Aubrey's office and got out. The windows of the former TV repair shop were clean on the outside but dusty on the inside. Rhodes was a little surprised no one had opened a new business there, since it was a good location, but new businesses were risky in Clearview, no matter where they were.

Looking through the window of the real estate office, Rhodes saw that Aubrey was inside at her desk, talking on the telephone. It was an old landline like the one in Rhodes's office at the courthouse. He went on inside, and she waved him to a seat with her free hand. He sat down to wait until she finished the call.

It didn't take long. She hung up, folded her hands on the desk, and asked what she could do for Rhodes.

"I was wondering if you'd thought of anything else that might help me," he said. "When you talked to Jake, he must have made conversation about things not related to the theater now and then."

Aubrey looked almost at Rhodes, but he thought it was more likely that she was looking out into the parking lot. "I don't remember that he did."

"Nothing about his old friends, people he knew when he was growing up, his sister who died in an accident?"

Aubrey looked thoughtful. "He may have said something about what the building was like in the old days, now that you mention it. I think he went to the movies there with his friends."

That was possible. Jake would've been just old enough to see a movie there before the place closed down for good, but he'd have been too young at the time to remember much about it. There wouldn't be any connection to what happened to his sister.

"He didn't mention seeing any of those old friends lately?" Rhodes asked.

Aubrey looked directly at him. "Sheriff, why are you asking about his friends? Do you think one of them killed him?"

"I don't know what to think. That's why I'm asking."

"I see. You've put me in a bad position. I don't want to get anybody into trouble."

"It's not like we're talking about a parking ticket," Rhodes said. "This is a lot more serious."

"I know, but still . . ."

"Nobody will ever know it came from you," Rhodes told her.

"All right, then. I remember now. He did talk about at least one of them."

Rhodes was used to this kind of circuitous conversation, thanks to spending so much time around Hack and Lawton.

"Which one?" he asked.

"Ed Hopkins."

"Did Jake mention what they talked about?"

"It was the building," Aubrey said, and stopped.

"What about the building?" Rhodes asked after a second or so.

"Ed was upset because Jake hadn't come to him and asked about finding the heirs and making the deal."

"Ed mentioned to me that he needed a sale," Rhodes said.

Aubrey nodded. "So did I. You might have noticed that Clearview's not growing a lot. Any sale we can get is a sale we need."

Rhodes wasn't disappointed that Ed had lied to him. He'd gotten used to being lied to. People nearly always lied to the law if it served their purposes, and their purposes were often to keep from being suspected of a crime. Ed was likely to have been the one who'd called Glenda Tallent. Maybe he'd asked her not to say anything about his having talked to Jake.

"So you got a good price for the building," Rhodes said.

"Not really. It's old and in bad repair. I didn't do too badly, though. The fact that Jake really wanted it helped."

"He didn't mention having talked to any of his other old friends? What about Al Graham?"

"He works on cars, doesn't he?"

"That's him."

"Jake wouldn't need him. He always had a practically new car."

Rhodes thought about that. He asked a few more questions but got nothing useful in return. It appeared that the only person Jake had been in touch with, or at least the only one that Aubrey knew about, was Ed Hopkins. Rhodes figured it might be worth his time to have another little chat with Ed.

He thanked Aubrey for her time and drove to Ed Hopkins's office. This time Ed was sitting at his desk as Rhodes walked in. Ed didn't look pleased to see Rhodes, which wasn't surprising. Nobody liked to have even one visit from the sheriff, and a second visit within a couple of days was even less likely to be welcome.

"Sheriff," Ed said.

It wasn't much of a greeting, but Rhodes took it as an invitation to have a seat. When he was more or less comfortable, he said, "I've been talking to Aubrey Hamilton."

Ed fiddled with some papers on his desk and said nothing, so Rhodes continued. "She tells me that you've talked to Jake recently. I seem to remember that you said you hadn't."

Ed looked up from his papers. "Did I say that? I don't remember. I might've talked to him, but if I did, it wasn't about anything of any consequence."

"I think it might have been consequential. You argued with him about the building. You were upset that he'd gone to Aubrey and hadn't come to you."

"I told you I could've used the sale. I didn't think it was important that I'd mentioned it to Jake. If I did."

"I asked about that specifically, but we'll let that go for a minute. I want to know how long you talked and how upset you were by the time you finished."

Ed shoved his papers aside. "Now just a damn minute, Sheriff. Whatever Jake and I said to each other is my own personal business. It was just between us. You don't need to know about it."

"Jake's dead," Rhodes said. "I believe somebody killed him, and I'm conducting a murder investigation. So I do need to know about what you said. I can't force you to tell me, but it's going to make you look pretty bad if you don't. I'll bet you know that."

Ed leaned back in his chair and sighed. "I know how it must sound. That's why I didn't tell you in the first place. I knew you'd think I had something to do with Jake's death, and I didn't. I haven't even been in that theater since they started work on it."

"If that's true, you don't have a thing to worry about," Rhodes said. "Tell me something. Where were you the morning Jake died?"

"Right here in this office, working, as usual."

"Nobody else was here?"

"Well, what do you think? I've told you how slow business is. About the only person who's been here this week is you. I was working on contacts that morning, figuring out who might be selling and who might be buying and how I might get in on something. Not that it did me any good."

Rhodes wondered why Ed didn't just retire. Like the others who'd known Jake, he was old enough. Maybe business had never been good enough for Ed to build up any retirement funds or to have much coming in from Social Security.

"Not much of an alibi," Rhodes said.

"It's what I have. I'd lie if I thought it would do me any good, but you'd figure that out. Then I'd really be in trouble, wouldn't I?"

"You got that right," Rhodes said.

Rhodes decided to stop by the theater before he went to see Al Graham. Being inside the building again might give him some ideas, although he already had a lot of those. He just didn't know how the bits and pieces of the puzzle that were jumbled in his head all fit together, or even if they *did* fit together. He didn't want to go to the courthouse to think things over because of Jennifer Loam's aggravating habit of tracking him down there and asking about his investigations. The theater would be more private unless someone saw the Tahoe parked in front. Even that wouldn't matter, because he was going to lock the door.

The only problem was that he'd have to stop by the jail. The sheriff's department had keys to all the downtown buildings, and they were kept where whoever was on duty could get one if it was needed. Retrieving one meant seeing Hack again, and while Rhodes didn't mind *seeing* him, he didn't have time for a long-winded conversation about chocolate chips or anything else of that nature. But he needed the key, so he'd have to chance it.

He got lucky. When he entered the jail, Hack was on the phone to someone about some kind of dispute between neighbors. Rhodes couldn't tell what kind of dispute, and he didn't want to know. He grabbed the key and got out of there before Hack could try to send him to solve the caller's problem. Hack would just have to dispatch one of the deputies. Rhodes didn't have the time.

When he got downtown, it occurred to Rhodes that he could park in the lot across the street from the theater. That was the lot for

Randy Lawless's law offices, and even Jennifer Loam wouldn't be suspicious to see the Tahoe parked there. Rhodes and Lawless could be discussing some of the finer points of the law for all Jennifer would know.

After he parked the Tahoe, Rhodes looked around to be sure no cars were coming. When he saw that no one was around, he got out of the Tahoe and hustled across the street. He got across and into the theater quickly without being seen, at least by anyone passing by. Someone in another building might have caught a glimpse of him, but that didn't matter. Rhodes unlocked the door, went inside, and locked the door behind him.

In the lobby, he felt sure he could smell popcorn again. Funny how the imagination could play tricks on a person. The power of suggestion. Most ghosts were probably a result of the same thing. What you expect is what you get. Rhodes didn't expect to encounter any ghosts.

It was colder inside the theater than it had been outside, and the ghost light threw some odd shadows around the empty stage. Rhodes walked down to the front row and sat in the same seat he'd taken when he'd first talked to Aubrey Hamilton about Jake's fall. He thought about the theater's locked back door, and he looked up at the grid where the boards had broken. Pieces of the boards still lay on the stage, and Rhodes remembered how he'd felt as he dangled from one of the boards before he'd managed to get back on top of the grid. He was glad the board he'd had hold of hadn't broken, and he wondered what Jake had thought just as he fell. Or did he even have time to think?

Rhodes considered what Seepy had said about Jake's ghost trying to kill him by causing the boards to break. That was ridiculous, of course. The boards had just been rotten. Why would Jake want to kill him, anyway? He was trying to find Jake's killer. Jake's ghost should have appreciated that.

Seepy would probably say that Jake didn't want his killer to be found, but that didn't make any sense.

Or maybe it did. As Ivy had pointed out, Jake might've let the killer into the theater by opening the back door. If the killer was one of his sister's old childhood friends, would Jake want to protect him? Or her? That didn't make any sense. Jake had been out for revenge, and he was about to get it. That's why he'd been so happy lately.

Or so Rhodes had thought. What if he was wrong about Jake's motives for restoring the theater and presenting the play? That was always a possibility. Rhodes started rearranging everything he'd learned or guessed at so far, but even with the new scenario in mind, nothing fit together.

Rhodes stood up. Thinking things over had just confused him. Talking to Al Graham might clarify a few things, though, so Rhodes would give it a try.

As Rhodes started up the aisle, the ghost light moved and shadows flickered over the walls.

"Just the wind and nothing more," Rhodes said, and although there was no wind in the theater, he made himself believe it.

Chapter 23

▼

When Rhodes walked through the wide door into A+Auto Repair, Al Graham was bent over under the hood of a car. Rhodes had no idea what he might be doing, but he supposed he was replacing a part that the computer had told him was defective.

Graham appeared to be too busy to acknowledge Rhodes's presence, so Rhodes looked around for Graham's son. He didn't see him. He was either taking the day off or had gone after a part for the car his father was working on.

Having nothing better to do, Rhodes walked around the garage, looking at the grimy concrete floor with its years of accumulated grease and dirt embedded in it. Rhodes didn't know how long Al had been in the building, but it was easily more than forty years.

Rhodes glanced at a chain hoist that hung from an iron beam and at an area of tools and parts that was separated from the garage by chicken-wire fencing that Rhodes was sure provided no protection from theft. It was more decorative than secure. Rhodes wondered if the chain hoist had been used anytime within the last few years. He doubted that anybody pulled an engine anymore. He wondered if that could even be done with the way cars were built now. A large electric heater with a fan inside a housing sat at the end of the garage opposite the door, but while it was a bit cool in the garage, the heater wasn't turned on.

"What do you want?" Al Graham asked from behind Rhodes.

Rhodes hadn't heard Al walk up. His rubber-soled shoes didn't make any sound on the concrete.

"Not much," Rhodes said, turning around. "Just wanted to talk a little about Gwen Marley."

Al held an adjustable wrench, the kind mechanics called a knuckle-buster, in his right hand. He lowered the knuckle-buster to his side and looked at Rhodes. "I've said all I have to say about that."

"That's fine. Let's talk about you instead. You must have liked cars even when you were young since you decided to make a living by working on them."

"It was something I was good at. Back then, anybody could work on a car. Lots of guys had old cars that were easy to fix when something went wrong with them. Change the spark plugs, put on a new muffler, put in a new thermostat. Start off small and work up to something harder, like putting on a new radiator. It wasn't like work. It was fun."

"You didn't work on Gwen's car, I guess."

"What's that supposed to mean?"

"You mentioned something about how it might not have been in good repair."

"Yeah, well, if it wasn't, I didn't know it. I didn't work on other people's cars then. Just mine."

"You drove yours pretty fast," Rhodes said. "Too fast sometimes."

Al raised the knuckle-buster and tapped the business end of it into his left palm. "You've been checking up on me."

"A little bit."

"I don't like that," Al said. "That's stuff that happened when I was a kid. Means nothing now."

"It might've meant something to Gwen."

"I don't like what you're implying, Sheriff." Al tapped the wrench against his palm again. "I have work to do, and I think you might as well leave now."

"I'd like to talk to you some more about the night that Gwen died before I go."

"I don't care what you'd like. This is my place of business, and you need to get out of it."

Rhodes knew Al didn't want to talk, but he needed answers. "You say you and your friends didn't see Gwen the night she died. I don't think that's true. I think—"

Rhodes didn't get to say what he thought because Al swung the wrench at his head. Rhodes didn't have the fastest reaction time in the world, but Al was older and even slower. Rhodes dodged out of the way. The wrench missed his head, but it did hit his upper arm, not very hard but hard enough to sting.

Rhodes backed away and bumped into the chicken wire of the cage he'd seen earlier. Al came after him and swung the wrench again.

Rhodes moved more quickly this time, since he was expecting Al to be aggressive. The wrench missed Rhodes completely and went right through the flimsy wire, proving him right about how insecure the cage was, not that it mattered to him at the moment.

Al pulled the wrench out of the wire. "You get out of here, Sheriff. I don't want to hurt you."

Rhodes didn't think that was true. He moved away from Al, but Al came right on after him. Rhodes was near the chain hoist, and he wondered how smoothly it would slide down the beam. Pretty smoothly, it if had been maintained. Al's garage was greasy but neat, and even if he didn't use the hoist, he must have kept it in good working order. As Rhodes passed the hoist, he grabbed the load chain, turned, and slung the hoist toward Al.

The hoist slid smoothly on the beam, and the chains smacked into Al before he could jump out of the way. He wasn't hurt, but he was momentarily stunned. More important, he dropped the wrench.

Rhodes pushed Al out of the way and picked up the wrench as Al staggered aside. For a second Rhodes was afraid that Al would fall, but he was able to maintain his balance. When he came to a stop, he stood quietly.

"I'm sorry for coming after you, Sheriff," he said. He had a hangdog look. "I guess I got a little upset that you wouldn't leave me alone. I didn't mean to act like that. Are you gonna arrest me?"

Rhodes thought it over. "Maybe not. What I want are some answers. If I got those, I wouldn't need to arrest you."

Al shook his head. "You're asking for something I can't give you."

"I don't see why not," Rhodes said. "I'm here, you're here, and we're talking. Just tell me what I need to know."

"Let's go in my office," Al said. "I need to sit down."

Rhodes wouldn't mind sitting down himself. He followed Al into the office, but first he put the wrench on the floor beside the car Al had been working on.

Al sat behind his desk, which was just as cluttered as it had been the previous day, and Rhodes took a seat in a well-worn wooden chair. He stretched out his legs, crossed his ankles, and waited for Al to start the conversation.

Al looked around the little room for a few seconds, avoiding Rhodes's eyes. "I know what you think," he said after a while.

Rhodes grinned. "You read minds?"

"No," Al said, "but I've been talking to a few people. You know who I mean."

"You'd better tell me, just so I'm sure. I'm not like you. I don't read minds."

"Okay, but you do know who I mean. It's Ed Hopkins, Ron Gleason, and Glenda Tallent."

"I thought you folks weren't talking to each other. That's what everyone's told me."

"We don't talk, usually, but we don't usually have the sheriff coming around and asking us questions, either. We figured we needed to talk it over."

"Who got the talking started? That might be important."

"It was Ed who called us. He thinks you have some kind of idea that one of us killed Jake and that maybe it was because of what happened to Gwen. You've been asking all of us about that night."

"I just ask questions," Rhodes said. "I don't have a lot of ideas."

"Yeah. Well, that's not what Ed thinks. He's worried about how all of us are supposed to be in that play Jake wanted to do. He says it's all about the past and the future."

"The present, too," Rhodes said.

Al grimaced. "I don't read a lot, but I think I saw a movie of it once. Anyway, it might seem to you like Jake was trying to say that one of us was the killer. That's just not the truth."

"Then what is the truth?"

"I can't tell you."

"Why not?"

"It's not mine to tell. I guess you could say it's all of ours."

Rhodes started to stand up. "Then I guess I'll have to put you in jail."

"Sit down, Sheriff. Let's talk about this."

Rhodes sat back down. "I don't know what more there is to say."

Al pushed aside some papers, braced his forearms on the desk, and leaned forward with an earnest look on his face. "Maybe we can work something out."

"Like what?" Rhodes asked.

"Like maybe getting you to leave us all alone. We didn't have anything to do with what happened to Gwen. It's just like we've all told you."

Rhodes didn't believe that any more than he'd believed that Al didn't want to hurt him.

"That's not true," he said. "You told me you're protecting a secret, and now you're saying you've told me everything I need to know. One of those things isn't true."

"You don't get it," Al said, sighing and leaning back in his chair.

Rhodes stood up. "Come on. I'm taking you to jail and filing assault charges."

Al gave Rhodes a stubborn look and didn't move. "I can't go to jail. I got to fix that car out there."

"You should've thought of that before you swung the wrench. Let's go."

"Wait a second, Sheriff. I need to think about this. Just give me a minute."

"A minute's all you get," Rhodes said. He didn't sit back down.

Al sat silently. After a little less than a minute, he said, "I need to call everybody. Make some arrangements to see if we can talk to you about this."

"By 'everybody' you mean Ed and Ron and Glenda."

"Yeah. You might as well sit down and listen. I mean, if you want to talk to us about it."

"Will I get any more from all of you than I know so far?"

"Maybe," Al said. "I can't make any promises for the whole bunch, but I'll try to get them to keep me out of jail."

Rhodes sat back down, and Al pulled the old-fashioned dial phone closer to him.

"Bet you don't see many of these," Al said.

"I have one in the courthouse," Rhodes said, "and I saw one earlier today in Aubrey Hamilton's office."

Al looked disappointed.

"Those have pushbuttons, though," Rhodes said, "not a dial."

Al brightened a little and started to dial. Rhodes listened to the clicks as the dial rotated. It was a sound that had been quite familiar at one time, but now it was just a part of history.

Al was able to get all three of his friends on the first try, and while Rhodes listened in, he explained the situation to them. He left out the part about the wrench, saying only that he was in trouble and that Rhodes was about to arrest him. He assured each person he called that he hadn't told Rhodes anything, and only Glenda Tallent seemed skeptical.

"He's sitting right here, listening," Al said. "You want to ask him for yourself?"

Glenda must not have wanted to, because Al didn't hand the phone to Rhodes. He continued his spiel instead. The gist of it was that he thought it was time for the four of them to get together and talk to Rhodes, who needed to be convinced that they hadn't all been lying to him.

Glenda must have had quite a bit to say about that, because Al listened for a while, looked at Rhodes, shrugged, and listened some more.

"Look, Glenda," he said after she was done with him, "either I'm going to have to tell him or we're all going to have to tell him. I think it would be better if we all did, but if I have to, I will. I don't want to go to jail."

Glenda started in again. Al looked shocked.

"I hadn't thought about that," he said when she paused. "Who do you think—"

Glenda cut him off and talked some more. Finally Al said, "All right. I think he'll go for that. You call Ed and Ron and set it up. Ed's office is the biggest. We can meet there. How about half an hour?"

Glenda must have agreed, because Al said, "Okay," and hung up.

"What is it that I'll go for?" Rhodes asked, although he had a pretty good idea.

"A meeting," Al said. "Me and Glenda and Ron and Ed, in Ed's office. We'll talk to you together. Would that be okay?"

"Yes," Rhodes said. "That would be okay. Now tell me what you hadn't thought of before."

"Glenda asked me, what if one of us was guilty."

"Of what?"

"Of killing Jake."

"It's about time one of you thought of that," Rhodes said.

As it turned out, Ed had a small meeting room in the back of his office, and it was just about the right size for five people. It was furnished with a wooden table and six chairs, so they could've squeezed in one more person if it had been necessary.

Rhodes had stayed with Al until it was time to drive to Ed's office, and Al hadn't said much. He did ask if it would be all right if he went out and closed the big door so that nobody would bother his shop while he was gone, and Rhodes let him do that.

"Son's taking a few days off," Al said when he came back into the office. "His mother-in-law up in Abilene's sick, and he took his wife up there."

That was all he had to offer until it was time to go, when he asked if he could drive to Ed's place in his own pickup.

Rhodes could understand the request. Hardly anybody ever wanted to ride with the law if they didn't have to. Someone might see them and get the wrong idea. Or the right idea. He said it would be all right for Al to take his own pickup as long as he promised to behave. Al promised, and Rhodes followed him to the real estate office.

When everyone was there in the little meeting room, Rhodes stood at the head of the table and waited until they were all seated. They settled in and looked at him expectantly.

"Well?" he said.

Nobody responded.

"Who's the spokesperson?" he asked.

The four people at the table looked at each other, and Rhodes looked them over while they were at it. Glenda Tallent was dressed almost as spiffily as she'd been when getting ready for church. Ed Hopkins had on a suit and tie, and his balding head had a little shine in the fluorescent lights. Al was a bit grimy. Ron Gleason was relaxed and comfortable in jeans and a flannel shirt.

"Well?" Rhodes asked.

"Al called the meeting," Glenda said. "Let him do the talking."

Al glanced around the table. Ron nodded. Ed said, "Go ahead. Maybe it's time this was out in the open. It's not going to hurt us now."

"All right," Al said. "I'll start."

Rhodes sat down to hear what he had to say.

"You're right about one thing, Sheriff," Al began. "We all saw something the night Gwen was killed. We were pretty close friends, and we'd been to a movie that night. Not all of us together, but we met up there and sat together."

Rhodes knew where they had to have been, and maybe it fit in with Jake's death.

"At the opera house," he said, just to make it clear.

"That's right," Al said. "It was the last week the theater was going to be open, so we all wanted to go one last time. I don't remember what the movie was."

"Something with Jerry Lewis," Ron said. "I liked those Jerry Lewis movies. Hardly ever missed one."

"Could've been Jerry Lewis," Al said. "Doesn't matter. After the movie we all went out to the Dairy King. You remember the Dairy King, Sheriff?"

Rhodes didn't, but the others did.

"Sort of like the Dairy Queen, only with a better jukebox," Glenda said.

"I'm not so sure about the jukebox part," Ed said.

"Does the jukebox have anything to do with the wreck?" Rhodes asked.

"No, it doesn't," Glenda said. "I'm just giving you some details."

"Why don't we get to the important details, then?" Rhodes asked, and Glenda gave him a huffy look.

"I guess I'm putting it off," Al said. "Here's what we've been holding back for fifty years or more."

He paused and looked around the table. Nobody said anything. After a second Glenda nodded.

Al took a deep breath. "Jake was there," he said.

Chapter 24

▼

The room was so quiet that Rhodes could hear the others breathing.

"Go on," Rhodes said to Al. "You've started it. Tell the rest."

Al opened his mouth, then shut it. He looked down at the table, then waved a hand as if to say he couldn't talk any more.

"I'll tell the rest," Glenda said. "You know that in those days you could get a license to drive when you were fourteen? Jake had been practicing his driving out in the country, and he begged Glenda to let him drive home. She didn't want to, but we—all of us—told her she should let him do it. She finally gave in. Jake is the one who had the wreck, not Gwen. We don't know how he got out of the car and away from the accident, but he must have run home. He might even have called in the report. We don't know what happened because he never talked about it to us. He never said another word about it. Maybe he dodged a jackrabbit or a possum."

Just like Latham, Rhodes thought. One quick irreversible bad decision was all it took, and a life was gone.

"Maybe he was just speeding and misjudged the curve," Glenda continued. "It didn't matter. He started missing school and becoming more and more withdrawn. We knew why, but we weren't going to say anything. It's not that we were at fault, you understand."

She paused as if hoping that Rhodes would exonerate her. He didn't speak.

"We were just kids," she said. "We were scared. We didn't know the law. So we kept quiet. Jake didn't tell anyone, either, as far as we knew. Maybe he told his parents. They had to know he was out that night with his sister, but he might not have told them he was driving. The sheriff might've known, but if he did, he wasn't saying. The Marleys had enough pull to hush things up."

Rhodes wondered about that. It would explain a lot. The sheriff must have known how unlikely it was for the driver of the car to wind up where Gwen had been. He might well have spoken to the Marleys, who could have used their money and power to keep their son out of jail and to keep his secret. Rhodes didn't like to think that one of his predecessors would have sold out like that, but he knew it was possible, even likely, no matter how unappealing the thought was to him. The Marleys had more than enough power in town to keep things out of the papers as well. As far as anybody knew, Gwen was alone in the car. If anybody saw her and Jake at the Dairy King or the movies, they hadn't spoken up.

"Sheriff? Are you listening to me?" Glenda asked.

"I'm listening. I had to think about a few things."

"I can see why. I believe that's all I have to say on the subject. You can tell him the rest, Ron."

Ron shifted in his chair. "We know you think one of us killed Jake, Sheriff, but why would we do that? He's the one who had something to hide, not us. I don't know why he stuck all of us in that play of his. I'll admit it. That had us worried, all right, but not worried enough to kill him. We don't have anything to lose anymore. Not our jobs. I'm retired. Al and Glenda and Ed can retire anytime they want to. Probably should have already. We're not worried about our reputations. Nobody cares about a bunch of old people like us. If anybody thinks about us at all, it's to wonder if we're still alive."

Rhodes looked at Glenda. "What about you? Do you think one of this group killed Jake?"

Glenda smiled. "I considered it, but I couldn't think of a motive. Can you?"

"No," Rhodes said. "I can't."

No one had anything to say to that, and Rhodes realized that everything he'd thought about Jake's death had been wrong. As often as he'd warned against reaching a conclusion before all the evidence was in, that was exactly what he'd done. All the evidence had seemed to point in one direction, so that was the direction he'd taken, forgetting that there might be other possibilities. Now he had to start all over and look at everything in a different way. He wasn't sure what different way there was, however. It would take him a while to move all the pieces around and create a new picture.

That was too bad, because he'd liked the old one. He'd especially liked the way he thought it was about to end, with all the suspects gathered in a room for the final confrontation, the way it was in the old movies he'd seen on TV years ago. It would've been a fine ending, and it was too bad that things hadn't worked out.

"Well, Sheriff?" Ed said. "Are we all under arrest, or is this little meeting over?"

"It's over. I appreciate your help, but I wish you'd told me this story earlier."

"Maybe we should have," Ed said, "but you know how it is. Jake was sort of redeeming himself and doing good things. We didn't want the story about the accident to get around and sour people on him and his project. Do you think people have to find out now?"

"Maybe not," Rhodes said. "We'll see. You can all go now. I won't be bothering you again."

"It's okay, Sheriff," Ron said. "You were just doing your job, and we were just covering our asses."

"Such language," Glenda said, but she was smiling. "If you ever need insurance, Sheriff, you know who to call."

She left the room, followed by Ron. Al asked if he and Rhodes could have a minute, and Ed went on out to the front office.

"What about it, Sheriff?" Al asked when Ed was safely out of earshot. "You gonna arrest me?"

"I'm not," Rhodes said. "You were under a lot of pressure, and now I know why. It wasn't smart to come at me with that wrench, though."

"I know it. I lost it for a minute. Now that you've heard the story, do you see what I meant about how there was a secret but there wasn't anything else?"

"I do. There's no connection between the past and Jake's death. Maybe he just slipped and fell."

"I bet that's it," Al said. He put out his hand. "I apologize again for trying to hit you."

Rhodes shook the grimy paw. "Just don't try it again."

"You don't have to worry about that, and I sure thank you for not taking me to the jail and locking me up. Anytime you want your Edsel worked on, you bring it around."

"I'll do that," Rhodes said.

Al grinned. "I'll do you a good job. Be fun to work on a real car again. See you, Sheriff."

He left the room, and Rhodes followed him. Ed was sitting at his desk, and Rhodes asked if he could use the meeting room for a while.

"I need a place to sit and think," he said.

"Take all the time you need," Ed said. "I'm sorry we held out on you, but we were upset and worried. We still haven't figured out why Jake wanted us to be in that crazy play of his."

"Me, neither," Rhodes said.

The little meeting room was a good place to sit and think things over. It was as quiet as Rhodes's office in the courthouse, and Jennifer Loam would never find him unless his Tahoe parked out front gave him away.

Because Rhodes still thought the play had something to do with Jake's death, he thought about calling Harry Harris for some English-teacher advice. Symbolism had never been Rhodes's strong suit in English class. He tended to take things too literally. He'd gone along with the ideas about the characters in the play and their relation to Jake, and he'd been too quick to jump on the idea that Jake was going to use the play to expose them, as had been the case in the Shake-speare play. Now he had to start all over, and there was no way to know if he was right, no matter what he came up with. He couldn't very well call Jake up and ask him.

It seemed simple enough now, though. Jake could very well have been happy because he was going to expose the person responsible for Gwen's accident. He'd been the person, and could use the play to admit it. He was Marley, after all, the one hauling around the chains, which represented not so much the people he'd hurt but the guilt he'd carried for fifty years or more.

And what better place to make his confession than in the theater where it had all started? That was a lot of symbolism, but it made sense to Rhodes. Jake had wanted his friends in the play because he knew they shared his guilt to a certain extent, and he wanted them to have some relief, too. He'd wanted Rhodes there as representative of the law so that justice could be served. Just what Rhodes was supposed to do at this late date was an open question, but the idea also made sense.

What didn't make sense was why anybody would kill Jake. Rhodes started going over everything he'd heard and seen, even the little things that hadn't meant anything at the time.

He wasn't sure how long he sat there since the meeting room didn't have a clock, but after a while he came up with an answer. He wasn't sure it was the *right* answer, but it was an answer.

Rhodes left the meeting room and went to Ed's office. Ed sat at the desk reading a book. Rhodes could see the title: *A Christmas Carol.*

When he saw Rhodes, Ed laid the book on the desk. "I read it a long time ago. I didn't remember much about it. I thought it might give me some ideas about Jake and what was going through his mind."

"Did it?" Rhodes asked.

"Not a one, but it's a good story. Did you get any ideas while you were in my meeting room?"

"Just one."

"Is it any good?"

"Better than nothing," Rhodes said.

In the parking lot, Rhodes got into the Tahoe and called Hack.

"I'm going to Wesley," he said. "Don't call me unless there's an emergency."

"What level emergency we talkin' about this time?" Hack asked.

"Same as last time."

"You gonna tell me what you're goin' to Wesley for?"

"Nope," Rhodes said.

"That's what I thought. Keep the old dispatcher in the dark. I'm used to it, though. I don't even care anymore."

"I don't believe you," Rhodes said, "and I'll fill you in later just in case I'm right about you."

"Prob'ly read all about it on the Internet before you tell me anything."

"Not this time," Rhodes said.

Driving down the hill to Wesley, Rhodes thought things over again, remembering what Elaine had told him on his prior visit. At one point he should've pressed her, but she'd changed the subject, and he'd let her get away with it. He'd made a lot of mistakes in this investigation, but so far nobody had been hurt by them. He was thankful for that, at least.

The sun had been shining earlier in the day, but now the sky was overcast with thin gray clouds. The fields beside the highway looked even more barren than usual. The weather was in keeping with Rhodes's gray mood, so he tried to lighten it up by turning on the radio to KCLR, which sometimes played music and sometimes had talk shows. He got lucky. It was a country music hour, and Dolly Parton was singing "Jolene," an oldie that wasn't overly chipper. That didn't matter. Just hearing Dolly's clear mountain voice cheered Rhodes up a little.

When he arrived at the Tunstall house, he saw that Harvey had finished breaking up the sidewalk and had hauled off the broken concrete. He'd built a form so he could pour the new walk, but he hadn't done that job yet.

Rhodes parked the Tahoe and walked up the dirt walkway. Harvey opened the door but not the screen before Rhodes knocked.

Harvey didn't have a welcoming look. "What're you back here for, Sheriff?"

"Just wanted to talk to Elaine again," Rhodes said. "I thought she might've remembered a few more things about the other morning."

"She's been taking her meds," Harvey said.

Rhodes nodded. "This isn't about her meds."

"I guess you can come in, then," Harvey said, opening the screen and standing aside.

Rhodes went past him into the house and found Elaine sitting on the couch, watching TV again. She was so intent on the screen that she didn't notice Rhodes.

"Sheriff's here to see you," Harvey said at Rhodes's back.

Elaine looked away from the TV and saw Rhodes standing there. "Hey, Sheriff," she said. "You ever watch *The People's Court*?"

"Never seen that one," Rhodes said.

"You oughta watch it, you being in law enforcement and all. It was better in the old days when Judge Wapner was on, but this Judge Milian is all right. She's tough but fair, just like Judge Wapner was."

"Tough but fair is always a good policy," Rhodes said. "Harvey, would you mind letting me talk to Elaine for a few minutes, just me and her?"

Harvey looked at Elaine. "That all right with you?"

"Sure. I like to talk to the sheriff."

"I'll be in the kitchen if you need me," Harvey said, and he left the room.

"You have a seat, Sheriff," Elaine said. "What did you want to talk to me about?"

Rhodes sat down. "It's about when you were in Clearview the other day," Rhodes said. "We talked about that, remember?"

"I remember."

"You told me that you drove around a little before you came to the Beauty Shack."

"I'm real sorry about what I did," Elaine said. "I just love Lonnie to death, and I'd never do anything to hurt him or his shop. This haircut's not really so bad, either."

"I like the haircut," Rhodes said, "but that's not what I want to talk about."

Elaine picked up the TV remove and muted the program. "What is it, then?"

"I asked you if you saw anybody downtown, and you said you didn't remember. I thought maybe by now you'd have thought of something."

"Like what?"

"Like something you saw."

"I didn't see anybody."

"Maybe not on the streets. I thought you might've seen someone in the alley behind the theater if you happened to glance down that way. If not a person, a car or truck."

Elaine looked down at the coffee table. "I guess maybe I did see a car."

"Tell me about that," Rhodes said.

"I guess it'll be all right," Elaine said.

"I'm sure it will," Rhodes told her.

Chapter 25

▼

Glenda Tallent's office was on the highway leading to the Walmart but much closer to town than Aubrey Hamilton's. It was a neat brick structure only a few years old. Rhodes figured the insurance business was doing pretty well. Even in a small town like Clearview, everybody needed insurance. The office was only a block from the McDonald's, a location that Rhodes liked. He could've used a Quarter Pounder right then, in fact, but he thought he'd better postpone eating. Seeing Glenda was what mattered at the moment.

When Rhodes parked and got out of the Tahoe, he caught the scent of burgers. He wondered why he seemed to be smelling food so often these days, but this time it wasn't his imagination. His stomach rumbled a little, but it quieted down by the time he reached the door of Glenda's office.

He opened the door, and a little bell rang. It wasn't necessary for it to alert Glenda, however, as she was sitting at her desk.

"What a pleasant surprise, Sheriff," she said. "Twice in one day. I feel honored."

"You shouldn't," Rhodes said. "This is still business."

"Your business or mine?"

"Mine, I'm afraid."

"Well, have a seat and tell me how I can help you."

Glenda's visitors' chairs were brown leather armchairs, and Rhodes settled down in one.

"I thought you were through with us this morning," Glenda said. "I can't imagine what you could want with me."

"Just a couple of things," Rhodes said. "I have a few questions about the inspection report for Jake's building before you insured it."

"We don't always inspect," Glenda said, "but with a building as old as the theater, I thought it was necessary."

Once again Rhodes wondered if everyone in town had forgotten how to answer a direct question. Maybe there was something in the water.

"That's not what I asked," he said, something he'd been saying a lot in the last few days.

"I know it wasn't." Glenda didn't snap, but she gave him a cold look. "I was giving you some background."

"You mentioned that Rick Shepherd did the inspection. Is he honest?"

"I said I'd used him before. He's always been fine."

"The building has some real problems," Rhodes said. "Some dangerous ones. Were those noted on the report?"

Glenda smiled. "You're trying to trick me into something, Sheriff. There were no dangerous items listed. Just the usual things. The building is structurally sound."

"The structure might be sound. What's inside it isn't." Rhodes had found that out the hard way. "There's something wrong with that report."

Glenda's lips tightened. "I wouldn't knowingly accept a false report."

"You wouldn't know it was false if you didn't check it out for yourself, and why do that? After all, you trusted Rick. He'd always done a good job before."

"He certainly had. I don't know what you're implying, Sheriff."

"I'm implying that he overlooked some things, on purpose. I think you suspected as much, but you didn't question the report."

"I don't think I like the way these questions are going."

"That doesn't matter. I need some answers. You even hinted to me about a reason Rick might fudge the reports. Feminine wiles. Remember?"

"It's possible that Rick could have been susceptible to a little feminine charm," Glenda said. "His wife died several years ago. Breast cancer. He's a fairly young man. Young single men can be susceptible."

"I know," Rhodes said.

Glenda frowned. "I assured you I didn't use any feminine wiles."

"I'm not talking about you."

Glenda leaned forward, and her voice was strained. "It wouldn't do me much good with my company if I signed off on a report that I knew was falsified. You understand?"

"Let's say you couldn't have known. Suspected, maybe, but not known. Tell me about it."

"Aubrey Hamilton's an attractive woman," Glenda said. "She might have convinced Rick to take it easy on the inspection so Jake would buy the building. She wouldn't want to call in a second inspector, so she would've told Jake to show me Rick's report. Not that there was any way I could've known there was any hanky-panky going on."

"Just tell me what you did know."

"I knew that Aubrey and Rick had a date or two. I knew that the building was old and in bad shape. But Rick's a licensed inspector, so I had to trust his report."

Had to? Or did she just need the business? Rhodes didn't care. He'd let the state go after Rich Shepherd if it wanted to. He had another crime in mind. He might have to use Rick to bolster his case, but he wasn't going to arrest him. He stood up.

"That's what I wanted to know. Thanks for your help."

"That's all? Nothing more about Rick?"

"You can report him if you think you should."

"I'll have to think about it."

"You do that," Rhodes said.

Rhodes was pretty sure he had the whole thing now. Maybe there were a few rough edges on the puzzle pieces, but he thought he could sand those off and make them fit. He was sorry that things had turned out as they had, but you couldn't always get what you wanted. Hadn't someone said that sometimes you could get what you needed instead? Benjamin Franklin? It didn't matter, not as long as things worked themselves out one way or the other. That was the way his job went.

Rhodes stopped at the courthouse to visit a judge before going to Aubrey Hamilton's office. It didn't take long, and he was on his way again.

Aubrey's car was still parked in the same spot in front of her office. Rhodes parked beside it and went into the building.

"Hello again, Sheriff," Aubrey said, folding her hands on the desk. "To what do I owe the pleasure of this visit?"

"I'm afraid it's not going to be a pleasure," Rhodes said.

"I don't know what you mean."

"I think you do. You killed Jake Marley, and I'm arresting you for his murder. I'm going to read you your rights now."

Rhodes recited the Miranda rights while Aubrey sat and stared at him. When he was finished, she pushed back from her desk and said, "You're wrong. I didn't kill Jake. He fell from that grid."

"He fell, all right, but he had help. Jake called you about the inspection report on the building. You'd told him everything was fine, but he'd found some problems. He wanted to point them out to you, personally." That was guesswork, but it was based on other things Rhodes had surmised. "You parked in the alley behind the theater. No need to deny that. Someone saw your car." Elaine Tunstall. She might not be the best witness in the world, but Rhodes was sure she was right.

"You may have had a key to the back door of the theater, since you were the Realtor who sold it, but that wouldn't matter. Jake would've let you in. He wanted to show you some of the problems with the building. One of them was the rotten boards in the fly loft. I'm sure there were others."

"This is just crazy," Aubrey said. "I didn't kill Jake. I'm the one who reported that he was dead."

"You had to, in case anyone knew he'd called you. We might have checked his phone records and found out. After he fell, you climbed down from the fly loft, parked in front of the theater, and called my office. You were worried about the inspection report, though. What if someone happened to run across it in Jake's house? What if he'd left a note about it or written on it? You broke into the house to look for it. I don't know if you found it, but your fingerprints are all over his office."

That was another little lie, but Rhodes thought they could find her prints if they looked hard enough.

"I don't know what you're talking about," Aubrey said. "I was never in that house in my life."

"We'll find somebody who saw you," Rhodes said.

Aubrey was still calm. Rhodes had to admire her. She'd been very cool in the theater talking about Jake's death as well.

"I don't think you'll find anyone who saw me," she said, "because I wasn't there."

"I'm going to talk to Rick Shepherd about the report. He'll have a copy. He'll have to defend it. Or tell the truth about it."

For the first time Aubrey showed a bit of distress. "I had nothing to do with that report."

"We'll see what Rick has to say about that."

"Even if he filed a false report, that doesn't mean I killed Jake. Which I didn't. You don't have any proof of that, because I'm innocent."

Rhodes looked at her folded hands. "I noticed in the theater that you weren't wearing any rings. Both times I've visited you here, you've folded your hands, right over left. You've stopped wearing your wedding ring, and I can understand that, but you're wearing a ring or two on your right hand. You weren't wearing them in the theater."

Aubrey kept her right hand covered. "I don't have to show you anything."

"Yes, you do," Rhodes said. He reached into his pocket and pulled out a piece of paper. "I have a search warrant right here. You see, it doesn't matter how hard you scrubbed those rings, there's going to be a little bit of Jake's DNA left on them. You can't get rid of it."

That was the biggest lie Rhodes had told, but he hoped Aubrey watched a lot of TV. If she did, she'd probably believe him, considering the miracles TV cops could work.

She believed him. She slumped in her chair, and her voice broke when she said, "I didn't mean to do it."

Rhodes wondered how many times he'd heard that. He figured that it was something that most of the people who killed believed about themselves. In one second they made a decision that they couldn't take back in a lifetime, so they told themselves they didn't mean to do it.

"He was angry," Aubrey said. "He'd always been so nice to me before, but he was yelling about the boards and the plumbing and the roof. He knew those things would have to be fixed. I couldn't understand why he was so upset."

"Maybe because he thought he'd been misled."

"I needed the sale," Aubrey said, as if that excused everything. "He didn't understand that, but no wonder. He'd always had money. He didn't have any problems in his life."

Little did she know. "That was no reason to kill him."

"It was an accident! He was so upset that I thought he was going to throw me to the stage. He reached for me, and I swung my arm. I didn't mean to. It just happened. You said it yourself. He fell. I didn't kill him."

Just like Latham had dodged the squirrel and Jake had maybe dodged a rabbit or a possum, Aubrey had swung her arm. Reflex. The action of an instant that you can never reverse. Maybe it would be a good defense. Randy Lawless would do all he could with it.

"You'd better come with me now," Rhodes said.

That evening Rhodes sat in the theater with Ivy, Seepy, and Harry. The ghost light shone on the empty stage, and the shadows danced. It was cold in the building, but not abnormally so, not enough to convince anybody that a ghost was present.

Seepy's idea was that Jake's spirit might not be hanging around the theater for much longer now that his killer had been put in jail.

"He's free to wander now," Seepy said. "He may be gone already. We need to get in touch while we can."

"That's assuming he was ever here to begin with, which he wasn't," Rhodes said. He regretted that he'd let Seepy talk him into coming to the theater in the first place.

Seepy and Harry had tried their equipment and hadn't gotten any readings. The Ouija board hadn't done a thing. Rhodes thought that should've convinced them there was no ghost, but they were hardheaded.

"I don't know about the rest of you," Ivy said, "but I'm getting hungry, and these seats are really uncomfortable."

Rhodes stood up. "I'm hungry, too. Let's go."

Ivy stood up, but Harry and Seepy kept their seats.

"Would it be okay if we stayed just a little longer?" Harry asked, tapping the EMF meter.

Rhodes didn't think they'd cause any damage. "Just behave yourselves."

"You don't have to worry about us," Seepy said. "It's the ghosts who might cause trouble."

"I'm not worried about them," Rhodes said.

He and Ivy started up the aisle. They'd gotten almost to the door to the lobby when Rhodes felt a change in the temperature.

"Sheriff," Seepy called, "wait a minute!"

"Are you going to wait?" Ivy asked.

"Not a chance," Rhodes said.

As they walked through the door, the ghost light flickered, blinked, and went out.

"Sheriff!" Seepy yelled.

Rhodes touched Ivy's arm. "Just keep walking," he said, and they did.